WRITING THE WOLF

A WEREWOLF PARANORMAL ROMANCE

STEFFANIE HOLMES

BACCHANALIA HOUSE

1

ROSA

"As you can see," Margaret said, opening the creaking door, "it's a little sparse. But you mentioned you wanted something authentic and rustic, so I thought this was the perfect cabin for you."

Sparse? This wasn't *sparse*. It was the bloody grapes of wrath.

I glanced around the cabin, which didn't take very long, as the room was the size of a postage stamp and contained exactly five items of furniture – a bed, a small desk under the window, a chair for the desk, a long bench along the wall beside the door containing a sink and some shelves, and a faded armchair beside the fireplace. The tiny windows above the desk and beside the door let in a square of grey light, which only made the dark wood walls and low ceiling look even more gloomy.

I want to go home.

The thought hit me like a freight train, dislodging me from the present and sending me back in time, halfway across the country, to where I once had a nice Tudor cottage at the end of a quiet street. I planted window boxes and painted the front door bright red.

Margaret droned on about the plumbing and the handyman

and the sewage and the other quirks of the property. I nodded along, barely listening, lost in the grief steamrolling across my whole body.

It's no use wanting it. You can never go back. You don't have a home anymore.

My therapist, Nancy, said it was normal to grieve for a lost home the same way you would grieve for a person. I hated the grief – it made me feel so weak, so pathetic, pining away for all my *stuff*. I always thought I was pretty grounded, that I didn't place much value on possessions and things, that I could take whatever shit people threw at me and hurl it right back. But while I watched that fire consume everything I owned, I felt as though a piece of myself had burned up along with it.

All my photographs. The diaries I'd diligently kept ever since intermediate school. The furniture I'd collected from estate sales and elegantly restored. The paintings I'd bought at local art fairs. My computer with all my early story drafts. The piles and piles of books. The English Rose crockery Grandmother Mary left me. The gold bangles my mother gave me on my sixteenth birthday, made by craftsman in our ancestral village in Ghana. Who was I without these pieces of a life?

"You need a fresh start, Rosa," Nancy told me, after listening to another of my tirades about the fire. "If you really feel like a shell of a person, then take the fire as an opportunity to remake yourself. Do what you've always wanted to do. Be bold."

Be bold. That was my new mantra. I still wasn't sure it fit, but I was doing my damn best.

As soon as my insurance payout landed in the bank, I handed in my notice at my crappy administration job at the accounting firm in Old Garsmouth; the tiny, backward, completely white village outside of Leeds where I'd lived since university. My boss – the white, leggy Susan, who had done her bit to make my life miserable – at least had the decency to look pissed. "Going back to Africa, then? Going to go steal yourself a jigaboo husband?" she sneered, before informing me she wouldn't be paying me my last paycheque.

"You can keep it." I grinned at her, before walking out of there with my head held high, black curls bouncing over my shoulders. Susan could keep her stupid check. I had 300,000 pounds burning a hole in my pocket. And I knew exactly what I was going to do with it.

I googled "Remote forest cabin England." The first entry that came up was for a collection of cabins on the edge of the Crookshollow Forest. They were owned by an elderly woman named Margaret who rented them out to artists and yogis and any other weirdo who needed a tranquil place to think and create.

It sounded perfect, mostly because it was far, far, far away from Old Garsmouth and the charred remains of my life. I called Margaret immediately and gave her my credit card number for the deposit.

And now I was here, standing in the place I'd call home for the next year. Looking around the drab interior, I couldn't help but think I should have checked out the cabin first. So much for practising being bold.

Maybe bold doesn't work for you, I thought as I dropped my bag beside the battered armchair, sending up a cloud of dust that made me cough and splutter. Stuffing bulged from long gashes in the arms, and I could see more stuffing poking out from beneath the sagging seat. *Maybe you should have just got an apartment—*

No. Stop being so dismissive, Rosa. This is your new life. This is where you're finally going to write your book.

I wandered over to the window, pulled out the chair and looked down at the tiny desk, barely large enough to fit a cup of coffee and my laptop. When I'd come up with the idea of holing up in a cabin in the forest to write, I had visions of those cute cabins you see on the internet, all comfy beanbags by the fire-place and strings of fairy lights and plush couches covered in moroccan blankets placed around warm braziers. I pictured mosquito nets and bright-coloured rugs and a Japanese-style dining nook and little framed motivational quotes stuck to the walls.

This cabin barely had room for a beanbag, much less a Japanese-style dining nook.

Margaret was looking at me expectantly. "Is something wrong?" She rapped her wooden walking stick against the floor.

I realised I was frowning. Quickly, I plastered a smile across my face. "It's lovely, really. It's just a little ... bare."

"It's yours for the whole year, dearie. Feel free to decorate it as you like. JK Rowling used it for the whole summer a few years back. She put up some lovely cream curtains."

That made me beam. *If it's good enough for JK Rowling, it's good enough for me.*

"I'll leave you to get settled in." Margaret hobbled down the front steps. "Don't forget what I said about the plumbing!"

"I won't." I waved, frantically replaying our conversation in my head to try and figure out if I remembered hearing anything about plumbing. "Bye, Margaret."

Alone at last with my insanity. I dumped my suitcase beside the bed, and started pulling out the few possessions I'd brought with me, mainly stuff I'd bought since the fire. My clothes I had to leave inside the case until I could buy some drawers. The torch and ereader and books and drink bottle went beside the bed. A framed picture of my beloved cat, Lennox (after Lennox Lewis) took pride of place on the windowsill above the desk.

Poor Lennox. I'm so sorry.

Tears burned the corners of my eyes. *Oh no, you don't.* I was here, in my cabin, about to start the next phase of my life. This wasn't the place to get all hysterical again about shit that was in the past.

I slammed my laptop down on the desk harder than I'd intended, placing my new coffee cup, a pad of paper and set of new pencils beside it. This was it. This was where I'd write my novel. This was where I'd pour out all the hurt and pain and anger that had been brewing over the years.

This was where I'd make them all pay.

AFTER I FINISHED UNPACKING, I went for a walk around the cabin to admire the wonderland that would be my home for the next year.

Margaret owned a small parcel of land at the edge of Crook-shollow Forest, left to her by her first husband after his death. Her house – a beautiful, sprawling eco-lodge built from enormous rough-hewn logs – was up at the opening of the driveway, near the dirt road leading deeper into the forest. Right down the back of her land, some three miles from her house and not even accessible by car, were a collection of six cabins all made from wood felled from the forest by Margaret's second – also late – husband.

Each cabin stood several hundred metres from its neighbour, and the tightly packed trees and uneven ground made them practically invisible, hidden away like witches homes in fairy tales. The whole place had a fairy-tale vibe about it – small paths meandered off in several directions, one leading me down to a swimming hole in the stream, the others leading to lookouts or the day hikes through the forest mentioned on the website. Each cabin had its own letterbox – carved from wood in the shape of animals by Margaret's talented third – also late –

husband. Mine was a wolf. Maybe he would be my spirit animal, to go with my new mantra and my new life.

I headed for the nearest path, and wandered a little way. Branches swayed gently in the breeze, and the cool light of the moon shone between the leaves, creating bubbles of light that danced over the ground. In the distance, I could hear an owl hooting, and the rustle of some critter moving through the undergrowth. I stood silent, taking it all in, wrapping my body in an armour of peace.

Best of all, there was no one else around.

I could see the faint flickers of light through the trees, indicating at least two of the other cabins were occupied. But they'd come here for the same reasons I had, to get away from the world. My only company would be these tall, majestic trees – no one was yelling abuse at me, or telling me to go back to Africa, or threatening to cut me just because I was black.

I sucked in deep breaths of crisp, cool air. It felt *damn* good.

By the time I returned from my walk, I was in much greater spirits. I knew I could make this work. In the moonlight, even the dreary cabin didn't seem so bad. In fact, it had potential. I decided to visit town tomorrow and buy a few things to brighten up the cabin, as well as some groceries. I definitely needed groceries. When I returned from my trip, I could start writing.

As it was, I'd brought a few essential supplies to see me through the night. Dinner was tinned beans on toast, cooked over the little gas stove Margaret had provided. I had a bottle of red wine in my pack, and even one of Sam's old cigars. As I lit up the cigar and took a deep drag, I felt like a real writer.

As the moon rose higher in the sky, casting a cold haze through the trees, I poured myself a third glass of wine, stubbed out the cigar (what a disgusting thing. Why did I like it when Sam smoked them, again?), and picked up my ereader. A few pages into the latest Zadie Smith novel, I realised I desperately needed to go to the bathroom.

The bathroom. Where was the bathroom?

I hadn't given too much thought to it when Margaret had gestured at the rear of the cabin, but now when I went to hunt for the facilities, I couldn't find a doorway inside, which meant only one thing.

Don't tell me. Don't fucking tell me ...

Yup. I had somehow managed to rent a cabin that didn't even have a fucking indoor bathroom.

Cursing at my stupidity, I grabbed my ereader and held it out in front of me, using the screen as a torch as I fumbled my way across the porch and—

"Ow!"

I rubbed my knee. The ereader didn't make a very good torch.

Hobbling around the balustrade, I found my way to the steps at the end of the porch. Sure enough, when I descended them, I found myself facing a tiny wooden shack so small I secretly hoped it was a TARDIS, because if it wasn't bigger on the inside I couldn't see how my booty could possibly fit through the door.

I grabbed the handle and tugged. The door rattled on ancient hinges, but didn't budge. My bladder howled in protest. Squeezing my thighs together, I shoved the ereader under my armpit, gripped the handle with both hands, and yanked it back as hard as I could.

The door flung open, sending me sailing backward. My foot caught on a loose tree root, and I toppled over backward, my palms and ass stinging as they caught the brunt of my fall. My ereader clattered against a stone, and the light flickered out.

Great. This was turning out to be a real disaster. Tears pressed at the corners of my eyes, but I wiped them away with a stinging palm. I wasn't going to let the stupid toilet get to me. That wasn't *being bold.*

Look on the bright side, Rosa, I reminded myself. *At least the door's open now.*

I rolled over and got to my feet, brushing the dirt off my ass. I grabbed the door and walked into the dark closet, pulling it shut behind me, leaving a gap just big enough that the moonlight could give me some visibility. I sat down, did my business, and tried not to think about how many creepy crawlies were lurking in the shadows. I stood up, and grabbed the thin cord hanging from the ceiling to flush the toilet.

The toilet didn't flush.

You can't be serious. I am not doing this. I'm not living in a fucking cabin with a toilet that doesn't work.

I yanked the cord again, harder this time.

The loo made a gurgling sound, but nothing else happened.

"You've got to be kidding." I said aloud, my voice sounding hollow in the darkness. *Great. This is just perfect.* I should have listened more carefully to Margaret's warnings about the plumbing. What had she said, while I was busy thinking about the fire again?

Even when I was hundreds of miles away, Old Garsmouth still managed to fuck up my life.

Well fine, I wasn't going to deal with this problem in the dark. I'd call a plumber in the morning. I slammed down the lid, and turned on the tap to wash my hand. A tiny trickle came out, followed by nothing except a loud, thumping noise from the pipes.

"Aargh!" I pounded my fist against the wall. Something scuttled across my knuckles.

"Aargh!" I yanked my hand away and stumbled out the door, straight into a tall stranger who was standing on the path.

"Do you need some help?" A deep voice boomed in my ear,

with the familiar heavy vowels of a Scottish accent. Huge arms wrapped around my body.

"Aargh!" I flailed my arms about, tearing myself away from his grip. Who the hell was that? Why was some guy walking around my cabin at night?

And why did my body suddenly feel so strange? It was as though I'd stuck my finger in a light socket. All the hair on my body stood to attention. I could only imagine what the frizz on top of my head must look like. My heart thundered in my chest, but this wasn't fear – it was something else. It almost felt like … excitement.

I fought against the overwhelming urge to throw myself back into the arms of the stranger. *What is that about?*

I backed against the side of the loo, and studied the stranger. Even in the moonlight, it was obvious he was the world's most attractive man. Well, maybe not the most … Idris Elba was still alive, of course, and Sam Heughan. But this guy would certainly make top five. And he had the significant advantage in that he was in my immediate vicinity, although I still had yet to ascertain if that was a good thing or not.

He had long, floppy red hair that tumbled around his face in tousled waves. A line of dark stubble crossed his strong, square jaw, and the corners of his mouth lifted up into a cheeky half-grin. Eyes of blue ice looked me up and down with predator-like focus. Even with a thick leather jacket on, I could see the dark shapes of a tattoo poking out from the side of his collar. He carried a metal box in his hand. A gold ring dangled from the top of his right ear. God, I'd love to grab that with my tongue and—

What are you even thinking? This is nuts. That's a white guy, standing in the dark. Hot or not, he can't be there for any good reason.

I backed away further, trying to ignore the desire surging through my body. *Stay alert, Rosa. Ignore your body for the moment. It's probably having some kind of seizure. If he makes a move, turn and run for the path at the other side of the cabin—*

"Are you having some plumbing issues?" the stranger asked, taking a step forward.

I held up a hand. "What the hell do you think you're doing?" I demanded, in a voice that oozed the confidence I did not feel. "You're sneaking around my cabin in the middle of the night wearing all black, you scare me half to death, and the first thing you have to say to me is about the *plumbing?*"

He shrugged, a full-on wicked grin spreading across his face, the kind of grin that might move him from top five hottest guys on Earth into the top three. "Why not? I help lots of women with their plumbing."

"Don't be disgusting. Are you here to attack me? I warn you, I'm dangerous when provoked." I tried to make my feet move back, but they were frozen in place.

"Oh, I bet you are." There was that grin again. Cocky, self-assured. Sexy as hell. Damn this guy. "In all seriousness, though. I just came to see if you were all right. I've brought my tools."

He jiggled the box in his hand, which upon closer inspection did indeed look like a toolbox. Certainly not big enough to carry a body around in. That was some positive news.

I still wasn't buying it. "Do you just randomly walk around the forest in the dark, looking for plumbing disasters? You still haven't told me your name."

The guy set down the box, and held up both hands in a gesture of supplication. "My name's Caleb. Caleb Lowe. Margaret hired me to do some carpentry work around the place. I'm staying in the cabin just over there." He jerked his thumb at the trees behind us. "She asked me to come out and check on you, offer my services for whatever you need." Caleb grinned again. "Looks like I got here just in time."

My shoulders relaxed a little. Margaret had mentioned

something about a handyman. But that gorgeous, white face and the thrumming energy surging through my body still left me feeling off-guard. "How do I know you're not just some crazy dude *pretending* to be the handyman? I've seen a lot of horror films that started with conversations just like this, and they always end up with the heroine slashed across the throat and being dragged into some kind of dungeon torture chamber."

"You watch horror films that regularly begin with the protagonist and the serial killer discussing plumbing?" He raised an eyebrow. "Where are you getting your film recommendations, the National Plumbing Association Film Festival?"

"So you admit you're a serial killer."

Caleb grinned again, then leaned into the closet and tapped the pipe on the wall. "Let me guess, you don't have any water, right? But the pipe's making a gurgling noise?"

"Yeah, that's about the size of it."

"Too easy," he grinned.

A flush crept across my cheeks. Thankfully he wouldn't be able to see it in the dark. "Yeah, well, it's been a long day. If I'd known I'd be swapping *double entendres* with an itinerant fix-it serial killer, I would have taken the time to bone up a bit."

I wondered if he got realised that one was deliberate, but he burst out laughing, and I found my unease melting away. It didn't help that the strange energy was still flowing through my veins, and my hands were itching to run through his hair.

"Funny as well as gorgeous, you might be my new favourite neighbour." Caleb held up his toolbox like a peace offering. "I know what's wrong because the exact same thing happened to me the first day I moved in. I can fix this in a few seconds for you, if you like."

I was still a bit apprehensive, but the energy in my body screamed at me to accept his offer. Besides, I needed to have running water, and all I knew about toolboxes was that they provided a great surface for stacking books. I waved an arm dismissively at the toilet, as if the whole thing really wasn't that big a deal. "Yeah, sure. Knock yourself out."

Caleb set down his toolbox, and took out a couple of strange-shaped tools. He bent down beside the toilet, giving me an excellent view of his tight, muscular ass swinging in the air. A few moments later, his head popped back up again. He leaned in and turned the tap on. Water gushed freely into the sink.

I flinched a bit, sorry I'd been so suspicious. "Thanks so much."

That grin again. Damn, it made my knees weak. "Don't mention it. It was worth it for the excuse to come over here and meet you. It's been fun."

It's been fun. Oh, screw Idris, Caleb was the most attractive man I'd ever seen. Clearly, my body screamed for him. It had been so long since Sam Seymour, and there hadn't been anyone else since. I desperately wanted to be touched, and a guy like Caleb would know his way around a woman's body, of that I had no doubt.

I toyed with the idea of asking Caleb in to finish off the wine. As I opened my mouth, a hard thought stopped me.

Caleb was *white.*

I couldn't overlook that key fact. I wasn't normally attracted to white men. It probably had something to do with the fact that white men had been a source of much of the misery that had invaded my life, especially in recent years. The police never caught the arsonists who burned down my house, but I *knew* they were white. It was pretty obvious when you thought about it.

Sam Seymour, the biggest mistake of my life, had been white, too. After him, I'd sworn I'd never go there again.

And yet here was the most beautiful man I'd seen, and

instead of staring at me with disgust, or calling out some kind of slur, he was friendly, and dare I hope ... even a little flirtatious?

I was all alone here in the middle of the woods, in a forest known for strange occurrences. Only six months ago, Crookshollow had hit the national news after a reporter was found dead, torn apart by some kind of wild animal. There were some mysterious goings-on at an archaeological site, too, and before that, a dead rockstar showing up in perfect health, and some kind of altercation at an art gallery ... Clearly, this place attracted weirdos and freaks of the first order.

Maybe it would be good to have someone looking out for me.

I couldn't have a lover, much as I might want one, but maybe ... maybe, it would be good to have a friend. Especially a friend who knew his way around a toolbox.

Just friends, that's all. It's okay to be friends with a white guy, if you don't get involved. What's the harm, right?

Right?

I plastered a smile on my face. "While you're here, would you like to come in for a cup of tea?"

Oh girl, my brain berated me as I walked up the steps ahead of Caleb, trying not to let my hips sashay too much. *You are in for a world of hurt.*

2

CALEB

*W*hoah.

My whole body shuddered with hot lust. My feet shuffled forward of their own accord, inching me closer to the delicious beauty standing before me.

When Margaret browbeat me into agreeing to visit the new resident, I had no idea I'd be walking in on the girl I was destined to be with. Literally.

As soon as my skin touched hers, I *knew*. The knowledge surged through my veins like an electrical current, turning all my sense on high alert. The smell of her wafted all around me, spicy and rich and feisty, which from our short meeting seemed a perfect description for her. She was the one, my destined mate, the woman who would complete me.

Damn if the universe didn't know how to pick them. This woman – my mate – was *exactly* my type. Shapely legs that never seemed to end, bouncing breasts, one hell of a fine ass, and a smile that lit up the whole sky. Plus, she gave as good as she got. I could tell right away how much fun she'd be, in and out of bed.

Judging by the look of shock on her face when she slammed into me, she felt it too – the energy thrumming through her veins, the tug of the cord of destiny, winding us together. She looked surprised as she asked me in for tea.

There was no way in hell I'd refuse.

I followed her up the steps of the porch, sneaking a long perve at that gorgeous ass wiggling in her tight jeans. My cock was already pressing against my own pants, so while her gaze was turned away, I did a quick little adjustment, hoping she wouldn't notice.

Her cabin had the same layout as mine, except instead of the battered chair beside the fire, mine had a bright pink vinyl chaise lounge. "You take the armchair," she said, setting the kettle to boil, and moving the small desk chair over to the other side of the fire. "Sorry for the state of the place. I haven't had much time to customise it to my taste."

"The place looks great. Hey, nice cat." I picked up the frame on the windowsill and admired the wise little black-and-white face staring back at me. "Why didn't he come along, too?"

"He died," the woman said, her voice flat. Damn, that was the wrong question. Hurriedly, I replaced the picture. *Way to kill the mood, Caleb.*

"You still haven't told me your name," I said as I quit my circuit of the room and lowered myself into the chair. It sagged in the middle with a giant sigh, sucking my ass right down into it.

"It's Rosa. Rosa Parker," she said. "And before you laugh about it, yes, I was named for Rosa Parks, and no, my parents aren't immigrants. I'm third generation British, born and bred." Her tone had turned sharp.

"I wasn't going to ask that," I said, even though I was. "I was going to ask you what made a smart, sassy woman such as yourself choose to rent a tiny cabin in the middle of nowhere?"

"I'm writing a book."

I should have guessed. The laptop on the desk by the

window. The smashed ereader I'd picked up outside, and the teetering stack of paperback books beside the bed. "Oh yeah. What's it about?"

"Huh?" Rosa handed me a steaming mug of tea, and settled herself into the desk chair opposite me, clutching her own cup and crossing her legs to reveal more of her shapely thigh.

"The book. What's the story about?" I stared at her intently. "I don't know many writers, but I'd assume you have some idea about the plot?"

She stared down at her teacup. All traces of that sassy, sexy woman disappeared from her face. Her eyes betrayed a sadness so deep that I wondered if she even registered my presence any longer. After a moment, she shook her head and spoke, her voice hard. "It's a tale of revenge. A black woman suffers a great tragedy because of the ignorance and racism of others, and so she sets out on a mission to get back at the people who hurt her."

"Sounds brutal," I said, not sure what to say to that. Fuck, someone had hurt her *real* bad. This could be tricky. I didn't do drama. I didn't do commitment. I fucked and forgot – that was the way it had to be, for everyone's safety. My cousin Luke had the luxury of being free to marry his mate, but until our family pack was re-established, and our territories recognised, I couldn't do the same.

Although ... having a mate would have some definite advantages, especially when it came time for Luke and I to decide who was alpha ...

Watching Rosa's eyes harden, I couldn't help but wish I could find a way to help her, to sink my teeth into the person who hurt her, and tear out their throat. I rubbed the tingling palm of my hand. I'd had no idea finding my mate would feel like *this*. No wonder my cousin Luke was so much less grumpy whenever Anna was around.

Rosa squared her shoulders and sucked in a breath. After a moment, she turned to me, and the sadness in her eyes was gone, replaced by that same sparkling woman I'd been flirting with earlier. But it was too late. I'd seen it, and she knew it.

You're hiding something, Rosa Parker. You're hiding a hurt, way deep inside.

But now wasn't the time to call her up on it. Instead, I cleared my throat, wanting to say something to bring us both back into the moment. "How long are you here for?"

"Until the book is finished," she said. "I've booked the cabin for the whole year, but that was before I'd seen the place. I might go nuts and shoot myself in the head before then."

"Don't do that," I said. "You'll totally ruin Margaret's marketing spiel. Did you know JK Rowling stayed here?"

Rosa laughed. She threw her whole body into it, tossing her head back, the chuckle beginning deep in her belly and shaking her glorious tits as it rumbled right up through her chest. That was the sexiest fucking laugh I'd ever heard.

I crossed my teacup over my crotch, hoping like hell Rosa hadn't seen that hard-on pressing against my thigh. My little rearrangement earlier hadn't made much difference.

So Rosa Parker was going to be in Crookshollow for the next year. With Luke away in the US with his new wife Anna, I hadn't exactly been looking forward to staying in Crookshollow by myself. There was a lot of work to do re-establishing our old pack territory, and when the working day is done, I liked to have fun. "Fun" in Crookshollow meant winning the pie-eating contest at the village church fete. Not exactly what I had in mind.

But if Rosa Parker was going to be here, that was an entirely different story.

"I've been in Crookshollow for a few months now," I said. "I have some family business here. I'd be happy to show you all the crazy nightlife."

"Oh, yes? What crazy nightlife would that be?"

"Well, there's *Tir Na Nog*, the pub in town. And there's … absolutely nothing else."

Rosa laughed again. "I got that vibe as I drove through today."

"The vibe of, 'Why the hell did I come here?'"

"Exactly." Rosa grinned. "I came from an even smaller village near Leeds. I know what small towns are like. I'm really not too interested in getting to know people. I just want a quiet place to write."

"You've definitely found it."

"Yeah." She grinned again, a warm grin that made my heart beat a little faster. "I think I have."

We lapsed into a few moments of silence. I searched around for a new topic to discuss. Odd, I was usually so confident around women, but the sudden appearance of my mate had blown all my usual lines clean out of my head. "Hey, you should add some witches to your book, and a couple of goblins. This would be the perfect setting for it. You know Crookshollow is apparently the most haunted town in England?"

"That was in the brochure. I don't write fantasy. At least, not *that* kind of fantasy. What are you really doing here, Caleb?" Rosa asked, her fingers fiddling with the handle of her cup. "From your accent, I'd say you weren't born around here, and 'Family Business' sounds like a fake excuse if ever I heard one."

Baby, you have no idea.

"Are you a goblin hunter? Is that what brought you to Crookshollow?"

I shrugged. "I came down from Aberdeen about eight months ago to visit my cousin. He's in the US with his new wife now. I was going to wander around a bit, wherever I could find work, but this place has kind of grown on me. It'll be more fun when my cousin comes back."

"A vagabond. No fixed abode, no ties, no rules or schedules."

"I like my schedules loose," I said, barely able to keep the grin off my face. "Like my—"

"If you finish that sentence, I'm going to tip this tea over your head."

"Interesting. I've never tried Earl Grey foreplay before."

There was that laugh again, rumbling through her whole body. My cock strained against my thigh. Restraint was clearly not my strong suit.

We stayed by the fireplace, chatting for hours about stuff that didn't really matter – books and movies and favourite sexual positions – long after we'd drained the kettle of water. I fought every muscle in my body not to jump her right there, especially after the words "doggie style" fell so easily from her gorgeous lips.

But I couldn't forget that shadow that had passed through her eyes earlier, the darkness in her voice when she'd spoken about her book. I had a feeling that if I pushed things too fast with this girl, she'd bolt so hard.

The moon was high in the sky when I finally stepped outside and bid Rosa goodnight. She stood in the doorway, those dark eyes gazing into mine, daring me to make a move and, at the same time, begging me not to.

My fingers grazed her cheek. The energy pulsed through my skin, dancing across the palm of my hand and right down my arm. Rosa jerked her head back, rubbing her cheek self-consciously.

"Will I see you around, neighbour?" she asked, her voice a mixture of hope and accusation.

"Don't forget, I'm right over that ridge." I pointed east from her cabin. "Just follow the path behind your loo, and you'll find me, if you need me for anything, anything at all ..."

"I will. Thanks, Caleb."

"Seriously, if you need some help with your plumbing, I'll be over in a flash—"

"Goodnight, Caleb."

I flashed her one last grin, and she shut the door in my face.

I rounded the side of her cabin and started back on the path toward mine. I drank in the moonlight, my veins buzzing with the electricity of my encounter with Rosa. Fuck, I was practically skipping. Rosa Parker had me skipping like a giddy schoolgirl.

I passed an area on the path where the trees thinned out, and I got a glimpse of the moon. It was waxing, only six days until it was full. I was starting to feel the tug of my shift, the familiar beckoning of wild places and fresh meat that signalled my inner wolf's desire to take over.

Not yet, I admonished myself. *I get to be human for a few days yet. I need to know more about Rosa. I need—*

A smell stopped me short. A scent trail wafted across the track, so strong even my human nose picked it up. *Shit.* Fear knotted my stomach, quickly turning to anger.

I'd recognise that smell anywhere. But it shouldn't be here.

My inner wolf called to me, and this time, I obeyed, slipping into the transformation. I toppled forward, my hands hitting the damp, cold dirt. My nails curled over and gripped the earth, as the bones in my legs snapped backward. My ribcage cracked open, the sick churning in my stomach signalling my organs rearranging themselves. I gritted my teeth as my nose dislocated itself from my face, elongating and rebuilding into a completely new shape. Prickles ran along my arms and down my back as a thick pelt of hair burst out from my skin.

When the transformation had finished, the world blazed before me in a bold new pattern. Colours were muted, the moonlight no longer twinged with cool blue, the green of the trees no longer registering. Scent trails wafted across my nostrils, as distinct as though I were smelling the lines of a master painter.

Amidst the bird trails and rat pathways emerged two distinctly wolfish scents. Douglas' two finest warriors, skulking around Crookshollow forest. They passed this spot on the path only a few hours ago, while I was inside talking to Rosa.

Which meant they knew I'd return this way. They wanted me to know they were here.

I had no idea what had provoked them after all this time, but the Maclean pack were coming for me.

And that meant the beautiful Rosa Parker was in grave danger.

3

ROSA

*A*s I drove toward the village, I passed Margaret's cottage on the edge of the road. She was out by her letterbox (shaped like a squirrel, courtesy of the second husband), chatting to Caleb, who leaned over the handlebars of a monstrous bicycle. My heart flipped as I drove up to the road. He looked stunning with his tousled hair and his leather jacket pulling across his monstrous shoulders.

As I passed, I waved out the window. Margaret waved back. Caleb turned, and his eyes met mine. He flicked quickly away.

What's up with that?

He *deliberately* didn't acknowledge me. And he'd been so nice yesterday. I'd tossed and turned in the hard bed for hours last night, thinking about how nice he'd been and how naughty I wished I could be. I couldn't stop analysing the way I'd felt around him, and the sparks that flew when we touched. I'd kicked myself for keeping myself at a distance. I'd been wondering about heading to his cabin after I'd done my writing for the day and asking him out for a drink.

And he just ignored me? Why?

Maybe in the light of day, my dark skin was just too much.

Well, fuck him. *You hear that, Caleb Lowe. Fuck you.* I tapped the window angrily with my finger as the forest zoomed by around me. I was not going to let some guy get to me, even if he was a candidate for hottest guy of all time.

As my car sped into the village high street, I turned my attention to Crookshollow, trying to find a distraction from the disappointment welling up inside me. I'd read a little about the village on their tourism website after I rented the cabin, and it all matched what Caleb had talked about last night. According to poltergeist experts and ghost hunters, Crookshollow was the most haunted town in England. It was built on the crossroads of two key ley lines, which meant that throughout history, witches and vampires and other magical beings congregated on the town. That was, until witch hunters descended in droves in the 1700s and cleared the place out. More witches were burned in the town square here than any other town in Europe.

I drove down the high street past the very same town square, admiring the pride Crookshollow had in its sordid and spooky past. Crystal shops and tarot readers took pride of place in the row of shops, with window displays looking like something out of Diagon Alley. There was a bakery called *Bewitching Bites*, a haberdashery store called *Curtains & Curses* and, best of all, a tiny bookshop called *Spellbinding Books*.

I couldn't help but grin as I drove past a statue of a crooked old witch in the middle of the village greene. This place was ridiculous. I couldn't imagine a better setting from which to write my book.

Except ... I couldn't help but study the faces walking between the shops as I drove by. White, white, white. An ocean of grinning, happy white faces.

It doesn't mean it will be the same, I reminded myself, gripping the wheel harder. *It's just a function of English life, that small towns tended to be less diverse. You know that, you learned that in university.*

It doesn't mean it will be any different, either, my mind shot back. I glanced across to my rearview mirror. A pair of dark eyes ogled me back from a dark face. I was different, and every time I looked at a crowd of people like this, I was reminded of how different I was. I could never just forget, never blend in. And after what the white people of Old Garsmouth had done to me, the idea of being the same sickened me.

I saw the *Coles* sign up ahead. Groceries first, then I might stroll back along the main street and have a look for some things to brighten my cabin. *Maybe mosquito netting and fairy lights don't have to be just a dream.*

I turned into the parking lot and found a park near the front doors, so I could make a speedy getaway. Old habits die hard.

Inside, I quickly zoomed around with a trolley and picked up a few days' worth of supplies. Milk, bread, cheese, Jaffa Cakes, tonic water, lemons, salami, chicken ... down every aisle I walked, eyes burned in the back of my head.

White white white.

In the cheese section, two teenage girls were giggling and whispering to each other. They stopped abruptly and shuffled off when I approached. My face burned, and my heart started to pound against my chest.

You don't know if they were talking about you.

An older woman gave me a filthy look from over by the humus. Her scorn burned into my skin, another scar that I had to wear. I gripped the handles of my trolley so hard, my knuckles turned white, and started pushing it toward the counters. I couldn't remember my shopping list, or where I'd parked the car. All I could focus on was one single thought:

Get out before it happens again.

I joined a queue of people, all white, waiting for the register.

My whole body was tight and tense. I gasped for air, but it seemed as though my lungs had seized up. My chest ached. Fear coursed through me. *Please, don't let this happen today.*

I stared down at my trolley. The labels on the cans blurred together as the world spun out of control. My legs wobbled, and bile rose in my throat. I grabbed a Cadbury display shelf to steady myself, closed my eyes, and counted backwards, forcing myself to breathe slowly the way Nancy had taught me.

Not here. Don't break down here.

After a few moments, the panic attack had subsided enough that I could make a break for it. Luckily, my vision cleared enough to notice that at the rear was a self-checkout. I scanned my items, my chest burning, and raced out of the store without waiting for my receipt. I tossed the bags into the car and sank into the front seat. As soon as I slammed the doors shut and locked them, tears spilled down my face.

I'm supposed to be over this. I'm supposed to have moved on with my life.

I drew in deep breaths through my nose, releasing them slowly through my mouth. I reminded myself I was in a new town, far away from Old Garsmouth, and that people here weren't the same. I pulled out my mobile and punched in Nancy's number, my finger hovering over the call button. She'd said to call her if I needed to talk about anything.

You're just having a panic attack, Rosa, Nancy would say in her soothing voice. *It's perfectly normal after experiencing any kind of trauma.*

Well, I didn't want to be *perfectly normal*, thank you very much. I wanted to be the Rosa Parker who I was before Sam Seymour had walked into my life. But that wasn't possible. That woman burned up along with her house. But I could be the woman who was putting it all behind her, getting on with her new life. I wanted to be bold, but I didn't feel particularly bold right now. In fact, I felt pretty damn foolish.

Look at me, falling to pieces in a supermarket. This is ridiculous. I can do better than this.

After a few minutes of deep breathing, I felt calm enough to drive again. I shuffled through my playlist to find something upbeat. I had a really fun hip-hop list for just such an occasion. I was no longer in the mood for shopping, so instead I cranked the volume and took a scenic drive around the outskirts of the village, where several fine country homes sat back on luxurious sculpted grounds. I put my foot down, enjoying the way the grand houses flashed by.

Caleb's bike was no longer parked in front of Margaret's when I drove past again. Good. I couldn't handle another one of those cold stares.

I parked in my designated space, grabbed the bags and headed up the path toward my cabin. Having to make this trip every few days for food was sure going to keep me fit. I puffed along, the handles of my cloth shopping bags digging into my wrists.

After about half a mile, it dawned on me that I was been followed.

Twigs snapped in the woods, as though they were being trodden on by clumsy feet. My neck grew hot, as I sensed eyes watching it.

It's just one of the other cabin residents. You all use the same path to get in and out. You're bound to run into them occasionally. Stop making yourself crazy because you're hearing things—

Snap.

Okay, that really did sound like a footstep this time.

My fingers tightened around the handles of my bags. I wanted to get to my cabin, shut the door, and not talk to another person for at least a week. But my mother had taught me not to be rude. It's time I introduced myself to my stalker.

I stopped in my tracks, the burning sensation on the back of my neck intensifying. "Hello?" I called out, scanning the path for another person.

No one answered.

My heart pounded against my chest, the muscles tightening. My hands tingled, and the corners of my eyes were starting to blur. Shit, I was going to have another panic attack. I squared my shoulders and tried to force myself to remain calm. "Is anyone there?" I called out, making my voice as strong and confident as I could. "I'm from cabin three. It would be really nice to meet you, if you'd just come out."

From behind me, I heard a low growl.

I whirled around. There, sitting in the middle of the path, piercing eyes locked on mine, was a wolf.

I jumped. *That's not possible. There are no wolves in the United Kingdom. It must be someone's big dog off its lead.* I'd seen notices posted along the roadside warning about authorities cracking down on dogs in the forest. Maybe this was why.

The dog in front of me sure looked like a wolf. In the gloom of the forest, his creamy fur appeared to grow. A patch of brown fur ran across its forehead and down its spine, blending through to cream on its chest and legs. Pointed ears flattened back against its head. A long, bushy tail swung from between its hind legs.

But what held me frozen, mesmerised, was its mouth. Its jaw hung open, revealing rows and rows of razor-sharp teeth. The dog ground its teeth together as it growled at me.

Please don't let it be rabid. Please don't let—

"Nice doggie," I whimpered, fear clutching my chest. Rabid or not, if that dog jumped on me ... I wouldn't be able to over-power it. And I was miles from medical care. Blood roared in my ears, and I could feel the fear creeping through my body. The trees started to warp and wobble, the leaves blurring together as the dog's eyes burned into mine.

No, Rosa. Stay focused. Think. I was carrying raw meat in my shopping bag. That might even be what made it attack me in the first place. If I could just reach the package and throw it into the trees, that might distract the dog long enough I can run past and get to the cabin—

The dog growled again, baring its long, sharp teeth. Fuck, it really did look like a wolf.

From behind me, I heard another crunch, and a second growl joined the first.

Shit, there are two of them. How is this possible? Where are their owners? Don't tell me after everything I've gone through I'm going to die from a dog attack in the middle of a forest?

"Excuse me!" I yelled into the forest, as I slowly bent at my knees, setting my shopping bag down on the dirt and reaching inside, fumbling for the package of mince. "Is anyone out there who can hear me? Your dogs are here off their leads and they're about to attack me!"

Nothing. No one came running. It was just me and the two beasts. Great.

The wolf in front of me took a few steps forward. Panic rocketed through my body. My fingers closed around the package. I yanked it from the bag, and tossed it into the bushes on the side of the path.

"After it, boy!" I yelled. The dog lifted its snout toward the bushes, sniffed the air a couple of times, then turned back to me. He bared his teeth and gave me a long, terrifying growl. The dog behind me answered his growl with an even deeper, more guttural growl of his own. He sounded close, too close. They'd be on me in a moment. I'd have to take a chance and run—

Wait a second. What's going on?

The dog leaned back, raising itself up on its hind legs, revealing a lean, muscled body. The fur on the underside of his stomach was so light, it was practically white.

As I watched, frozen in fear and surprise, the dog's snout grew shorter, receding back into its face, its features flattening and widening. It kicked out its front legs, and the bones crunched as its limbs rearranged themselves, the elbows breaking and rejoining, the paws lengthening, the toes turning into long, thin fingers.

The grey hair retracted into the skin. The dog raised its forelegs and ran its new fingers over its face. I stared in horror. A man stood where the dog had been only a few moments before. He was naked, his tight muscles gleaming in the dappled sunlight. He was white, with short brown hair and a scar across his temple. His whole body was covered with tattoos, including an elaborate castle tower on his bicep, surrounded by the words VIRTUE MINE HONOUR.

The man glared at me with cold grey eyes, his mouth twisting into an ugly grin.

This can't be happening. This can't be real.

"Who the fuck are you?" I demanded, my fear registering as anger. From behind me, I heard another man chuckle. I whirled around, finally facing the second dog. Only, there was no second dog. Instead, another naked, muscled man advanced toward me, dark hair falling around his grinning face.

"That's not your concern, lass."

I whipped back to face the first dog-man, the one who had spoken. He had a strong Scottish accent and a deep, gravelly voice, the kind of voice that might be sexy if it wasn't coming from a guy who'd just transformed from a dog and who was staring at you like he wanted to eat you up.

"I'm nobody's lass," I shot back. "And I want to know why

you're following me, and why you won't let me past. Do you have something against women carrying groceries in the forest?"

I decided not to mention the whole "transformed from a dog into a human" thing, or the "running around naked in a secluded area" thing. Calling attention to these things seemed like a fine way of acknowledging that I believed them, and I wasn't quite ready for that.

Dog-man's gaze locked on mine. He stared me up and down, his tongue running across his lips like he was assessing a particularly juicy steak. "Aye, I can see why he chose you."

"*Who* chose me?" Suddenly, all my questions came tumbling out. "What's going on? Who are you? Where is the dog? Why are you wandering around the forest without clothes on? Are you some kind of new naked national-socialist group?"

"We ask the questions around here, girlie." The second man stepped even closer. I leapt away as he grabbed at me, backing up toward the trees. "Where is Caleb?"

The dog-men were after Caleb? The concept made even less sense than them being after me.

"I'm not his keeper," I said. "Try at his cabin or back at Margaret's house. Now, if that's all you need me for, I'll just be on my way."

Gulping back my fear, I took a step forward. The first man leapt in front of me, blocking my path with his huge, muscular body.

"You're coming with us, lassie," he said.

I can't believe this is happening.

"I don't think so." I balled my hands into fists. They weren't going to take me without a fight.

The second wolf grabbed my shoulder, his fingers digging into my flesh so hard I cried out. I swung my fist at his face, but he threw up his hand and blocked the punch easily, knocking me off-balance. As I reeled, he grabbed both my arms and pinned them behind my back.

My heart thundered against my chest. *This is bad. I have to—*

From out of the bushes, I saw a flash of grey and red fur. The first man leaned into me, his mouth open as though he was about to speak. His words turned into a yelp of pain as *another* giant dog crashed into him. The dog slammed my attacker against the ground, sinking its teeth into the man's shoulder. The man cried out, struggling against the dog's grip. But the dog held fast, each movement working his teeth deeper into the man's flesh.

"Get off, you stupid mutt!" The man growled, trying to throw off the dog. The second man dropped his grip on my arms, and dived into the fray. He grabbed the dog around the neck and tried to wrench its teeth free of his buddy's neck. This only made the teeth tear deeper. The man howled with agony, blood splattering down his toned chest.

Now's my chance. I knew I should be running as fast as I could back to Margaret's place, ready to call the police or the dog squad or the Avengers. But I couldn't tear my eyes away from the scene in front of me. As I watched, the two men changed; their bones snapping, their faces elongating, snouts growing from their noses, hair sprouting across their rippled chests. As they tumbled across the path in a vicious battle with the third dog, they were completely transformed from men into wild dogs.

How is this even possible?

The three dogs snapped their jaws at each other, rolling toward me in a tangle of limbs and tails and snarls. I backed away, grabbing my shopping bag handle and retreating backward down the path toward the parking lot, not wanting to take my eyes off the fight for a second.

The first dog, his creamy fur now stained by blood, let out an almighty whine as he tore his shoulder free. He and the other dog backed away, up to the edge of the path. The new dog snarled at them, gnashing his teeth and pushing them back, back into the trees. They snapped their jaws back at him, but their tails were lowered and they didn't attempt to regain any ground. The first dog had a large flap of flesh torn away from his shoulder, and he struggled to place weight on the corresponding foot.

The first dog let out one final, menacing growl, then turned on his heel and disappeared into the woods, his friend hot on his heels. The other dog gave a series of short, sharp barks, then backed away from the edge of the path and sat down. He stared up at me with icy blue eyes.

Why did that dog's eyes look so familiar? It was almost as though I'd seem them before. But that was impossible—

The dog started to change.

First, its ears shrunk, moving backward on its head. Its fur retracted into its body, revealing beautiful white skin covered with tattoos. Its legs bent at odd angles, the feet elongating to create a flat heel and sole that braced themselves against the dirt. Its muzzle collapsed inward, the doggish features disappearing, and a human face emerging instead. A very *familiar* human face.

It couldn't be ... but it was.

My head was spinning, my whole body trembling. Soon, I was going to pass out.

Through my blurred vision, the man's whole body came into view. Strong chin, tattoos across his chest – the curl of a tree branch stretching up across his neck – long red hair curling around his face, piercing blue eyes like razors digging into my soul.

"Caleb?"

Caleb crouched on the ground in front of me, squatting on

his bare feet, his legs parted and his nakedness very, *very* obvious.

Holy shit.

He broke my gaze for a moment, turning to the forest. "Get out of here!" he yelled into the trees. "She's under my protection, do you hear?"

He turned back to me, and stood up, giving me a full view of all his naked glory. Deep scratches covered his chest, one of them bleeding badly, smearing blood across his stomach and forearms. I opened my mouth to speak, but I couldn't make a sound. My legs wobbled. I couldn't believe what I'd just seen. What I was *still* seeing.

Caleb's hands gripped my shoulders. "Are you hurt? Did those bastards touch you at all, or mark you in any way?"

My knees buckled, and I sank to the ground amongst the strewn remains of my groceries. I couldn't process what I'd just seen. *None of this is possible. It's all some kind of dream. Any second now I'm going to wake up, and I'll be back in the cabin and I'll pour myself a glass of wine and laugh about what a fool I am for believing that I'd just seen Caleb ... seen him ...*

"What ... what *are* you?" I managed to choke out.

He looked up at me with those piercing blue eyes. "I guess I've got some explaining to do."

Those were the last words I heard before the dark, swirling void swallowed me up.

4

CALEB

"*R*osa! Rosa!"

Her eyes were glassy, unfocused. Her whole body had gone limp, and I thrust my hip out to catch her as she slumped to the ground. I laid her down in the dirt, cupping her soft face in my hand, trying to ignore the pull of our attraction as our skin touched.

Shit. What have those bastards done to her?

Her eyelids fluttered open. My heart stopped. "Wha ... what happened? I was dreaming and ..."

"Rosa, it's me, Caleb. You had a bit of a shock. I'll take you back to your cabin, and explain everything, I promise. Can you stand?"

"Yes ... no ... I think so."

Rosa was shaking as she stood up, gripping my arm for dear life. But when she hobbled around so she could see my face, her whole body shuddered. I offered a hand to help her. She swatted it away.

"Stay away from me," she snapped, her words barbs in my chest.

"I'm not here to hurt you." I held up my hands, showing her I was unarmed, and giving her a nice full-frontal while I was at it. It was always good to flaunt the body before telling someone that shapeshifters really existed. I found it helped people to have something decent to look at while their entire worldview was shattered. "I'll explain everything, I promise. We just need to get inside first."

"If what I just saw was true, you don't need to explain." Rosa narrowed her eyes at me, and staggered to her feet. "You turned into a dog, Caleb. Or was it a wolf?"

"It was a wolf."

"As in, a creature that isn't a human. A creature that isn't even supposed to exist in this country. And you fought those other two wolves."

"Yes, I did. Well, really I just fought off one of them. He was going to drag you away. The other one ... he just follows instructions."

"But why? What instructions? Why were they here at all? They said they were looking for you, and something about choosing."

"They know you're my—" I stopped myself just in time. *No, don't tell her yet. She's not ready.* She was still reeling from the attack, and from seeing what I really was, she didn't need to know about mating ... not just yet. I could explain it later, after we'd got to know each other a little better. Instead, I opted for a half-truth. "Because he's after me, and he believes he can get to me through you."

"Why?" Rosa scrambled after her groceries, her hands shaking so much she fumbled a block of butter four times before she managed to toss it back into her shopping bag.

"He probably saw us last night. He knows I like you. He thinks that if I see you're in danger, I'll obey him."

"Obey him in what?" Rosa's gaze was fixated on the ground,

very deliberately avoiding looking at me. It was annoying. I wished I could read her expression.

"In returning to Aberdeen, most likely." I grabbed her salami from where it had rolled to the edge of the path. "I think that's the last of it, unless you want to go hunt out that package of mince you threw into the trees."

"No, thank you."

"Then, let's go inside. You need to sit down and digest this. I'll fix us some tea. I promise I'll explain everything,"

"I'm not going anywhere until you tell me what I just saw! What the hell are you, Caleb?"

I sighed. Rosa Parker was one stubborn woman. "Fine. I'm a werewolf."

Her face pinched, like I'd just released some kind of toxic odour into the air. "I don't believe it. Werewolves don't exist. They're just characters in children's books and horror stories."

"You're a writer. You know better than anyone that all stories, no matter how impossible, contain a nugget of truth. Think about it. Think about what you just saw. Is there any other explanation that fits the facts of your own eyes?"

Rosa's eyes met mine, and I could see the fear there. "It's a trick," she whispered. "You're trying to play a cruel joke on me."

Her face had paled. For some reason, the idea of this all being a joke was more upsetting to her than the concept that I was a man who turned into a wolf. I wondered if that had something to do with what – or who – had hurt her, but now was definitely not the time to press.

"I swear to you that I am not tricking you." I lifted my arms, showing her the few strands of grey fur still peeking through my skin. "Sometimes they don't all retract properly. This is what I am, Rosa. It's what I've always been – a man and a wolf, sharing the same skin. There's nothing supernatural or horrible about it."

"Don't tell me that bullshit. Tonight's been pretty damn horrible."

"True. But if you come with me now, I promise you'll be safe. No other wolves will touch you now. You can trust me."

"Why should I trust you? You were so nice to me last night, and then this morning when I drove past Margaret's, I know you saw me."

"I did see you."

"Why did you act as though you'd looked right through me?"

I cringed. "Again, it's a long story. I was trying to protect you, dumb as it sounds."

"You're right. That does sound dumb."

"I smelled the two wolves on the path last night, when I was coming back from your cabin. I thought they might pull something like this, so I was going to try to keep my distance from you, to keep you safer. But when I saw your face, I felt like a fucking idiot for even trying it. I heard your car pull up and I was actually coming to apologise when I smelt Angus and Robbie."

"You *know* those guys?"

I sighed again. She was not going to like this. "They're my stepbrothers."

Big mistake. Rosa's eyes blazed, her whole body tensing again. "Figures. This is what I get for daring to think I could start over."

"I can explain everything."

She turned away from me. "Fine. Whatever. I've got vegetables to put away."

She stalked through the forest ahead of me, deliberately averting her gaze from my naked body. I wanted to make a joke about it, but judging by the set expression on her face, I knew it wasn't the best time.

When Rosa reached the cabin, she stomped across the porch, unlocked the door, walked inside and slammed the door shut behind her. I stopped myself before I slammed my face against the glass panel.

"Hey." I rapped against the window beside the door. "I'm still out here."

"I know that. Say what you need to say to me through the window." Rosa moved toward the kitchen, and started slamming her groceries down on the bench. Her hands were still shaking, but she managed to open the window a crack. "I'm not having you inside, not when you could turn into one of *them*."

"Could you at least throw me a towel or something? It's a little nippy out here and I'm afraid I'm not showing you my best angle."

The corners of Rosa's mouth tugged upward a little, but she didn't crack that gorgeous smile for me. She balled up the red duvet she'd spread over the bed, and shoved it through the door to me, slamming it shut behind her before I could get an arm through the gap.

I wrapped the duvet around my lower half, knotting the ends together. "Not quite the kilt I'm used to, but it's something."

"Don't try to be funny. This is serious. You're a werewolf. I was just attacked by two other werewolves. The werewolves that attacked me today – they're your stepbrothers, and they are after me to get to you for some reason that I'm sure to regret learning."

"That's an astute summary of the situation."

"I'm going to need more, Caleb. I'm going to need the full story." She slammed the kettle down on the stove, and turned on the gas.

"It's a pretty long story."

Rosa held up her cup and waved it at me. She folded her arms and leaned against the bench, one hip jutting out suggestively. "I'm listening."

I took a breath, trying to sort out what I should tell her. I decided to start at the beginning, with how I'd come to be in Crookshollow. "My werewolf family, the Lowe pack, originally came from Crookshollow. We're one of the reasons Crookshollow has the supernatural reputation it does – our pack has laid claim to this territory for hundreds of years. The pack lived in a cave deep in the forest, and they were the dominant wolf pack in this area. No other wolf dared to step over the boundary of the forest without permission of the Lowes. The last generation to live in that cave was my grandfather and grandmother, and their three sons."

"They lived in a cave? Did they spend all their time as wolves?"

"In those days, yes. It's dangerous to live in a populated area as a werewolf. As you've seen today, we're able to control when we shift. Most of the time, when I'm in my wolf form, I'm still me inside. I have the senses of the wolf, but the mind of a human."

"Most of the time?" Her eyes narrowed. "Does that mean you can lose control?"

I nodded. "When the full moon comes out, things are different. I can't control my shift. No matter where I am or what I'm doing I'll become a wolf, and I operate only on my wolfish instincts. I no longer have control. This is very important for you to know. When the full moon approaches, which is in about five days time, you can't be near me."

"I'm not sure I want to be near you now." The kettle whistled, and Rosa took it off the element, and prepared her drink.

"Fair enough. You want me to keep going? You're handling this okay so far?"

"I'm handling it just fine." Rosa sipped her tea.

"Right. So ... my grandmother lived in the village, and she worked at the post office, and sometimes she taught at the school. My grandfather did odd jobs sometimes, but it got harder and harder for him to find work as the villagers grew hostile."

"How come your grandmother didn't live in the cave? Wasn't she a werewolf?"

I shook my head. "Now we get into the bit where things get a little complicated. Very few women are fully-fledged were-wolves. It's a genetic trait that is dominant on the male genome. However, women are the carriers of the genes. A pack will only survive if the alpha wolf mates with a woman who has the correct genes."

"So you have to go around DNA-testing every potential part-ner?" Rosa rolled her eyes. "How romantic."

"Not exactly." A giant moth flew in front of my face and flapped its wings against the window. "We have ... a sense, I guess you could call it. When we're in the vicinity of a potential mate, we get a feeling. Our pheromones go into overdrive. Any wolf can immediately sense that a woman has the potential to be a mate." I paused, but decided to press on. "Sometimes, a wolf will meet a mate who is a perfect genetic match. The combination of their genes would produce the strongest wolves, and their love for each other forms the perfect bond – we call that a fated pair. Once they lay eyes on each other, they won't even be able to look at anyone else. It's very rare, but when it happens, it's magical. My grandparents were fated mates, and that's why Lowe blood is considered so pure."

"That sounds ridiculous."

A second moth joined his friend on the window, their wings overlapping. They fluttered in unison, climbing over each other in a scrabble of insect legs and wings. Grinning, I jabbed a finger at them. "These moths don't think so."

"Don't female moths eat the male after they've finished impregnation?"

"That's spiders. Female moths attract their mates by

excreting pheromones."

Rosa wrinkled her nose. "Who needs dinner and a movie when you have excretions."

"Don't knock it until you tried it. Our moth friends are certainly enjoying it."

"Can we get away from the moth porn and back to the subject at hand?"

"*Moth porn?*" I snorted with laughter. Through the window, Rosa cracked a smile too, which she quickly wiped away.

Her eyes darted to the moths again, and then settled back on my face. "Is this why you came to see me, Caleb? Because I'm carrying the werewolf gene and you can smell my excretions?"

"Oh yes. You're a carrier. To me, you are bloody irresistible, and not just because of that fine ass. Unfortunately, my brothers can sense it, too. I think that might be why they attacked you. But we're skipping ahead."

"Right, yes." Rosa took a huge gulp of her tea. "Let's keep things linear, just jumping around like a David Mitchell book."

"Where was I? Aye, so my family lived at the cave. However, many people in the town didn't appreciate their presence, and over time, the unease at having wolves nearby grew into all-out hostility. About fifty years ago, a vindictive priest decided to use that anger to establish his own position of power. He incited the townspeople to form an angry mob, and they came to the forest and killed my whole family."

Rosa lifted one perfectly manicured eyebrow.

"Or so they thought. My mother was mated to Amos Lowe, the eldest Lowe son. At the time of the attack, she was visiting her family in Crooks Crossing. She was carrying me inside her. She returned to find her mate and his whole family slaughtered. The Lowe pack was no more, which meant she had no protection. And you can't just walk into a hospital and give birth to a werewolf, if you get what I mean. She fled to Scotland, where she had some family, and she went in search of local were-wolves. Unfortunately, that put her in the line of sight for the Maclean clan."

"Clan? As in, a Scottish clan? Werewolves dancing around in tartan?"

"Not quite. The packs in Scotland like to affiliate themselves with the traditional Scottish clans. They like the battle cries and the family loyalty and shit." I turned my arm to show her the tattoo of a tower and the words *Virtue Mine Honour* across my bicep.

She gasped. "That wolf had the same tattoo."

"Yup. It's our clan heraldry."

"It all sounds very official."

"They like that, the legitimacy, the sense of history, but it's all a farce. The wolf clans are only as virtuous as their alphas. And in this case, my mother was mated again to Douglas Maclean, alpha of the Maclean clan, the most infamous pack of scoundrels and criminals in the north."

"You mean, like a gang?"

"Not *like* a gang, they *are* a gang, responsible for drug trafficking and violent crimes up and down the Scottish highlands. They're also the only family I know."

I watched her face carefully for a reaction. I was admitting that I was a criminal, part of an organised crime family. But Rosa didn't betray her thoughts. I pressed on.

"My mother Maria raised me with the other cubs as part of the Maclean pack, but Douglas never accepted me as his own. He had two other sons by his previous mate; Angus was five years older and the heir to the clan. He was even more brutal and dismissive of authority than his father, and of course, Douglas encouraged his crimes. Robbie was two years younger than me, and he was a bit slow at times. It took him a long time to understand his lessons, and he'd often muddle up instructions and numbers, which would mess up the business and make Douglas wild. Robbie was always trying to get the crime side of things right, desperate for the approval of his father and brother. I was desperate too, but not so desperate I wanted to hurt innocent people or rob already struggling farmers."

"You refused to do these things?" Rosa's eyes were wide.

"Mostly, and my mother would back me up. Every time, it made Douglas hate me a little bit more. But don't get to thinking I'm some kind of saint. I did a lot of shit for the Macleans that haunts me. By rights, I should be in jail by now. But I really didn't want to hurt anyone."

"Why didn't you just leave?"

"It's not that easy. Pack loyalty is paramount in shifter society. Leaving means basically becoming a traitor, an outcast. You won't get any help from another pack, and there's no pack in this country who would dare take in a wolf who ran away from the Macleans. If you desert your pack, you're on your own. We call these wolves *rogues,* and there are very few around, fewer still after an explosion here in Crookshollow killed several."

"What?"

I waved a hand. "That's another story for another time. It's not important right now."

"Explosions are usually important."

"Not this one, trust me. *Anyway,* eventually I did leave, about eight months ago. I read about an archaeological excavation going on in Crookshollow. It was a cave site, where some paintings had been found. It was my ancestral home. I couldn't stop thinking about it or looking at the picture in the paper. Maria wasn't interested when I told her about it. She said she wouldn't leave Douglas to go searching after ghosts. I think she knew I would go. I didn't have anything keeping me in Aberdeen, and I needed to see what the archaeologists had dug up about my family.

"So I came here, intending to re-enter the caves once the archaeologists were done and claim my own territory in the forest – the last surviving member of the Lowe pack. Having that kind of a legacy attached to my name – even as a rogue – would've been enough to help me re-establish some of my old family lands. I thought I might've been able to attract some other rogues to the area, and together we could form a new pack.

"But another wolf got here first – my cousin, Luke, although I didn't know that at the time. I thought he was just a rogue wolf looking to take advantage of the Lowe name attached to the caves. It turned out, Luke's father, Walter Lowe, had been over-looked when the village brutally murdered our family. He and I defeated another wolf that was bugging his mate, Anna, and together we established boundaries of our own pack – the Lowe pack, version 2.0. So far it's just the two of us in the whole of the Crookshollow forest. But Anna's pregnant, and we're open to other recruits."

"Right, fine. So I've got your entire family history. But that doesn't explain why your stepbrothers are here."

"The truth is, I don't know the answer to that yet. My guess is, Douglas has heard about the Lowe pack by now. He either wants me to come back to Scotland, or, more likely, he can't bear the insult of having me establish another pack, and wants to fight me to the death."

"And me?"

I nodded. "That's my fault. I've put you in the middle of this. They saw me with you, and now they think they can use you to force my hand. I won't let them do it. I'll protect you."

"This is nuts. I didn't ask for this." Rosa set her cup down. Her hands gripped the side of the bench so tight her knuckles turned white.

"No, you didn't." I flashed her my grin. "Look at it this way. It'll give you lots of fodder for that novel."

"I already have quite enough inspiration, thank you."

"I bet Hemingway wished he was targeted by vengeful werewolves."

"Hemingway blew his brains out," Rosa said. "I don't really want to make him a role model."

"Right."

"He's also white, and a man. You could pick a different writer. Or do you only read books written by old, white men?"

Whoah. Where did *that* come from? "It was just an example. Look, I don't really want to argue about writers with you through the window, especially since that's not the pressing issue here, and you're a writer so I am totally going to lose. And I *really* hate losing. Can I come in now?"

"No."

"It's going to be difficult to keep you safe if I'm stuck out here. Not impossible, just more difficult." I flexed my arm muscles. "I'm up for the challenge."

Rosa gave me an odd look. "You're really going to sit out there all night and keep watch?"

I pulled out the chair at the porch table and sat down, wrapping the duvet around my shoulders. "Yup."

Her eyes softened. She opened and closed her mouth a couple of times, and moved toward the door. I stood up, letting the duvet drop to the floor. *She's going to let me in. She's decided to trust me. I'm finally making some progress with this girl. I'm finally—*

Rosa opened the door a crack. I took a step toward her, but she shoved something out to me. A cold cheese-and-onion sandwich.

"Enjoy your dinner," she said, and slammed the door shut again.

5

ROSA

*T*rue to his word, Caleb stayed outside the door, keeping guard all night long.

I knew this because I did not sleep for the entire night. I spent a couple of hours in front of my computer, agonising over the first three sentences of my novel and trying to pretend I wasn't sneaking a look outside at him every few minutes.

The first time I looked out at him, I noticed he'd transformed into his wolf. I guessed his fur – the beautiful grey pelt with a line of fiery red fur along his back – was warmer than the duvet.

Each time I glanced over, there was his grey body with the flash of red, turned away from the window, the ears pricked back, eyes alert for movement in the night.

I couldn't work with him sitting out there staring like that. I shut down the computer, went to the bathroom (where Caleb sat outside the door. It took me twenty minutes just to do my business because I was trying so hard not to make any noise he could hear). I came back into the cabin and went to bed, where I tossed and turned for hours, my mind whirring over everything Caleb had told me.

I met a werewolf. An actual *werewolf*. He rescued me from two other werewolves who were trying to kidnap me in order to force him to do something he doesn't even know what yet, for some shapeshifter gang that's apparently been operating for years without ever hitting the news.

Now this selfsame werewolf was outside my door, standing guard like a watchdog ... wait, that was probably the wrong analogy.

And the reason these wolves were after me was because I was a mate. I had wolfish genes. I almost wasn't surprised. My mother always said I had a wild streak.

If only she knew.

Actually, *did* she know? Did my mother have these genes, too? I'd never met my father. She'd told me he was a vacuum cleaner salesman she'd met in the bar she worked at, and he'd been charming, but forgettable, but was that a lie? Could he be a werewolf, too? I mean, *vacuum cleaner salesman? Really?*

Don't think about it. Go to sleep.

But I couldn't. Every time I closed my eyes, I saw those two wolves circling me, their teeth bared, their bodies poised to attack. My heart pounded in my chest, and my eyes flew open again, checking every corner of the room for glowing eyes.

My gaze fell on Caleb's sleek, wolfish visage – a silhouette in the moonlight, just visible through the kitchen window. Just seeing him there made my heart beat faster, but in a good way. My personal protector. It was kind of cool, actually.

I can't believe you just thought that. This is a serious situation. You are literally the female lead in a horror film right now. And you may have the sexy werewolf guarding the door right now, but all he needs is for the baddies to feed him a poisoned donut and then you're really in trouble.

You wanted something different from Old Garsmouth. Well, you got it.

My gaze fluttered across to the window again. Caleb stalked along the front porch, on a circuit of the cabin, then sat down in front of the window again, his long tongue panting against his teeth. As beautiful as his wolf form was, I kept remembering the taut muscles of human Caleb as he slammed into his brother. Goddamn, he was sexy. And funny, too. And nice. I mean, he *seemed* nice. I guess I didn't really know him, but he was standing outside protecting me. He didn't push me to invite him inside. That seemed pretty nice to me.

I *wanted* to invite Caleb inside, to beg him to protect me from a much closer proximity. But that would be foolish. And I was done doing foolish things for now.

It's nice of Caleb to stay with me. He doesn't have to do this. And the way he flirts with me …

Don't be ridiculous. He's not interested, and even if he was, you're not interested in him. He's white, and you know that's a recipe for disaster. Not to mention the whole werewolf thing. He thinks you have this gene, that you could be a potential mate. But that's ridiculous … whoever heard of a black werewolf …

I'm so confused … so tired … and I can't sleep …

My eyes fluttered open. Daylight streamed through the tiny window above the desk. My sheets were balled up around my torso. I'd been asleep, probably for hours.

I rubbed my eyes, adjusting to the sudden influx of light. A shadow moved across the end of the bed. A man, completely naked, stood over me, holding a square object in front of my face. A bomb? A weapon?

My heart leapt into my throat. I tried to scream, but I was still half asleep. All that came out was a frightened squeak.

"Ah," Caleb's voice said. "You're awake."

It's just Caleb. Relief flooded my body, along with another feeling I was going to do my best to ignore. I sat up, ready to admonish him for coming inside the cabin, but he pressed a warm mug of tea into my hands. He sure knew his way to an English girl's heart.

"What time is it?" I fumbled for my mobile.

"About ten," Caleb said, giving me that sexy grin. "I heard you tossing about last night, so I thought I'd let you sleep late. I figured you could do with it."

"Yeah ..." My eyes adjusted to the bright sunlight, and Caleb's naked body came fully into view. He wasn't even wearing the duvet. My gaze flickered over his lean figure, the elaborate tattoos dancing across his chest, the taut muscles of his thighs, the V of his abs leading down to ... to ...

Oh god. It was *huge*. He was hung like ... like an animal. My stomach churned. I was only two minutes into my resolution to ignore my desire for him, and already it was a raging failure.

"You like what you see?" Caleb's voice snapped me out of my trance. My face flushed with heat. *Oh crap,* he saw me looking. And he was half hard. *Oh crap, oh crap.*

Thinking fast, I threw a pillow at him. He caught it easily, damn him. "You're disgusting. How did you get inside?"

"The window above the desk was unlatched. You're a bit shit at this whole hiding-out-and-keeping-safe thing."

"I haven't had much practice." I sipped my tea. He'd made it perfectly, damn and god bless him.

"Luckily, you have me." Caleb sat on the edge of the bed, his thigh brushing against mine. The touch of his skin sent an electric shiver through my whole body. Why, why did he make me feel like this? Was it just my genes reacting to his pheromones? Was this just nature's way of trying to make me have his strong, sexy wolf babies?

I rubbed my head. These thoughts were going to give me a migraine. "Yeah, *lucky*. Lucky to be a prisoner in my own cabin with two homicidal werewolves on my tail. Lucky is exactly what I'd call myself right now."

He tossed the pillow back at me. I grabbed it before it knocked over my tea.

"They're not *homicidal*, technically. They're just in the market for a kidnapping."

"That makes me feel so much better." I finished my tea, feeling more alert already. "What do I do now? Are they still after me?"

Caleb nodded. "Yeah. Robbie's outside right now, hiding in the trees. I don't think he'll attack – he's just keeping watch, making sure we don't leave the area, waiting for me to leave you alone so they can strike."

"If it's you they really want, why don't they just try *talking* to you, like normal, non-homicidal people."

"Because they ken I wouldn't care about what they had to say. I think it's best if I move in here. I'll be able to keep an eye out for you."

"You're kidding."

"I am not kidding. If I let you out of my sight for a moment, those two are going to pounce on you."

"But ... but you can't move in here!" I gestured at the space. "It's barely big enough for one person! Where would you sleep?"

I can't have him in here. I'll never get any work done if an enormous, gorgeous wolf man is doing pull-ups on the door frame and bringing me cups of tea and sliding his hands all over my body—

"We'll top and tail." Caleb swung his leg up onto the bed beside me, his toes facing me, as if to demonstrate. Now his whole leg was pressed up against mine, sending another pulse of delight straight to my core. His crotch was open in front of me again. My eyes landed immediately between his legs, and my cheeks burned.

"That's not happening."

Caleb lifted one eyebrow. "... You have a better idea?"

This is ridiculous. We can't do this. I'm not going to last a day.

"Damn right I have a better idea. You can sleep in your own cabin."

"Only if you come with me." His face turned serious, his eyes boring into mine. "I don't want to tell you what to do, Rosa, but if my brothers get their hands on you, I can't promise you'll remain in one piece. The Macleans are basically the werewolf mafia. They won't hesitate to hurt you if they think it will get them what they want from me."

I gritted my teeth. I didn't want Caleb here, in my space, being all gorgeous and distracting while I was trying to write my book. But with the werewolf mafia involved ... an image of his brother's bared teeth flashed before me. I shuddered.

"Fine. I guess we're roommates." *I am so going to regret this. But at least I'll be alive to regret it.* Caleb started to say something, but I cut him off. "We're *just* roommates. And I have a few rules."

"Lay it on me."

"One, you have to wear clothes while you're in your human form. Duvets and towels don't count."

"You're going to deprive yourself of all this?" Caleb gestured to his body. My stomach flipped as my eye travelled along his sculpted chest.

"I know it will be tough for me, but I'll live," I said sarcastically, although I was a little sad about it. I patted the pillow he'd placed on the bed. Pouting, he arranged it over his crotch.

"Number two, you have to be quiet. No talking at all during the hours of nine and three."

"A strange rule, but sure, whatever."

"It's not strange. I came to Crookshollow to write this book. Why did you think I chose a cabin in the middle of the woods? Did you think I have a fetish for cockroaches and malfunctioning plumbing? I wanted a quiet place to work, away from people, *especially* away from white men. So far, you and your werewolf family have robbed me of a day of productive writing. That won't happen again."

"Fine. I'll be as quiet as a mouse. Any more rules?"

I jabbed my finger at the overstuffed chintz chair in front of the fire. "Yep. You're sleeping in that chair."

Caleb looked incensed. "No way. That thing is like sitting on a cactus. I'd rather sleep on the floor."

"That works for me, too." I shoved his leg off the side of the bed.

Caleb made a face. "Can't we share the bed? I promise I won't hog the blankets."

"That's not going to happen, so get it out of your head, wolf-boy."

"Is that all the rules?" Caleb gave me a wicked grin. "Will you discipline me if I disobey?"

I sighed. "I need breakfast."

"Ah, now that I can help with." Caleb swept off the bed and practically skipped to the kitchen. "One breakfast, coming up!"

After a breakfast of bacon sandwiches made by Caleb – and after I made Caleb chip the burnt bacon off the top of the toaster – I walked with my wolf protector over to his cabin so he could collect some of his things.

Caleb travelled in his wolf form, so he could quickly dart into the trees if one of Margaret's other residents walked past. I kept staring at his glossy red and grey coat, unable to believe it was really Caleb beneath that fur.

Inside his cabin, Caleb transformed into his human form again. His naked body moved through the cluttered space, collecting up clothes and supplies into a black backpack. The place was identical to mine, except that there was a hideous chaise-lounge instead of the chintz chair, and Caleb's kitchen was a mess of dirty dishes and buzzing flies.

I sat on the edge of his bed and waited, my nostrils breathing in the heady scent of him that clung to the cabin. An image of Caleb's naked legs dangling over the side of my bed danced across my vision.

How am I going to survive with this guy living in my space? How are we not going to end up in bed together – an event that, as much as my body wants to deny it, would be a bad, bad idea?

I was just going to have to be strong. Strong and bold, like Nancy said.

"All set." Caleb slung the rucksack over his shoulder. He was wearing dark jeans and a brown work shirt that made his hair look even more red and wild.

"Won't you need your mattress?" I pointed to the thin mattress sitting on his bed.

"What for?"

"For sleeping on. The floor is going to be pretty uncomfortable without it."

"I'm still hoping I'll be able to convince you to share the bed." He raised on eyebrow, and flashed me that wicked grin. "Kidding. I'll abide by your rules. I just don't plan on doing much sleeping."

"That's awfully presumptuous of you."

"'Presumption' is my middle name."

"Bring the mattress." I folded my hands across my chest, hoping he didn't see my nipples standing out through the fabric of my shirt.

Caleb shook his head. "Joking aside, I don't think you understand that I really don't need the mattress. I can't let my guard down for a moment. If I go to sleep, I'll be leaving you vulnerable."

I couldn't believe this. He'd known me for exactly two days, and he was going to forgo sleep just to protect me. A lump rose in my throat. I'd never had anyone try to protect me before.

There were so many times when I'd wished I had someone who I could count on, a friend who would tell the bullies to fuck right off. When all the white kids threw their fruit at me at the fancy school my mother had scrimped and saved to send me to. When a random guy at the pub punched me and called me a stupid black slag because I wouldn't go home with him. When Debbie Seymour and Susan and all their cronies attacked me in the local press, and everyone in town ignored me or talked about me behind my back ...

I'd always been alone – the one black girl in an ocean of white. I couldn't walk into a room without immediately knowing I was different, and that I was considered *lesser than*, just because of the colour of my skin. My skin was a weapon to be used against me, and I had no one on my side. And yet here was Caleb. How easily he had stepped into the role of my friend, my protector, and I had let him.

I didn't want to believe this, didn't want to trust that I was this lucky. But I couldn't help the surge of hope welling up inside me, a feeling that this time had nothing to do with how hot he was.

You're going to get hurt so bad, girl.

"Rosa ... hey, Rosa?" Caleb waved his hand in front of my face. I blinked. He must have been waiting for me to say something.

"I was just ... concerned about you not sleeping. All creatures, even ..." My voice caught on the word. "Werewolves ... need to sleep."

"I can get by on a few hours, until Luke gets here."

"Who?"

Caleb held up his mobile. "I've sent a message to my cousin, informing him of the situation. He's going to take the first flight back from New York. I just have to survive until he gets here, and then the two of us can take turns protecting you. We may be a small pack, but we look after our own."

Great, there was going to be two of them in my cabin.

"I'm not one of you, though. And I've never met this Luke."

"You're in this, babe, which means you're one of us. You're part of the pack, as far as I'm concerned."

Part of the pack. I'd never been a part of anything before, unless I counted the Women's Society at university, but those girls were way too intense for me. They wanted to protest something new every week, but I didn't want my face all over the school newspaper. That would've made it even less likely I'd find friends. I dropped out of the Women's Society after one semester.

"And you'll like Luke," Caleb was saying. "He reads a lot, mostly science fiction. Just don't get him started on Heinlein, or you won't get any sleep, either. Right." Caleb patted the bag on his shoulder. "Let's go."

Back at my place, Caleb dumped his rucksack beside my bed, and arranged his cans of beans and stew on the bench in the kitchen. I watched him move around my tiny cabin, his things making a mark on the space that was supposed to be just mine. For some reason, it didn't make me nearly as upset as I'd expected it to. In fact, seeing his bag on the floor and his razor on the windowsill beside my toothpaste was kind of ... exciting.

Caleb glanced at his watch. "You'd better get to work, if you want to get a few hours of writing in before I'm allowed to talk your ear off again."

"Like that's going to happen."

"I promised, remember?" Caleb held his fingers to his lips. "As quiet as a mouse. Just pretend I'm not here."

Right, sure. How was I going to pretend an enormous, delicious man wasn't at this very moment occupying my very tiny cabin?

"Fine." I sat down at my desk, and flipped open my laptop. Caleb flopped down on the bed, one leg crossed casually over his bent knee. He pulled out his phone, turned it sideways, and opened some loud, shooting game.

I turned back to my computer, taking a few deep breaths and trying to force out all the weird conflicting feelings swirling around in my head. This wasn't what I imagined when I dreamed about my writing cabin in the woods – that right behind me the world's hottest man would be playing some obnoxious, beeping game on his phone. But I had come here to write, and if I didn't get started, that meant the werewolves – and by extension, all of Old Garsmouth – had won.

And *that* wasn't an option.

I opened my novel file, and placed my fingers over the keys. I sucked in a deep breath, and closed my eyes, taking myself back to Old Garsmouth, to the night I drove around the corner of my street and saw the sky alight with orange flame as my precious house burned down with my beloved Lennox inside ...

"Yeehaw!" Caleb whooped from behind me.

"Could you keep it down, just a little?" I snapped, my fingers frozen over the keys. "Some of us are trying to work."

Caleb grunted a reply. I gritted my teeth, and forced my fingers to type a sentence, just to prove that I could do it.

As Nellie stared into the orange flames engulfing her house, her heart stopped.

There. It wasn't exactly Pulitzer material, but I could edit it later. I'd started. I was doing this.

My fingers started to move faster. With just a few sentences I was back there, back in that horrible place where the local paper had run stories about how I was going to hell, where people spat on me in the street, where I'd watched the giant plume of smoke devour the little cottage I'd worked so hard to buy.

> *A firefighter emerged from the blaze, carrying Nellie's beloved kitten, Lennox, folded in his arms. His protective jacket had fallen open, and the moonlight glinted from his sculpted and tattooed chest. Nellie couldn't help but wonder what it would feel like to run her hands over*

No, no, no. I deleted the last paragraph. That wasn't the story I was writing. There wasn't a sexy kitten-saving firefighter, or a hot best friend waiting to swoop in and rescue the heroine. She had to do all the rescuing herself. That was the *whole point.* That was the story I was destined to tell.

Dammit. Caleb was getting inside my head more than I realised.

I forced my way through the rest of the scene, recalling all the details of the fire, and adding in a crowd that stood at the end of the street, jeering and hurling racial abuse. I had to delete a second paragraph where the hot fireman showed up again and threatened to blast them with his hose if they didn't go away. But apart from that small diversion, my fingers flew over the keys, and the world outside faded away as the words tumbled out.

This was it. This was exactly what I wanted. My rustic writing cabin in the woods, where I could be completely alone with my characters.

"Take that, you filthy space pirates!"

Alone, that is, except for my roguishly handsome werewolf protector.

Sometime later, I emerged from Nellie's world, brought back

by the smell of something hot and delicious happening behind me. A plate clattered on the desk beside me.

"Dinner, ma'am," Caleb intoned in a posh voice. I peered at my plate. He'd presented me with a perfectly seared steak, a side of crispy-skinned garlic potatoes, and steamed green beans. Beside the plate, he'd placed a glass of red wine.

"It's dinnertime already?" I rubbed my eyes. Outside the window, it was already dark. No wonder I was having trouble reading the screen.

"Oh yes. You've barely lifted your head all day." He grinned. "I tried to interrupt you to give you a cup of tea, and you grunted at me."

"I didn't!" I had no recollection of that.

"You did. A very sexy little grunt it was, too. I've been debating whether to interrupt you for the last ten minutes, but I figure even Stephen King himself has to stop for dinner."

My first instinct was to admonish him for choosing yet another old, white, male writer. But the smell of the food wafted across my nostrils, and my stomach rumbled. "This looks delicious," I said, turning around to accept the glass of wine he handed me.

As I did, my eyes caught the scene in the kitchen. It was a bomb site. Oil stains splattered across the element. Dirty dishes were stacked on both sides of the sink. There were garlic peelings scattered across the floor, and a giant smear of ... something ... up the wall and across the ceiling.

"What happened?" I cried out. How had all this chaos ensued and I hadn't even *noticed?*

Caleb glanced over his shoulder at the carnage. He shrugged. "I'll clean up," he said, as if it was no big deal.

"That's right." I bit into a potato. "You will."

Caleb held out his own glass of wine. "To new roommates, and sexy grunts."

Oh, for Chrissake. "To new roommates, and not getting my throat torn out by the werewolf mafia."

We clinked glasses, and I couldn't help but smile as I watched Caleb eat with gusto, balancing his plate on his enormous thigh and gulping at his wine like he'd just come out of the desert.

I hadn't smiled this much since ... well, since Sam started paying attention to me. Ever since, my life had spiralled into a nightmare worthy of a literary novel, which, funnily enough, was exactly what I was writing.

Nancy hated my novel idea. "I'd rather see you write something that lifted you up," she said, twirling her pen through the ends of her hair. Nancy's hair was similar to mine, but somehow she managed to make the ringlets bounce and glisten. Mine was just a giant frizzy mess. I wanted to ask her for tips, but ours wasn't a relationship where I was allowed to ask questions, not even about hairdressing. "Do you really want to dwell in the horror of what happened? Do you think that fulfilling your revenge fantasies on paper will give you closure? You're incredibly funny, Rosa. Funny and clever. Why don't you write a comedy?"

I'd scoffed at the idea, but now the conversation came back to me. Why *didn't* I write a comedy?

Because the first rule of writing was 'Write what you know,' and there was nothing funny about someone burning down my house because my skin was a different colour. And now I could add "wanted by the werewolf mafia" to that list.

Despite the absurdity and very real danger of my current situation, I was actually enjoying Caleb's company, especially all our flirting. The flirting had been the fun part about being with Sam, too – him stopping by the office under some pretence, leaning over my desk, his bright green eyes dancing as he complimented my dress or casually discussed what he'd like to do to me when we next had the chance to share a hotel room.

It had been so much fun to feel adored, until it all went horrifically wrong. Until I found out who he was – the town mayor, a man with a wife and two young girls at home.

But Caleb's not the mayor. He doesn't seem to have any family apart from this cousin. So far, everything he's told you has turned out to be true.

Caleb was exactly the kind of guy I would fall for ... if only he wasn't white. I couldn't go through that again. It didn't matter that he was different from Sam. It mattered that I couldn't deal with anything like that right now, and probably never again.

While Caleb bustled around, dumping dishes in the sink and wiping furiously at the walls, I leaned back in the uncomfortable chair with a book. I was just settling into the latest Colson Whitehead novel, when my phone beeped.

I picked it up, expecting to see my mother's name flash across the screen. I didn't get many messages these days.

Instead, the SMS had come from an unknown number. I opened it up.

I know who you are, you black bitch. He won't protect you forever.

My phone clattered from my hand. Blood rushed to my head, and my dry tongue froze to the roof of my mouth. How had the werewolves got my phone number?

"What happened?" Caleb was at my side in an instant. "Rosa, answer me!"

I know who you are, you black bitch ... black bitch ...

"It's nothing." I passed him the phone. "Your werewolf friends sent me this text."

Caleb's face changed, his expression darkening as his eyes flicked over the message. "Those fucking bastards," he hissed.

"It's fine, Caleb. I'll just ignore it. I'm used to it—" This was the third phone I'd had since the fire. The Old Garsmouth lynching mob were pretty adamant that they would force me to leave however they could, and Susan never had any problem passing out my personal details.

But Caleb was already calling the number. "It just clicked straight to voicemail," he said. He snarled into the phone. "Listen, Angus, you son of a bitch. I already said I wasn't going to be part of your stupid fucking turf war any longer. If you lay a finger on Rosa, neither you, nor Douglas, nor the entire fuckin' Maclean clan will be safe. Don't fucking contact this number again."

He hung up, and dropped the phone on the table. "There. That should stop them."

I reached out and grabbed his arm. When my skin met his, the strange zinging pulse darted through my veins. "Thank you," I said, my voice cracking. Tears sprung in the corners of my eyes. I looked away, blinking rapidly. I wasn't going to cry. That was stupid. All Caleb had done was leave a screaming message on someone's phone. That's all. If anything, he was overreacting. The message wasn't even that offensive, when compared with some of the insults others had thrown at me.

It was just him, sticking up for me, trying to protect me. I'd always had to look out for myself, and I'd never known until I'd met him how good it felt to have someone I could count on, someone who believed I was worth fighting for.

"Hey, don't mention it." Caleb's voice was hoarse, gravelly. He leaned forward, his face only inches from mine. His cheekbones stood out in high relief, sharp enough to cut glass. "Rosa, you okay in there?"

The urge to kiss him overtook me. I forgot everything, who

he really was, what he was doing here, my promise to never go for a white guy again. *Be bold,* Nancy's voice echoed in my head.

I leaned forward, pressing my lips against his.

He responded immediately, pressing himself against me. He took control, teasing my lips apart, slipping his tongue inside mine. Fire leapt through my veins as the electricity that had been dragging us together for the last two days shot a fully-fledged jolt right through my system.

Caleb's hands reached up, his fingers tangling in my hair. I ran my own hands across his cheeks, deepening the kiss as I explored the beautiful structure of his face. His skin seemed to sizzle under my touch, as though the strange energy had wrapped itself tight around us, binding us together.

Caleb's hands moved down my shoulders, over my arms, his fingers brushing the edges of my breasts. I moaned against his tongue as my body flared with heat, leaning forward so he could—

"Yoohoo." Someone rapped on the door. "Anyone inside?"

Caleb and I sprung apart. His knee banged the desk, and my wineglass toppled over the side, crashing to the floor. Red wine sloshed across the wood.

"I'll clean this up," Caleb mumbled, grabbing for a sponge. I nodded, my heart pounding against my chest. "You get the door."

"Yoooooowhoooo, Rosa?" Ruth tapped her nails against the window.

"Hi, Ruth." I flung open the door, my cheeks burning with heat. How much had she seen through the window? "Wh-wh-what brings you out here at this time of the night?"

"I hope it's not too late in the evening, but I like to walk in the forest when the nights are warm like this. I was going to drop your mail in the box, but then I saw your light on and thought I'd just deliver it in person and see how you were getting on." She held up a couple of letters and a book catalogue.

"Oh, I'm great. Thanks." I took the mail from her, noticing my lawyer's letterhead on one of the envelopes. *It could be about the investigation.*

"You're welcome, dear. Hello, Caleb." She gave him a wave.

"Hey, Margaret." Caleb smiled back. "It will be a couple of days before I can get to the wood-cutting, I'm sorry. I've had some other work come up."

"That's fine, dear." Margaret grabbed the doorframe. "I'll be on my way then."

"No!" I dropped the letters on my laptop, slamming down the lid. If Margaret went, I'd have to face Caleb, and that kiss ... and since I was clearly out of mind to even consider it, I needed time to work up the fortitude to refuse him. "I mean, why don't you stay for a glass of wine? Caleb and I were just talking about Crookshollow's history. Some of the legends about this place are just crazy. I'm sure you know a few."

Caleb looked at me, his blue eyes blazing. I didn't blame him – his kiss still burned on my lips, and I wanted nothing more than to pick up where we'd left off, when it was about to become something more ... but Margaret's arrival had shocked me out of my stupor. I had to resist, before we took things too far. I couldn't believe I was inviting a chaperone to keep us off each other, but I needed the distraction. The energy still hummed through my veins. I couldn't trust myself to be alone with him right now.

"Oh, alright then." Margaret settled herself into the chair by the fire. "How about I'll tell you about my fourth husband, god rest him, who used to be the caretaker for a vampire."

"Sounds perfect," I said, handing Margaret a glass of wine. I thought for a moment, then poured myself another glass, and raised it to my lips. Across the room, Caleb's eyes burned into mine, his mouth a silent question. *Why?*

I'm sorry, Caleb, but this is for your own good. I know you can sense some werewolf pheromone on me, and it's making you think with your dick instead of your head. But you and I, we're too different. We're never going to work, and the sooner you realise it, the better off we'll both be.

I believed that, truly. But as Margaret chattered on and Caleb's eyes bore into me from across the room, an incredible sadness washed over me. Why was it that the things I wanted most were always things that could never be?

6
___

CALEB

*I*t was II p.m., an empty bottle of wine, six pots of tea, and thirty-five rambling stories about Margaret's various late husbands before we finally had the place to ourselves again. The moment Rosa and I shared earlier had well and truly passed.

I didn't want it to pass. I'd had one taste of her, and I wanted *more*. All evening, I'd had to keep a magazine open in my lap so Margaret wouldn't notice just how much I wanted more of Rosa. Those ruby lips slid so forcefully over mine. Her skin against me made my whole body surge with energy. I'd never felt like that about any woman before, ever.

You kissed me, I tried to send my questions to her. *Why did you change your mind? It can't have been the kiss. That was one damn impressive kiss. Was it because of whatever happened back in your old village?*

The door clattered shut. Rosa was back from brushing her teeth in the bathroom. She rearranged her toiletries on the windowsill to make more room for mine. I decided to just come out and ask her. "Rosa—"

"I don't want to talk about it." She kept her face down, deliberately not looking at me. A lock of her hair flopped over her face, and my fingers itched to brush it away and feel the electricity of her skin once more.

"But—"

"Please." Rosa looked up then, and I could see her eyes were filled with pain. "Just let's go to sleep and forget it ever happened."

Why? Why do we have to forget? I don't want to ever forget anything about you, Rosa Parker. But I could tell something had her freaked, and that now was not the time to ask, so I shrugged and gave her my best attempt at a smile. "Sure. Whatever."

Rosa crawled into bed and made a big show of pulling off her clothes and putting on an old t-shirt while under the covers. My cock throbbed as I finished the washing up and pretended I wasn't watching her.

Fine. She said she wanted to forget it. Well, I'd give her something to forget. Grinning at her, I peeled my clothes off, giving her a full view of exactly how much I wanted her. "This is how much I don't want to forget," I growled.

"Goodnight, Caleb," she said, flicking out the light. Her eyes gleamed at me through the darkness, reflecting the light of the moon. "Thanks for everything."

"Babe, you ain't seen nothing yet." I transformed into my wolf, and went to take up my spot by the door.

It wasn't long before Rosa was making adorable snoring sounds. I sat on the kitchen bench, looking out into the forest, at the dappled moonlight splashed across the porch. I could see why Margaret liked to walk around at night, although I'd have to talk to her in the morning about not doing that in future, lest one of my stepbrothers decide they need a snack.

Something moved at the edge of the trees. I sat up, scanning the area, my nose prickling. I couldn't smell much through the window, but I pressed my nose against the glass, and the faintest scent wafted across my nose.

Robbie.

I'd recognise my youngest stepbrother's scent anywhere. Growing up, I'd always tried to befriend Robbie, but he idolised Angus, even though Angus was mean to him about his learning difficulties. He followed his brother everywhere, fetching whatever Angus wanted, bringing him the choicest cuts of meat, giving Angus his favourite toys even though Angus would just break them. Robbie always took Angus' side, *always,* even when I could tell he disagreed. Later, as Angus got deeper into the family business, Robbie became his errand boy, always putting his ass on the line to help Angus score his next deal or win turf from the Bairds.

Now he was here, watching me for Angus, still doing the dirty work.

I know you're out there, I sent the thought out. Werewolves communicated telepathically with each other while we were in wolf form. It enabled us to still articulate human thoughts along with our wolf signals and body language. *I'm not going to let you take her, so you might as well go home.*

Caleb. Robbie's thought appeared in my mind, the words dripping with malice. *Come outside, and we can talk.*

We can talk just fine right here. What do you want, Robbie? Why did you come all the way to Crookshollow and try to kidnap Rosa?

You have to come back to us. Dad needs you.

No, he doesn't.

Dad doesn't want us to take no for an answer. He told Angus to use whatever force was necessary. Things will be easier for you if you just come with us. We won't hurt the girl, we promise.

No can do.

She's your fated mate, isn't she? There's this really intense smell from her that—

That's none of your business. I'm no longer part of your pack.

You haven't yet claimed her. Angus wants her. He wants to claim her for his own.

Rage bubbled inside me. Angus would be able to sense my connection to Rosa, but clearly he didn't care. It was considered highly offensive in shifter society to attempt to go after another wolf's mate, especially a fated mate. Granted, I'd done it to Luke in the beginning, when I'd first smelt Anna's scent. She wasn't my type at all, but I was so desperate to establish a pack and I didn't exactly have much to lose. I gave up as soon as I figured out Luke was family.

Granted, I hadn't claimed Rosa as my own yet, but that shouldn't matter. If anyone else in the Maclean pack tried to take another's fated mate, they'd feel the sting of Douglas' teeth in their back. Even gangsters have their standards.

But Douglas had said *by any means necessary*, and it seemed Angus was taking that to heart. Angus had to have the best of everything. If my mother gave me a treat, or a special toy, Angus would make me give it to him, or break it or hide it. I was never allowed to have anything of my own. And now he was trying to take Rosa, the one bright spark that had come into my life.

I damn well wasn't giving up Rosa to these pricks.

She's mine, I growled, baring my teeth.

Not for much longer, was his reply.

Is this what you're stooping to, now? Is Douglas really so desperate he'd let Angus piss all over his rules just to get me to return? Why does he need me so much, anyway? I'm only one wolf. What possible difference can I make?

The Bairds have taken your mother.

I sucked in a breath. *Shit.* My mother Maria – Aberdeen

university librarian and matriarch of the Maclean clan – was one powerful hostage. I hoped like hell she was all right. The whole thing sounded very odd. I'd had dealings with Irvine Baird, the young alpha in charge of the Baird clan, and kidnapping seemed out of character. He was shrewd and level-headed, and this seemed like a move of desperation more than anything.

At least I knew the Bairds would pay for this. Douglas may have been a scoundrel with no love for me, but he did love my mother with all the ferocity he possessed, and he would make them bleed for this offence.

So go and fight them and get her back. I still don't see why he needs me.

They want an exchange. You for her.

That made no sense whatsoever. What on earth did the Bairds want with me? I was nobody important – the forgotten adopted child of their biggest rival. I wasn't an heir, nor did I have a particular knack for being a criminal mastermind, nor was I privy to any of the secret details of Douglas' crime empire. And if they really wanted *me*, why didn't Irvine Baird just come and get me himself? Something didn't add up here.

Why? Why do they want me? They've never shown any interest in me before.

Dunno. Robbie pawed the ground. *Dad has no idea, either. But he doesn't have any choice. We either show up with you, or they're gonna start sending chunks of her back to us until we comply. He can't just go in and get her. You leaving has destabilised his power. Wolves Dad thought he could count on are nowhere to be found. He doesn't think he has the numbers to stand up to the Bairds.*

I had no idea my leaving would have such a huge impact.

It's the precedent you set. Now everyone thinks it's okay to walk out on Douglas Maclean, or kidnap his mate. Dad has to show them all it's not okay.

Has he ever thought about not treating his pack like shit? That might get the desired effect and I'd never have to see his face again.

This isn't time for jokes. Your mother's life is at stake here.

Oh, no, I completely agree. We passed the jokes portion the moment you threatened Rosa. My mother will be fine. She's tough, and the Bairds won't hurt her if they need something from me. Irvine know me better than that. Tell him to come down here if he wants to talk to me so badly.

He says that's not an option.

Then you're on your own. Douglas needs to sort his own shit out. When I left, I left for good.

Robbie sighed. *I know you don't believe this, but I'm not actually here to fight you. I'm giving you this one chance, Caleb. Come back to your family, and we'll leave the girl in one piece.*

You want me to go back to committing all manner of crimes in Douglas' name, and Rosa becomes Angus' broodmare? That's not a deal, Robbie. It is a fucking joke.

Robbie sighed, a strange sound coming from a wolf. *Have it your way. Don't say I didn't try.*

With that, he turned and stalked off into the night.

I stayed by the window, staring after him, replaying the conversation over in my head. Something about it was very odd – odder than the fact the Bairds had taken my mother in order to get to me – and it took me a few minutes to realise what it was.

Robbie had come here alone, and tried to bargain with me. Clearly, he was shit at it, but the fact was that he'd tried to solve this thing without bloodshed. Angus would never have bothered trying. His motto was, "Bite first, ask questions never."

Everything Robbie had said ... *"I'm giving you this chance ... "* implied that he was offering me this boon of his own accord. That meant Angus didn't know he was here. Which was ... odd.

Robbie never did anything unless his father or Angus told him to. He wasn't exactly known for his lateral thinking skills.

The fact that he *was* here, bargaining with me, was completely out of character.

Was my younger stepbrother finally stepping out on his own? Did he have a different idea of how a pack should be run?

More importantly, was my mother okay? And what in the world did the Baird clan want with *me?*

7

ROSA

I can't take it anymore.

For three hours, I'd stared at the ceiling, trying not to listen to Caleb moving around the cabin and growling out the window. Every time his claws tapped against the wooden floor or his powerful silhouette passed in front of the window, I replayed our kiss over in my head. The way his hands were all over me ... the warmth of his tongue wrapping around mine ... the way he made my whole body hum with energy ...

I couldn't sleep knowing the possibility of another kiss like that was out there, and I wasn't taking advantage of it. As the minutes and hours ticked by, my protests grew smaller and sillier.

Desperate for a distraction, I leaned over to grab my glass of water. In the dark, my hand missed the glass and knocked off a stack of books. They clattered to the floor, the sound like gunshots in the silent cabin.

Caleb was by my side in a flash, his wet nose nuzzling my hand. His fur felt so soft and warm.

"I'm fine," I said, patting his head. "It was just the books."

Caleb leaned his head against the bed, his mouth open

slightly, revealing rows of sharp teeth. He panted, his big blue eyes staring into mine. I stroked the top of his head, scratching between the ears, the way I knew dogs loved. *I can't believe I'm patting a wolf. A real live werewolf.*

It's not too late. You can still back out. Just tell him to go back to his post, and—

Nope. Three hours of staring at the light fixture on the ceiling had convinced me that whatever I felt for Caleb, it wasn't going to go away by just ignoring it. Maybe it was a stupid idea to be with him, but it certainly wasn't the first stupid idea I'd ever had. Plus, as a writer, I had to seek out new experiences. And being with a guy like Caleb ... that definitely fell into the "new experiences" category.

"Caleb." My throat caught on his name. I coughed, and tried again. "Caleb, why don't you change into your human form?"

He lifted his head, staring at me with wide eyes. *Why?* he seemed to be asking me.

I lifted the edge of the duvet with shaking hands, and patted the sheet beside me. *I can't believe I'm doing this.* "You can guard me just as well from in here."

Caleb's eyes locked with mine. I swore I saw the corners of his mouth turn up into a grin.

My heart pounded. *I shouldn't be doing this. I shouldn't be doing this ...*

But the ache between my legs had a mind of its own. My body was screaming for attention that only Caleb could give me.

The wolf's face contorted, the fur falling away, revealing tone, muscled limbs. A few moments later, a very naked Caleb was crouched beside the bed, his icy eyes locked on mine. "Are you sure about this?" he asked.

"I've been staring at that light fitting for three hours, thinking about you. Yes, I'm sure."

Caleb stood up and swung his body on to the bed, straddling me. The weight of him against me lit my whole body up. His hardness pressed up against my legs. I ran my hand over his shoulder, surprised to find the skin smooth, no sign of a bite.

"Angus bit you when you fought, didn't he?"

Caleb nodded. "Our bodies heal fast. It's one of the benefits of having these particular genes."

"I'm not looking for a genetics lesson right now."

"Then what are you looking for?"

"You."

"I thought you'd never ask," he said, grinning.

His lips locked with mine, and all thoughts of dissent flew from me. Fire spread through my body, flaring in my veins and between my legs. He forced my lips apart with his knee, and his tongue wrapped around mine, exploring my mouth. He tasted hot and earthy.

Caleb leaned me back against the bed, his fingers cupping my cheeks. I ran my hands across his naked skin, admiring the tautness of his muscles, the vivid colours of his beautiful tattoos. Between our bodies, sparks flew.

Our kiss deepened, our tongues searching out each other's mouths, hungry for each other. His hands cupped my neck, fingers in my hair as he held my head against his.

Caleb grabbed the edges of my shirt, his hands locked in a war with the fabric. His eyes blazed. "You sure you want this?" he whispered against my lips. "Because I'm damn close to losing control here."

"I want this," I told him, firmly. "Bring it on, werewolf."

Caleb tore my t-shirt, the fabric ripping up the seams. He flung the scrap away, and stared down at my body. "God, you're so fucking beautiful."

The words replayed over and over in my mind. No one had ever said that to me before. *Ever.* And the way he was staring at me, biting his lip like he was trying to resist taking a bite out of me ... hot damn.

He cupped one of my breasts in his hand, lifting it slightly, his fingers gliding over my skin, leaving trails of heat in their wake. His light skin contrasted against my dark tone, looking at once strange and also beautiful.

Caleb bent his head down. His tongue circled my nipple, sending a shiver straight to my core. I arched my head back. Oh, but that felt *good*.

He sucked and swirled until the little bud stood as hard as a rock, then moved to the other one. His eyes remained locked on mine the whole time, watching my enjoyment. Every time I moaned, he sucked harder, sending me closer to the edge.

Just when I didn't think I could take anymore, Caleb dragged his tongue from my nipple, slowly trailing a wet line across my stomach. He kissed the flesh above my panties, trailing his fingers lightly over me through the fabric. I moaned as he hooked his fingers under the fabric and tugged them down.

His tongue trailed across my thigh, getting closer, closer ... his fingers made circles on my skin, making all my hairs stand on end. I lifted my thighs, driving my ache toward him, but still he continued to touch and stroke me everywhere except where I wanted him most.

"Stop teasing me, wolf," I moaned. "Get down to business, or I'm kicking you out of this bed."

Caleb gave me his widest, most stubborn grin. Then he buried his face between my thighs, his tongue lapping expertly at my clit. The heat from our joining bodies consumed me, as though my veins pulsed with liquid nitrogen.

His tongue darted in all directions, changing rhythm every few strokes. It drove me wild in a matter of minutes. I gripped the sheets as he continued to lick and swirl relentlessly. One hand snaked up and twisted my nipple, sending a sharp pain through my chest that only enhanced the pleasure his mouth was giving me.

His eyes burned into mine, the pleasure on his face increasing as he pushed me closer. He was loving this as much as I was. Knowing that he wanted to watch me made this even more intense, more erotic.

Caleb pressed his finger inside me, curling it back to stroke me in time with his tongue. He lapped faster, building up a pounding ache inside me, a wild animal clawing at my stomach, bursting to be free.

My body tensed. Heat rushed to my face as the orgasm tore through me. My limbs went slack. My vision blurred. Red stars danced across the ceiling. Whole worlds were born and died inside the celestial wave of pleasure that washed through my body.

Oh. My. God. That was amazing. Sam never made me feel like this.

Hang on, why am I thinking about Sam when I have this incredible, sexy werewolf in my bed?

Caleb leaned over me, his self-satisfied grin a mile wide. Just this once, it was pretty damn justified. "How was that, then?"

"It was okay," I croaked out, reaching up to stroke his cheek.

"Just okay?" He tilted his head to the side. "That was a lot of screaming you did for it being 'just okay.'"

"I screamed?" I had no recollection of doing that. I'd *never* done that.

"Oh yes. Good thing we're in the forest, or we'd have noise control restrictions to contend with."

"If your head gets any bigger, it will fall off your shoulders."

"Luckily, I've got you here to catch it." Caleb stroked my cheek. "I just want to make you happy. Are you happy?"

"I don't know if I can move my arms." I grinned up at him. "You were watching me the whole time."

"Doesn't everyone watch?"

I shook my head.

"That doesn't make sense to me. I need to see your reactions. I want to watch you writhe, your lips open slightly, your eyelids flutter. I need that, need to know I'm doing something right." His eyes clouded over for a moment, and his grin slipped a little. But then he was back, the same old cheeky, sexy Caleb.

"You're doing everything right," I whispered.

"Good. I need this, Rosa. I need you. I've been alone for so long."

Desire welled inside me again. I wanted more of this, more of him, and I didn't think I just meant in my bed. But while I had him here ... I leapt at Caleb, grabbing his shoulders and sending him reeling backwards. Before he could protest, I climbed on top of him. "You're not the only one who needs this," I said, as I grabbed a condom from my wallet beside the bed and slid it over him. Caleb tensed as my fingers stroked him, his cock jerking in my hands. I grabbed his shoulders, and forced myself down on his shaft.

I was so slick and wet from my orgasm that his huge length slid inside me with one single stroke. I sighed as I filled up with him, our bodies becoming one.

I rose up on my knees, drawing myself up along his whole length, before slamming my body back down, grinding him deep inside me. Caleb grabbed my thighs, his forearm muscles tightening as he controlled my movements, gliding his glorious cock up inside me as I slammed my pelvis down against him. I struggled to hold his shoulders as we bucked against the bed, my breath coming out in short, sharp gasps.

This was unlike any sex I'd had before. This was wild, primal, *wolfish*. I wasn't lying back, letting the man take control. Instead, I was on top, forcing him to go harder, faster, deeper.

And the way Caleb was looking at me, his eyes heavy with lust, I could tell he was loving every minute of it.

I rode him hard, and he rose to the challenge, reaching up to stroke my breasts as he slammed his cock inside me. The bed creaked dangerously as he pounded against me.

The ache inside me swelled again, leaping through my limbs, rising right through my body and pounding against my skull. My pleasure roared in my ears, a beast that could not be tamed. I dug my fingers into Caleb's shoulders as a second orgasm tore through me, the ache becoming a roaring fire as it burned me up in his arms.

When I could focus on Caleb again, his face was tight with concentration, his jaw set in a determined line. His hands gripped me hard, and I could feel his muscles tensing. He was close. I grinned down at him. "Come for me, Caleb," I cried, surprised at myself. I sounded like some movie harlot, and I loved it.

His eyes grew wide, and he clenched his jaw as a shudder rocketed through his body. Inside of me, his cock tensed, jerking as he came.

Caleb's face relaxed, and his grip on me softened. He collapsed back against the pillows, and I collapsed against him, my body spent. He wrapped one strong arm over my shoulders, his fingers tracing circles on my back. Delicious shivers followed the trail of his touch.

"That was ..." he huffed, squeezing my shoulders.

"Yeah." I leaned my cheek against his shoulder, draping my arm across him, my dark skin standing out against his tattooed chest. We looked like we fit together.

So *that* was sex with a werewolf. Apparently, I had no idea what I'd been missing.

8

CALEB

*R*osa's eyelids fluttered shut, and in minutes she was snoring on my shoulder, a thin line of drool extending from her mouth onto my chest. That was totally adorable.

This woman is amazing. I can't believe she's mine.

My own eyelids grew heavy, but I couldn't allow myself to sleep. That's exactly what Angus and Robbie were waiting for. I wondered if Robbie was still outside, peering in the window at us. If so, we'd given him one *hell* of a show.

I stared at the ceiling, counting the nails in the timber frame, and thought about how bloody lucky I was.

I'd never expected to find my mate. Many werewolves went their whole life without meeting theirs. It was pretty hard to date women when I had to constantly hide in the wilderness in case I accidentally bit them. I'd fucked a lot of girls, had a lot of fun, meaningless sex, but I never stuck around afterward. I'd never actually wanted to talk to those girls. This ... *this* was something else.

Now that I had Rosa, I wanted nothing else but to be with her constantly. At least, thanks to my stepbrothers, I was able to do just that. I just wished it wasn't at the expense of a price on her head, or my mother's head.

I hope you're okay out there, Mum. I knew she couldn't hear my thoughts over this distance, but I hoped all the same. *I know you're tough, but whatever the Bairds are planning, it's not gonna be good. I'll find a way to get out of this, I promise you.*

Moonlight streamed across the bed through the curtain-less window. Now that all the sexual tension had been released from my body, the wolf within me itched against my skin. The full moon was only three nights away. Would I be able to remain by her side in my full wolf form, or would I be a danger to her without my human emotions? When I lived with the Macleans, we always stayed away from humans during the full moon shift, even mates, with good reason. Once, Robbie was late back from a drop in Aberdeen, and he got caught on the road during his shift, crashed his bike into a tree, and nearly devoured the kind old couple who stopped to help him. Douglas had to go threaten the couple so they wouldn't talk to the press.

Harsh, yes, but that was the reality in a werewolf gang. It was a pretty lonely existence, especially if your pack didn't accept you.

My mother wasn't even safe around us. She kept a small flat near the university in Aberdeen where she and the other mates would stay during the moon. But then, she wasn't Douglas' fated mate. She was a widow with a werewolf cub, and he was a powerful alpha whose previous mate had been killed in a gang fight. He needed a woman by his side to maintain his power. Their marriage was a bond for survival, for both of them.

So I had no way of knowing what would happen to Rosa when the full moon took me, and I had to find out soon, because I couldn't exactly leave Rosa alone while I answered the call of nature.

This was the kind of question I wished I could ask my father.

But of course, I didn't have a father. Never really did. I wasn't even born when he died, and Douglas treated me more like a thorn in his paw than a son.

Luke will be here today, and Anna is his fated mate. I can ask him then, when Rosa isn't listening, of course.

I glanced down at Rosa, wondering again if I should tell her that she was my fated mate. It would be better for her to have all the information, especially if my stepbrothers got their hands on her.

They won't get her. I won't allow it.

I remembered the hurt in her eyes when I'd asked her about her cat; whenever she talked about her previous life. I knew someone had cut her so deep, she didn't know how to heal. Telling her we were destined to be together was *not* the way to heal her. It would send her running faster than a wolf in heat.

I clutched Rosa tighter. That was the last thing I wanted.

The sun rose, and the pull of the moon faded a little. It was always easier to ignore it during the day. I slid my body out from beneath Rosa, leaving her to sleep while I grilled bacon and made eggs in the tiny kitchen. As I was cracking the eggs into a bowl, one slipped through my fingers and splattered on the floor, half of the sticky insides going all over my bare foot.

Screwing my face up as egg ran through my toes, I stepped back, right onto Rosa's shirt that I'd thrown across the floor last night in what now turned out to be a very misguided gesture of passion.

My other foot flew out from beneath me, and I went down. I landed hard on my ass on the floor. As I was still holding the egg carton at the time, it popped open. I watched three eggs sail in the air above my head before all three crashed down around me, splattering their wobbly contents across the floor.

I hope Rosa didn't see that.

Behind me, someone clapped slowly. I whirled around. Rosa

was sitting up in bed, grinning that wild grin of hers. Her hair stuck out in all angles from her head, like some kind of voodoo goddess. She'd seen every glorious moment. Of course she had.

"Breakfast *and* a show." She smiled sleepily as I picked myself up.

"Eat quickly." I handed her the one intact plate of food, and started to mop up the mess. "We need to go pick up Luke from the airport."

"Did he bring Anna?" Rosa asked, her eyes widening. She forked a huge piece of bacon into her mouth and chewed. "I would love to get another woman's take on dating a werewolf."

"Are we dating, are we?"

Rosa's face reddened. She put down her plate, and stared at her hands. "That wasn't what I meant to say," she mumbled.

"No taking it back now. We can be dating, if you like."

She shook her head. "No, we can't. Don't get me wrong, Caleb. Last night was ... well, you know what it was. But I can't be with anyone right now, least of all a shapeshifting werewolf."

Disappointment surged through me. I thought that after last night – which she had initiated, much to my surprise and delight – we'd be able to move onto something more serious, and she'd be able to open up to me about her problems, and then maybe I could tell her about us. But it appeared I'd misjudged the situation.

You let me into your bed, Rosa, and it was fucking amazing. Why won't you let me into your heart?

"Okay, fine." I shrugged, making my face impassive, trying not to let her see that I was hurt. "Whatever you want. Fuck buddies, then. Isn't that what the kids are calling it these days?"

"I prefer, 'It's complicated.'" Rosa picked up her plate again and took another huge bite.

Complicated was right. I'd finally met the woman of my dreams, but she didn't want to be with me.

AFTER BREAKFAST, we walked down the forest path to Rosa's car. I kept my nose in the air the entire way, parsing the nocturnal activities from the scent paths in the air.

"Are they still here?" Rosa whispered, her hand seeking out mine.

"Robbie is," I whispered back, squeezing her hand. "He's about fifty metres behind us, in the trees. Don't turn around and look at him, though. I don't think he'll attack us, not by himself. But I don't want him to know we know he's there. Let him think I'm an idiot; it makes things much easier for us."

The conversation I'd had with Robbie replayed over in my head as Rosa drove us out of Crookshollow toward London. The more I thought on it, the more certain I was that he was making that offer of his own accord. What had made him do that? It was so completely out of character for my little stepbrother. Was he trying to stand up to Angus?

London was a nightmare, as usual. We hit the M25 during a huge traffic jam. My wolf blood bubbled beneath my veins. It hated being trapped in a car like this, hemmed in on all sides by people honking and shouting. Someone tried to cut in front of us, and I growled out the window so ferociously he pulled right back in again.

Rosa patted my knee. "Down, boy. We're not far away."

"I fucking hate London," I growled.

"Newsflash – everyone on this motorway hates London. Now, come on. We're going to see your brother. That's exciting, isn't it?" She turned down the off-ramp toward Heathrow and immediately slammed on her brakes as she joined a long line of traffic.

"We should've made him rent a car and come up to us."

"Now, now. Wolves who behave get a treat at the end of the

day," Rosa cooed, her hand snaking up my knee, between my legs, stroking me through the thick fabric.

Oh, fuck. Just the feel of her hand made me hard. "Shouldn't you concentrate on driving?"

"We're not going anywhere." With one hand, Rosa undid the zipper and took out my cock. She wrapped her hand around it, swirling her finger around the tip, collecting the pre-cum that had already leaked out. She used that to lubricate her hand as she stroked me slowly, taking her time as she inched the car forward a few feet.

This is so fucking hot. All those fools sitting in their cars around us, no idea that the hottest fucking lass in the world was giving me a handjob right beside them.

"The light's green," I moaned, as the car behind us honked loudly.

"Fuck!" Rosa let go of me and drove through the lights, rounding another corner and then we were back to idling behind another long line of traffic turning into the Heathrow carpark. "Where was I?"

"Your hand was on my cock and you were—" Words failed me as she wrapped those long fingers around my shaft and continued her slow, steady rhythm, watching the road carefully as we crept up to the lot. Her grip never faltered, and the steady rhythm sent heat rushing all through my body.

Rosa pulled into a park and turned the car off. "Now you can have my full attention." She grinned, bending down. Her lips wrapped around my head, sliding down my shaft as she took all of me into her mouth. She felt hot and wet and so, *so* good.

I gripped the car seat as she worked me like an expert, applying just the right amount of pressure, her hand working my shaft while her tongue circled my head. She changed her grip, drawing me right back into her throat. Her hair bounced up and down as she sucked me right back, and I could feel the warmth of her mouth all around me.

Her wild hair bobbed up and down in my lap, obscuring my view of her. I kept my eyes straight ahead, trying to keep up the pretence I was just one of them, not the luckiest guy in the world, getting a blowjob in the middle of the Heathrow carpark. People wheeled their luggage and chased after their children in front of our car, completely oblivious.

This was the hottest thing I'd ever experienced.

The heat in my body rushed towards my cock. My muscles tensed, my stomach sank.

"Rosa ... Rosa, I'm about to—" She increased the pressure in her hand, and let out a little mewling sound in the back of her throat. It was too much. I groaned as I came in her mouth, shuddering as a wave of pleasure coursed through my veins.

"Rosa," I moaned, my hand falling against her hair. That was the best head I'd ever had. Hands down, no contest.

She sat up, wiping the edge of her mouth with a tissue from the dispenser on the dashboard. She'd swallowed everything.

"Hopefully now you'll have at least one good memory of London traffic," she said, grinning.

"Get in the back," I growled.

"But why—"

"I want you. Right now."

"What about your cousin?"

"He can wait. Get in the back." My cock was already getting hard again, just thinking about her naked and writhing beneath me on the backseat.

"Don't be silly." She opened her door and swung her luscious legs out of the car. "We don't want to keep Luke waiting."

"Rosa—" The word came out more whiny than I'd intended.

"Chop chop!" She was already trotting across the parking lot, smoothing down her maxi dress over her gorgeous ass.

"You—" I frantically zipped up my pants and scrambled out of the car after her. Rosa laughed as she darted away from me. "You devil woman!"

"Keep up, wolf-boy!" Rosa yelled from over by the pay machines. I heard her deep, thundering laugh, and it made me break out into an enormous smile. I raced after her, not wanting to let her out of my sight for a second.

Now that I've found a girl more awesome than I ever dreamed of, I'm not about to let her get away, even if she doesn't realise it herself yet.

Even though the airport was insanely crowded, and foreign elbows kept finding their way into my ribcage, and a family was walking at a snail's pace in front of us with not one but *three* bawling children, I didn't even care. It was as though I was walking through a fluffy cloud. That's what being with Rosa did to me.

We only had to wait twenty minutes at the arrivals gate before I saw Luke running toward us, a small rucksack slung over his shoulder. He was wearing a Yale University sweatshirt, and his dark hair was pulled up beneath a Yale baseball cap.

"You getting a cut of the Yale merchandise, bro?" I asked as we did that macho-half-hug-back-pat thing.

He grinned. "Anna, of course. She's pretty excited about being at an Ivy League university. Try to tell her there is anything outside of Yale, and you'll wish you'd never opened your mouth. I think our baby is going to come out singing the Bulldogs' fight song."

"How far along is she?"

"Five months, thirteen days, seventeen cases of extra spicy chorizo, which she eats with peanut butter." Luke wrinkled his nose.

"I've heard that if a pregnant woman craves spicy food, you're more likely to have a boy," Rosa piped up. That was just the right thing to say to Luke. He beamed, and stretched out his hand to greet her.

"This is Rosa Parker," I said. "We're ..." I wanted to tell my brother what she was, but I couldn't, not in front of Rosa, not when she wasn't even comfortable with the title of "girlfriend." "... my friend. She's the one I need your help to guard."

"Nice to meet you." Luke shook her hand. "Let's get back to Crookshollow. I'm dying to see the old haunt again. You can tell me more about your wolf problem in the car. How are the caves?"

"They're still there, but unfortunately, so are the archaeologists." Luke had left me responsible for keeping watch over our ancestral home. So far, I'd marked several of our territorial boundaries around the forest, but I hadn't been able to get near the caves again. The archaeologists who'd found the cave paintings that caused me to come to Crookshollow in the first place were convinced that more important Neolithic treasures lay buried inside. I patrolled the area as best I could. So far, no other wolves had come to challenge our rights to the area.

"They'll leave at the end of the summer, when the season finishes," Luke said. "Then we'll have the place to ourselves. Anna and I are going to come back when the baby's born, and have a naming ceremony on the site. I'm hoping Clara will perform it for us."

"I'm sure she'd love to." Clara was an old witch who ran a crystal and witchcraft shop on the Crookshollow high street. She made all sorts of potions and pills to help werewolves manage their shifts, and she'd helped Luke identify the mysterious black wolf that was terrorising his Anna. I'd been visiting her regularly since I came to Crookshollow, and was even friendly with her two fox-shifter sons, Ryan and Marcus.

During the ride back to Crookshollow, Luke sat in front. I wanted to tell him what Rosa and I had done on that seat, but it seemed a rude thing to do to a jet-lagged man who'd just travelled halfway around the world to help us out. In between arguing about which radio station to listen to (Luke liked drum 'n bass, I wanted heavy metal), I filled him in on the situation with the Maclean pack and Angus and Robbie's attack. Rosa kept her eyes on the road. Her hands gripped the wheel a little tighter when I mentioned my stepbrothers' plan.

"Why do these Bairds want you, cousin?" Luke's brow creased.

I shrugged. "Beats me. Part of me wants to go and find out, but most of me suspects it's a trap."

"Will your mother be safe with them?"

"I think so. Dead hostages make for very poor bargaining power." As I said it, a shiver ran through my body. I hoped like hell I was right.

Maybe I should go, just to check she's okay …

No. That's exactly what they all expect you to do. They did this exactly because they know she's your weak spot. Not anymore. Mum will be fine. I'm not part of the pack any longer, so it's not my problem.

I'm sure I'm right. I just have to live with myself if I'm not.

We pulled in at Margaret's place and parked up. Luke hopped out of the car and breathed deeply. "It's so good to be back in the forest again," he said. "I could hug a tree, I've missed them so much."

"Isn't the Yale campus famous for its trees?"

"Oh, sure. The famous Yale trees. Every tree has several volumes of history written about it, where some famous poet has written a sonnet about the leaves, or a famous person sneezed on it." Luke patted the trunk of an oak. "I've been desperate for some good old fashioned humble British trees. No celebrity spittle here."

I sniffed the air as we walked back along the path. Angus' scent was thick. He was somewhere close, which made me nervous. Robbie I could handle – he talked tough, but I was confident I could easily overpower him if it came down to a fight. Angus was a whole different breed of wolf. He was born and bred to take over as pack alpha upon Douglas' death, and he had no problem using cruelty to get what he wanted. I didn't want him anywhere near Rosa.

"Walk quickly," I said, pushing Rosa between Luke and I. She stared up at me with a terrified expression, but I didn't elaborate. We took off at a trot, flying down the path as fast as we could while staying close together. Angus' scent wafted through the air, sending my nerves on edge. From Luke's grim expression, I could tell he smelt it, too.

Thankfully, Angus didn't show himself, and we made it to the cabin without any kind of incident.

Rosa unlocked the cabin, and practically dived inside. She slumped down in her desk chair, rubbing her arms, where goosebumps had raised on her skin. Luke and I piled in after her, and I shut and bolted the door.

"I can feel his eyes on me." Rosa's lip quivered. When her eyes met mine, I could see the fear there. I went to embrace her, but she held up a hand, telling me to stay away.

Okay, fine. Hugs are a boyfriend thing, I get it. Instead, I folded my arms across my chest, and made my face impassive.

"He didn't attack, at least. I suspect Luke's presence made him think twice."

"We'll get the bastards," Luke said. "No one touches my cousin's ma—"

I shot him a desperate look, and his eyes glinted with recognition. He broke down into a hideous coughing fit, covering up the rest of his sentence.

What a goon, but it seemed to work. Rosa didn't seem to

notice what he'd almost said. Luke stopped coughing, and gave me a look that clearly said, *We'll talk later.*

"I can see Caleb's been cooking." Luke pointed to the coating of mashed potatoes and egg bits caked to the wall.

"I resent that," I said. "I've been feeding Rosa extremely well. Haven't I, Rosa?"

"I never said you wouldn't. You cook some of the fluffiest pancakes I've ever eaten. It would just be great if you didn't coat every surface in crap while you're playing Master Chef."

"It's great to see you again, little cousin," I growled, pushing him towards the door. "Don't be a stranger now."

Rosa laughed her beautiful deep laugh, breaking the tension in the room. I relaxed, letting go of Luke's arm, and gave him a pat on the shoulder. It really *was* great to see him again.

When Luke and I first met, we were both used to being alone. Luke and his dad had lived as recluses in different forests all over Europe. He spent most of his life avoiding contact with the outside world, and I'd spent most of mine trying to hide from my stepfather and brothers. When we first met, we didn't exactly trust each other. In fact, I was ready to fight him for Anna, his mate. I'm glad I didn't, because Anna was lovely and all, but Rosa was something else.

I'd only just got used to calling Luke *family,* and talking to him about the future of our pack, and then he went off to the US and left me alone again. I didn't realise it until I'd seen him again today, but ever since he'd left, I'd been feeling lonely.

"I can see I'm going to have my hands full with both of you," Rosa said.

"First things first." Luke pointed at the bed. "Caleb, go to sleep."

"Don't be ridiculous. You're not taking the next watch. You must be jet-lagged to hell—"

"No buts." Luke turned to Rosa, who had picked up her notebook from the table, and was scribbling down something. "When was the last time he slept?"

"He's been awake for the last two days, at least," Rosa said, not looking up from her writing.

"I'm not tired—"

"Bed, now. No arguments." Luke crossed his arms. "You're no good for any of this if you're sleep-deprived. Rosa and I are going to head into town and get some supplies, and we're gonna barricade this place up like a German bunker ... hey, what are you writing?"

Rosa's face flushed. She dropped her pen and covered her notebook with her hands.

"Just fleshing out my plot," she said. "All this talk of kidnapping and gang wars gave me an idea."

"Rosa's here in Crookshollow writing a book," I told Luke. "A tale of bitterness and revenge."

"Sounds dark." Luke grinned. "Are there any space cowboys?"

"No."

"What about an android with a heart of gold?"

"None of them."

"Diabolical villains hell bent on ruling the universe?"

Rosa grinned. "I might add a couple of those, but I haven't decided."

"Are you sure you know how to write a book? I think you're missing some key elements."

I could feel my eyelids drooping already. Luke loved to read, but his tastes ran to old school science fiction writers, not the kind of highbrow literary fiction that cluttered Rosa's cabin. They were going to argue for hours about the literary merits of *The Martian.* Which was great, because I was about thirty seconds away from the land of Nod.

I sank down onto the mattress, Luke and Rosa's voices fading away. I was asleep before my head even hit the pillow.

WHEN I OPENED my eyes again, moonlight streamed through the window above the desk. My wolf form pressed against my skin, begging to be released. It was less than three days now until the full moon, and both Luke and I would need to go deep into the forest. We needed to ensure Rosa's safety before then, or we could have a serious situation.

I jerked upright, my eyes scanning the cabin. *Luke ... Rosa ... where are they?*

The cabin was empty. There weren't even any dishes in the sink. Panic seized my stomach. Had Angus managed to get in here? Had they both been taken, while I slept?

I saw something shift at the window. I bolted out of bed, my senses alert. I pressed myself against the door, and peeked outside.

Rosa and Luke sat side by side on the porch, a stack of books and a line of empty beer bottles covering the table between them. Luke was saying something and Rosa was laughing her wonderful laugh. They looked like two old friends.

I beamed. At least my cousin approved of my mate. If only she would actually agree to *be* my mate, and my maniacal stepbrothers stopped pursuing her, then everything would be perfect.

First things first, we had to get her safe. And that meant, somehow, neutralising my stepbrothers.

I pushed open the door and stepped outside. "What time do you call this?"

"Hello, sleepyhead." Rosa beamed, her smile making my body flush with heat.

Luke checked his phone. "It's a little after 3 a.m."

I leaned against the porch balustrade, and sniffed the air. My stepbrothers' scents lingered in the night, but the trails were a few hours old.

"They're not here," I said.

Luke shook his head. "The scent has been fading for a while. I think they saw me and figured it was pointless making a move tonight with two of us on duty, so they've gone somewhere to get some shut eye."

"Maybe they've given up?" Rosa said, her voice a little louder than usual. I wondered how many of those beers she'd had.

"I wish that were true." I rested my hand on her shoulder, my fingers trailing along her neck. "There's so much else I'd rather be doing than watching over my shoulder all the time."

Rosa grinned, flipping her hair over her shoulder. Her eyes were glazed from the alcohol. "So, what's the plan?"

"We need to find where they're hiding," I said. "Attack them before they make a move on us. For all we know, they could be expecting reinforcements from Scotland at any time. Luke and I need to attack them first, before they have enough wolves to overpower us."

"Why do you have to attack them at all?" Rosa asked.

"Because that's the only language Angus understands." I flexed my muscles. "This is not a problem that's going to be solved with a polite discussion over tea. I'll go after them. You guys stay here and continue your night."

Luke shook his head. "We'll go together. There are two of them, and two of us."

"But what about Rosa?"

Luke turned to Rosa. "Do you have any friends in the village you can stay with for the night? They won't attack you if you're around other people, and risk exposing the existence of werewolves to the world."

Rosa's face grew stormy. The subject of friends seemed to make her upset. I put in quickly, "Rosa's only just arrived in Crookshollow. She doesn't know anyone apart from me."

"That's no problem," Luke sad. "I know just the person." He glanced at me, and I nodded, knowing exactly who he was thinking of. Luke frowned at my bare chest. "You might want to put on a shirt."

"And spoil this view?" I gestured to my stomach. "Unlikely."

"Fine." Luke grabbed Rosa's jacket and tossed it to her. "But don't say I didn't warn you."

TWENTY MINUTES LATER, after assuring me several times she'd only had a couple of beers several hours ago, Rosa was driving around the streets of Crookshollow, following Luke's barked directions. He told her to drive right to the end of a dark cul-de-sac, the quaint workers' cottages on either side of the street all dark. "Pull in there!" He jabbed his finger at a bright blue cottage, the window boxes bursting with herbs and a front garden filled with all kinds of hilarious ornaments.

"Why are we at this house?" Rosa's brow wrinkled in concern. "Whoever's inside is probably asleep."

"Unlikely." Luke leapt out of the car before Rosa had even parked, and rapped on the door.

A few moments later, it swung open, revealing a short old lady wearing layers of black shawls and several crystals dangled from a chain around her neck. Her waist-length-hair was dyed a jet black. Intelligent brown eyes sparkled with recognition as they darted from Luke's face to my own. I smiled. Luke may be the younger and less handsome of the Lowe pack, but he did occasionally have some bright ideas.

"Clara." Luke threw her arms around her. She beamed as she

hugged him back, her tiny arms barely able to reach around his shoulders.

"It's nice to see you again, Luke." She turned to me as I came up the path, shirtless and all. "Caleb, you're as wild as ever, I see."

I ran my hand through my hair. "I'm not sure if that's a compliment, coming from you."

"It is a compliment, of the highest order. And you must be Rosa." Clara took Rosa's hands and held them between her own. "You're every bit as beautiful as Luke told me."

Rosa's face pinched. "Who are you?" she demanded.

I elbowed her. "Hey, don't be rude."

"I'm not being rude. I'm trying to find out what the *hell* is going on."

"Clara is our friend," Luke explained. "She owns the local witchcraft shop, and she helped us out when a rogue wolf threatened my mate. She also supplies Caleb and I with special pills to help us control our inner wolf during the full moon."

"I'm going to ignore the bit where you said she's a witch," Rosa spluttered. "How is she going to help us?"

"Why would you ignore that?" Clara asked kindly. "That's the most interesting thing about me. I make a delicious love potion, tastes like cherries."

"I don't need a love potion, *thank you,*" Rosa said through gritted teeth.

"Don't worry, Clara." I patted her shoulder. "Rosa isn't usually this rude."

"I'm not being rude, I'm sorry. I'm just ... trying to put this together." Rosa gestured toward Clara. "She's a tiny old lady. What's she going to do if a vicious wolf shows up on the doorstep? Beat him off with her walking stick? No offence or anything," Rosa added hastily.

Clara just grinned. "I see you boys have done a wonderful

job of explaining everything. Come inside, all of you. I've got the kettle on. Ryan and Marcus are here as well."

Ryan and Marcus were Clara's twin sons, and they were fox shifters, although Marcus was a mutt (a shifter with genetic defects which meant he didn't have as much control over his shifting as he'd like). Between them and Clara, I knew Rosa would be safe.

"A cup of tea sounds great," Rosa said. "And an explanation." She glared at me.

I shrugged. "I like to keep my women on their toes."

"No time for tea, unfortunately," Luke said. "Caleb and I need to find these wolves. Are you sure you're going to be safe, Clara? I hate bringing all this to your doorstep."

"I've cast a protective spell around the whole property," Clara said. "Between the magical barrier and my two boys, they're not getting in here."

"Right. We have to go." I made to turn away, but Rosa squeezed my hand.

"Be careful, Caleb."

"I'm always careful."

"You're not. I've seen you cook. Be *super* extra careful. I want you back in one piece."

I pulled her body against mine and kissed her, breathing in the scent of her. There was no way in hell I was going to let Angus ruin this thing we had.

"Caleb," Luke warned. "We can't stay here."

"Right." I brushed Rosa's hair out of her eyes, and pressed my finger to her lips. She let go of my hand, her eyes begging me to stay. But I couldn't – Luke and I had to take this chance to find Angus and Robbie. I gave Rosa a final wave, and turned to head back down the path.

Luke and I didn't get back into the car. Instead, we turned down the side of Clara's cottage, heading for the forest that bordered her property. Already, the scent of the trees and fresh air tugged at my inner wolf. I stripped off my shirt as I followed Luke, who was discarding his clothes in the same way. We dumped our clothes in a pile at the end of the path, and raced for the trees. The moonlight drenched my skin, more intoxicating than any wine.

As Luke and I ran toward the forest, I caught a glimpse of a fox sitting beneath one of Clara's box hedges. It nodded as we passed, and the thought landed in my head, *We'll protect her.*

Thanks, Ryan. I owe you one.

Once we reached the forest, Luke and I shifted. My wolf was so close to the surface, snarling and snapping to be loose in the moonlight, it took very little energy to draw him up, and less than a minute later, I had all four paws on the ground. My vision had dulled, colours fading away into blurred shades of grey. Now, the world mapped itself before me in trails of scent. The movements of a hundred tiny animals crisscrossed the trees like telephone wires, connecting the whole forest in a network of snacks and predators. And I was at the top of the food chain.

Luke met my eyes, his grey pelt shimmering under the moon. Silently, we passed back and forth the details of our plan, and then we set off.

We doubled back toward Margaret's place, running alongside each other, sniffing the air as we sought out Angus' trail. We caught it again in the parking lot behind Margaret's house, and followed it back to the now-empty cabin. The trail led us around the back, past the outdoor toilet, and along the ridge before diving deeper into the forest.

After a half hour of running northeast, we emerged into a small clearing. A cabin stood in the centre, similar to the ones Margaret rented out to her guests, but smaller and more dilapidated. A path had originally led to this cabin as well, but it was now completely overgrown. It was clear from the rotting wood and partially collapsed roof that this cabin was no longer in use.

There was no sign of any recent human visitation, but every square inch of the clearing reeked of wolf. In particular, of two specific wolves.

My stepbrothers are here, I called to Luke. *Get back!*

Luke and I darted back into the bushes, moving several feet downwind before our scent alerted them to our presence. We quickly formulated a plan of attack, then circled around to the back of the cabin, careful to remain low to keep our scent masked as much as possible.

The rear of the cabin was lower, the roof sloping toward it. There were no windows on this side, so anything we did would be invisible from the inside, which was exactly what I was hoping for.

I clambered up an overhanging tree, and checked out the situation from above. The hole in the roof was near the front of the cabin, just behind the door. It was an enormous hole, large enough for me to fit through in my wolf form. So far, everything was going our way.

Rain and wind would enter the cabin through the hole, but it was far enough forward that the whole back end of the cabin would be reasonably dry. I guessed my brothers were sleeping in that section. I signalled to Luke to move around the front of the cabin, keeping out of view of the side windows.

Wait for my signal.

As soon as Luke's tail disappeared around the edge of the house, I leapt from the tree branch. My feet thudded as they landed on the wooden shingles, and I scrambled for a moment before gaining a foothold on the steep slope. I hoped like hell the sound hadn't alerted my stepbrothers that I was there. Luckily, the wind was blowing away from the cabin, so they'd be unlikely to have caught my scent.

As silently and carefully as I could, I shuffled forward, over the ridge of the roof, and right to the edge of the hole. I crouched down just back from the edge, so the moon wouldn't throw my shadow on the floor below. Luke poked his head out from the end of the porch, and nodded at me. I nodded back. *Go for it.*

Luke started to howl.

Instantly, something squabbled awake beneath me. I could hear paws scraping against a wooden floor. I strained my mind to catch their thoughts, and my stepbrothers' messages fell into my own mind.

—*Caleb, I can smell him. Can you see through the window? How many does he have out there?*

There's only one wolf. It's Caleb's cousin, the other Lowe wolf. He must've followed us.

You told me they were at the cabin all night.

They were. I swear, Angus. They must've woken up after I left. I'm sorry, I figured they'd sleep for hours after all the—

Alright, I don't have to hear about it again. If the other wolf is here, it means Caleb probably isn't far away, which means my new mate isn't far, either. Caleb wouldn't leave her alone. You definitely can't smell any other wolves?

What do we do? Robbie sounded concerned.

There are two of them and two of us. It's hardly a successful ambush technique. You go out there and see what he wants. I'll hang back here, and I'll come out if you get into trouble.

But, Angus—

Stop arguing with me and get out that fucking door.

I watched as a white-grey wolf slunk across the floor beneath the hole. He was in the perfect position for me to get him, but I didn't want Robbie.

I was after Angus.

Robbie stood on his hind legs and opened the door with his paw. His whole body was trembling. He was terrified.

Sorry, Robbie, but this is what you get when you hang with Angus.

I raised my paw, and Luke rushed forward. Robbie had barely pushed the door open a crack when Luke pounced. Robbie didn't stand a chance. Luke pinned him against the rotting porch, and hissed in his ear, *Stay silent, or I tear out your throat right now.*

Robbie whimpered, but he didn't say a word.

Well, where are they? Angus demanded from the depths of the cabin. *I can smell Caleb's rank stench from here. They must be right on top of us.*

I grinned despite myself.

Answer me, you git. We don't have time to fuck around. Robbie? Angus' nails made a clicking noise as he padded across the wooden floor. *Click click. Click, click.* Any moment now and—

Angus' enormous, black head popped into view over the edge of the hole.

I pounced.

I flew through the air and landed hard on his back. Angus turned his head in surprise, but I'd already sunk my teeth into his neck, right on top of the wound I'd given him just two days earlier. Metallic blood filled my mouth as I sank my teeth deeper. The wound wouldn't kill him, but it would prevent him from tearing himself away from me without taking a huge chunk out of his neck.

Angus roared, rearing up onto his hind legs, and slamming back down again. I pitched forward, nearly losing my grip. But I dug my claws into his sides and held on tight. Angus tried to throw me again, but I managed to stay on, my teeth gnawing deeper into his flesh. Sweat poured down his back, mingling with the blood trickling from the wound, making his fur slick and hard to grip.

I'll kill you, bastard. His anger roared inside my head.

You wouldn't dare, I growled back, my own words thick with rage. *I'm the whole reason you're here, remember? I'm the one you have to bring back in one piece. It's gonna be pretty hard to do that if I tear your throat out.*

We're family. You wouldn't dare.

Oh yeah? I bit down harder, spraying Angus' blood all over the rotting wooden floor. *Try me. You threatened my fated mate. You tried to take her from me. That's no way to treat family, Angus. No way at all.*

She's too good for you, he growled.

And you're a better option? You think she was just going to submit to being the mate of her kidnapper? You really are delusional.

She's not even your mate yet. You haven't claimed her.

That's no excuse, and you know it. You're going back to Aberdeen with your tail between your legs, and when you get there you can tell Douglas exactly what it was you tried to do in order to get me to come with you.

Fine, Angus growled. *We go back, and when the Bairds find out you're not with us, they'll kill our mother.*

That stopped me short. I hated the fact that she was caught up in this.

So stop them. MacLeans don't solve their problems by giving into the demands of their enemies. Douglas is weak if he—

Father is not weak. Angus' eyes were practically on fire.

Whatever. I don't care. I'm not going back with you. You won't change my mind. My jaw was starting to hurt from gripping a mouthful of his fur.

Then hurry up and kill me, bastard. Listening to you talk is tiring.

I'm not going to kill you, Angus. I loosened my grip on his neck, only slightly, but enough for a river of blood to flow again. *You're *in my territory now, and I do things differently. You and Robbie will go back to Aberdeen, tell Douglas what I've just told you, and then you'll all put your ten brain cells together and find another way.*

Outside, I could hear crashing and cursing as Luke and Robbie fought. I dropped Angus' neck, planted my foot on his shoulder blades to keep him down, and shoved his head against the rotting floor.

Angus yelped. *But Mother—*

She's not my concern anymore. I have my own pack now. You worry about your family, and if you so much as look *at Rosa again, I won't be so lenient.*

Angus howled as I stepped across his head. I kicked him in the mouth as I trotted outside. Luke held Robbie against the porch, his claws buried in Robbie's fur and his teeth bared right in his face.

Luke! I called out. His head snapped up, and I saw that blood caked his teeth and chin. Robbie's face looked pale, and his tongue was panting furiously against his teeth. *You can drop him now. They're leaving.*

Luke growled one last time, snapping his jaws in front of Robbie's face. Robbie whimpered, and collapsed in a heap on the sagging porch. Luke jumped off him, and came to stand beside me.

Angus limped out of the cabin, his eyes blazing, his neck and the side of his face caked in his own blood. He looked stricken as he rushed to Robbie, and started to lick the slash marks Luke had made across his cheek.

Why are you still here? Angus glowered at me. *You've done enough.*

Right, like I'd trust you to just leave. We're going to escort you to the border of Crookshollow Forest, make sure you're safely out of Lowe territory. If you cross back over into my domain, I'm well within my rights as the alpha in this area to kill you on sight.

Angus glared at me, but he didn't say anything.

Good. We have an understanding. Let's go.

Angus nudged Robbie in the side. Robbie hunched over and whimpered. Angus licked at another wound, cleaning away the blood from his fur.

You hurt him, he growled.

Stop wasting time, I growled. Angus nudged Robbie again, and he clambered to his feet, his legs shaking. The two of them limped toward the trees. I fell in step behind them, the metallic taste of Angus' blood still coating my mouth. I marched them into the trees, heading north, toward the forest edge and the nearest boundary of our territory. Luke circled around to walk out to the side, preventing them escaping into the trees. None of us said a word.

The sun was rising over the horizon when we finally reached the northern edge of the forest. In the new morning light, Angus and Robbie looked even worse for wear than I'd realised. A flap of Angus' skin hang down from his neck where I'd torn it away, and one of Robbie's legs had swollen up to nearly twice its size. Deep gashes ran across his cheek. When those healed into scars, they'd make him look like a pretty mean critter.

I felt a flicker of sympathy for them, but it quickly faded when I remembered what they'd done to Rosa.

I raised my leg to a nearby tree, adding a fresh mark to the edge of my territory. I splashed a bit on Angus' foot. He backed away, growling, but Luke was right there behind him, pushing him back toward me.

I marched along the tree-line, ensuring the boundary was clearly indicated. *If you cross this line again, you will be directly violating my specific order. As far as I'm concerned, our familial relationship won't guarantee your safety. And you can tell the same to any other member of the Maclean or Baird packs that want to come down here and harass any members of my pack.*

You don't have a pack, Angus growled. *I've never seen another wolf in these parts. If we came back with reinforcements, you wouldn't be able to do a thing.*

Despite myself, fear flickered in my stomach. I'd made up the bit about being the alpha and having a pack. News of the return of the Lowe wolves had started to spread, and for all Angus knew, there *could* be more of us. But there wasn't, and if they did came back with more wolves, we wouldn't have a hope in hell.

Is that so? Luke growled.

I knew Luke was just playing along to help dissuade Angus. If we had an alpha, by rights it should be him. When I met his eyes, I was surprised to see a fire burning there. He looked as though he really believed in the Lowe pack.

Maybe ... I thought of Clara and her sons back in Crookshollow, helping me to protect Rosa. I thought of Luke and his wife Anna, and their coming cub. I thought of Rosa, and how badly I wanted her to be my mate.

I turned to my stepbrother, and all their faces swirled around me. They'd all done so much for me, and for Rosa ... For the first time in my life, I had people around me who were willing to stand up to this bully. I had friends who would stand beside me to protect my family. Pride beat against my chest. If that wasn't a pack, I don't know what is.

Angus and Robbie were already limping away through the trees. I yelled at their backs. *You think you can stand against the Lowe pack and all our might? I wouldn't be so sure if I was you.*

9

ROSA

I woke up in a bed of rose-covered sheets, to the smell of something amazing wafting under my nose.

"Rise and shine, dear," a kindly voice said. "Your wolf-men will be back any moment."

As my eyes adjusted to the bright sunlight streaming in the window behind her, it took me a moment to recognise the kindly black-haired woman who'd taken me in last night. As soon as she'd got me inside, Clara had made me a cup of herbal tea and ushered me up to bed. I'd expected not to sleep a wink, worried about Caleb out there in the forest, but as soon as my head hit the pillow, I was out.

It must've been *some* tea.

Now, Clara was standing in front of me holding a tray bursting with dishes. I rubbed my eyes and stared at the feast she'd laid out for me. A gourmet bacon butty on seedy wholemeal bread, covered in what looked like some thick homemade chutney. A lemon tart, the top glistening with a beautiful chocolate lattice, and a long doughnut dusted with icing sugar and bursting with fresh cream and jam. A fresh pot of tea and a beautiful rose cup and saucer waited on the edge. She'd even put a sprig of herbs into a tiny vase.

"Is that for me?" I gushed. "Thank you. I'll definitely stay in this hotel again."

Clara set the tray down over my knees, fussing with the curtains on the window. "The first thing you need to know about living in Crookshollow is that *Bewitching Bites* bakery is the only place you need go if you're ever in need of a sweet treat."

"I'll remember that." I picked up the cream doughnut and took a huge bite. Cream and jam spurted out the sides of my mouth, and I wiped them away with an embroidered napkin Clara handed to me.

"You slept well?" she asked.

I nodded, my mouth full of cream.

"Good. I see my tea did some good, then."

"Your ... tea?" I set the doughnut down, feeling suddenly suspicious.

"Yes, dear. The tea I gave you last night was a powerful sleep draught. I ground the herbs myself."

"You ... drugged me."

"Heavens, no!" Clara patted my shoulder. "I just made sure you didn't spend all night worrying about your wolf. I was worried about you. We all were." She leaned close, her eyes glinting. "That Caleb is a very nice young man, and rather hand-some too, wouldn't you say?"

I swallowed another mouthful, grinning at her despite myself. "He's available, you know. If you're in the market."

She chuckled, pausing on her way out the door. "Oh, I don't think he's available at all. When you're up and dressed, come down and meet my sons."

I finished off the bacon butty, cream doughnut and half the lemon tart, drowned the tea, and hunted around for my clothes. Clara had folded up my jeans, shirt, and jacket at the end of the bed. I lifted them to my nose. They smelled of lemon and grape-fruit. How had she washed and dried them so fast?

I remembered that Caleb had said she was a witch. But that's ridiculous. Witches don't exist. That's just new age nonsense.

But then, I'd always assumed werewolves didn't exist, and I'd been proved very, very wrong. And she did make me that tea, that definitely put me straight to sleep. Maybe Clara did have some magical powers. If she'd used them to ensure I had clean laundry, that was the kind of witchcraft I could get behind.

My phone on the nightstand beeped. Smiling to myself, I picked it up and clicked on the message icon, expecting something from Caleb. My smile froze when I read the anonymous message.

Don't think you can hide, you black bitch. I'm watching you right now.

The hairs on the back of my neck stood up. The phone clattered to the floor. I surveyed the room. Was someone hiding in here? Someone ... or some wolf?

My gaze fell on the window. I could see it was tightly latched, and it looked out over Clara's sloped roof, down onto her tiny back garden below, and the towering forest beyond that. There was no one out there, and no evidence anyone – or any wolf – had been there.

My phone beeped again. With shaking hands I read the next message.

You can't hide from me. You'll get what's coming to you.

My skin crawled. I felt eyes boring into me, watching my every move. But that was impossible. Who was watching me?

Sucking in a breath, I silently lowered my head over the edge of the bed, and yanked up the cover. I let out my breath when I saw there was nothing underneath except a couple of mothballs and a squeaky mouse cat toy.

I slid out of bed and threw open the narrow closet. No, no one there, either.

It's just those wolves trying to scare you. But Caleb said he was taking care of them ... did he not succeed? Is he out there, injured somewhere? Are the wolves planning to attack me the minute I leave Clara's cottage?

My stomach twisted with fear. I studied the tree line. Something flickered in the corner of my eye. Was that something moving between the trees? It could've been a bird, or the wind ...

A cold shiver ran down my spine. My hands shook. *I hate this. I hate feeling so exposed all the time.*

My hands started to shake, and the panicked feeling rose through my chest, consuming all of me. My head swam. My ears rang. *No, please, no. Don't have a panic attack here.*

My head pounded, and a wave of nausea swept over me. I sat on the floor, wrapping my arms around myself, focusing on steadying my breathing, until the sickening feeling faded.

This is silly. You're just overreacting. There's no one here. It's just Caleb's brothers, trying to scare you. Caleb will be here soon, and everything will be okay.

I got up slowly, my head still spinning, and pulled on my fresh clothing. That done, I padded downstairs, following the sound of masculine voices. I had to twist and flatten myself against the walls to avoid knocking over any of Clara's precariously perched knickknacks with my ass. Every spare inch of space was crowded with candles, crystals, statuettes, photo frames, jars of herbs and other unknown substances, and all manner of strange objects.

Even following the voices, it took me two wrong turns before I located the kitchen. The room was exactly how one would expect a witch's kitchen to look – shelves lined with mason jars filled with dried herbs. More sprigs of herbs and strings of garlic hanging from racks over the bench. Every surface crammed with lopsided, colourful ceramic bowls and plates and cups, and a large black cauldron sat on a dedicated shelf above the aga stove. I loved it instantly. It reminded me a little of the tiny kitchen and small wood-burner in my old cottage.

No. Don't think of that now. I was already fragile enough.

Clara stood behind the stove, stirring a pot of beans. Eggs and sausages sizzled in a pan beside her, and a tray of freshly-baked shortbread sat cooling on the windowsill. I half expected to see little birds darting around the kitchen, stirring the pots and popping toast in the toaster.

Two men sat at the table, each with muscles bulging from the sleeves of their tight t-shirts. The one nearest to me flicked a lock of pitch-black hair from his eyes, and smiled up at me. He had flecks of coloured paint all over his clothes and forearms. The other one – a blond with dark stubble across his chin – was frantically tearing into a huge stack of bacon sandwiches.

Clara beamed as she turned from the stove. "These are my sons. Ryan." She placed a hand on the black-haired man's shoulder. "And Marcus." The blond nodded at me, his mouth full of bacon.

"Hi." I sat down, and Clara placed a huge plate in front of me. My stomach protested, already full from the breakfast I'd eaten in my room. "I didn't see either of you when I came in last night."

"We were outside," Ryan said. "We've been guarding the house from those wolves."

"Did you see or hear anything?" I tried to keep my voice casual, as the words on the text message flashed across my memory.

Ryan shook his head. "Apart from a man walking down the

street earlier this morning, the place has been completely deserted. We didn't smell any wolves nearby, either. I'm pretty sure you're safe."

"Thank you." I pointed to the splatters on his arm. "What's that about?"

"Oh ..." Ryan looked down at himself, as though he'd only just noticed. It was then I saw he had flecks in his long eyelashes. "Yes, that. I'm a painter. It kind of comes with the territory."

"I'm very used to Ryan splattering around all sorts of colours around the place," Clara said, as she set down a plate in front of her son.

"Oh, you paint houses?" That must be how he got all those impressive muscles. He looked like a manual labour kind of guy.

Marcus snorted. Ryan grinned. I guessed I was missing some kind of joke.

"I must say, Rosa. I think you're handling this all rather well." Clara poured tea for all of us. "It's always interesting to see how people react when they find out shifters are real. Ryan's girl Alex was pretty level-headed, all things considered, but your Kylie had a bit of a panic about it, didn't she, love?"

"She's fine," Marcus growled, stealing a butty from Ryan's plate.

"If you do have any questions, we're happy to answer them. Your wolf has probably been too busy running around after your attackers to have a good talk about it."

"Oh, thank you." I toyed with the handle of my cup. "I guess ... I'm a little curious about one particular thing. From what Caleb's told me, there are plenty of other shifters living in England, not to mention all over the world. You're not supernatural demons, but a real species, effectively a minority with rights like anyone else. So why do you live in secret? No one should have to hide who they are. You could have politicians fighting for your rights, and celebrate your heritage, and educate humans about shifter society—"

"You have a very rosy view of humankind's capacity for dealing with something as different as shifters," Ryan explained. "We may not be supernatural, but to most people, we're demons. All the myths and legends throughout history about shapeshifters came from times when we did not live in secret, and our races were hunted down and killed because of what we are and what we represent. Near-extinction tends to make one a little camera-shy."

"I know a little about what that feels like," I said, staring at my black fingers wrapped around my cup.

"I don't doubt you do," Ryan said, his voice gentle. "Unfortunately, fighting for equality is the least of our problems. There are many shifters who want to end this vow of silence. Most of them are either mad or dangerous, or both. There was one such wolf here last year, by the name of Isengrim. His idea was to unite all the rogue shifters – those are shifters who don't have a pack of their own – into one great pack. Then, he would use a public event to shift into his wolf form and attack a prominent shifter, forcing that shifter to reveal his own identity as Isengrim killed him. His idea was that once the world knew we existed, he would already have demonstrated his power for all to see, and with his pack behind him, he would be the ultimate leader. It had nothing to do with what was good for shifters, but about how much power Isengrim could keep for himself."

"So you believe you should remain underground?"

"I do," Ryan said. "But then, I prefer to be on my own, hiding away in my house. I don't want people beating down the door asking for interviews or wanting me to go on TV. They do that enough as it is."

"They do?"

Ryan ignored my question. "If there was ever a really solid

case for it, a case that didn't support some megalomaniac, I would possibly support it. There's a lot of crime that goes on in the shifter world, a lot of territorial disputes that result in fatalities. When you're invisible, you can do whatever you want without consequence, like kidnapping people's mothers and terrorising innocent women."

I turned to Marcus. "And you?"

"Why should we hide?" Marcus said, his mouth full of sandwich. "I want to stand. If we were free, then it wouldn't be pureblood shifters like Ryan dictating how everyone was treated."

"I don't dictate anything."

"You don't disagree, though, *do you?*"

"You can't help what you are, Marcus. But that does come with certain issues that have to be controlled, or else you're a danger—"

Marcus shot me a look. "They said the same thing about segregation, didn't they? Even among shifters there are outcasts, don't forget that."

I remembered that Marcus was a mutt, whatever that really meant. I wanted to ask him more about it, but he seemed so agitated, I didn't want to risk further setting him off.

"So is shifter society a bit like the wizarding world in *Harry Potter*? Do you have your own schools and newspapers and weird sporting tournaments?"

The front door banged. "Honey, I'm home."

Caleb. He's okay!

My curiosity forgotten, I leapt from my seat and darted into the hall. I was so desperate to see him, I accidentally upset a bowl of crystals on the stand by the door.

"Oops." My face flushed red as tiny rocks skittered across the floor. A black cat leapt out from under the table and started batting them around.

"Don't worry about that, dear." Clara hunched over and started collecting the rocks. "Go see your wolf."

She didn't have to tell me twice. I bounded into the hall, where Caleb and Luke were pulling on their shirts over their bare chests. I fell into Caleb's arms, placing my hands against his skin, breathing in the woody, earthy scent of him. That grin of his melted my heart, and I realised how much I'd been worried that he wouldn't come back, especially since I'd received that text message. Caleb started to say something, but I pressed my lips to his, drowning out his words with my tongue.

"Now that's what I call a greeting," Caleb said, pulling away slightly to look at me. "You okay?"

"As okay as could be expected. I think you're right about Clara being a witch. She drugged me, and now she's trying to fatten me up, probably so I'll taste better in a pie."

"I think you'd taste delicious in a pie." He nibbled on my lip.

"That's the way to a girl's heart – cannibalism jokes." I stroked his cheek. "Seriously, though, are *you* okay? Did you find them?"

"We found them all right," Caleb said, his voice dark. "They've been holed up in an abandoned cabin only a few miles from yours."

"Did they—"

"Caleb, Clara's made food!" Luke's voice called from the kitchen.

"Great. I'm starving."

"Hence the cannibalism." I dropped his hand and led him into the kitchen, where Luke was already deep in conversation with Ryan. Clara shoved Caleb down into a seat and set a cup of tea and a pile of butties and sausages in front of him, but he didn't move to take them.

"We took them by surprise," Luke was saying as he shovelled down a mouthful of egg. "There was a hole in the roof of the shack, so Caleb climbed up there, while I went around the front and lured Robbie out. Caleb sank his teeth right into Angus' neck—"

"You didn't kill him, did you?" As much as I hated Angus for what he was trying to do to me and Caleb, I didn't want Caleb to be responsible for killing his brother.

"No. We just convinced them it would be in their best interests to leave our territory," Luke said. He turned to each person at the table in turn. "Caleb *may* have implied that he had a whole pack here ready to defend Rosa if they had to."

"Why would you do that?" I glanced at Caleb in surprise. "What if they come back? You don't *have* a whole pack. It's just you and Luke."

"Correction." Ryan set down his fork. "There's a few more of us than that."

Caleb looked at Ryan with an expression I can only describe as awe. "Really?"

"Really. If you'll have us." Ryan wiped his mouth. "I've decided I'm through hiding away for now. I've got Alex to think about, and whether I like it or not, she wants to be out in the world, and that means many eyes are on us. I don't want to be trapped and I want to know I have friends I can count on if anyone like Isengrim threatens her again. Marcus and I have already discussed it. If you Lowe boys will have us, we'd love to help you keep Crookshollow safe from the likes of the Macleans."

"And me too, dear," Clara said, setting down a second plate of bacon in front of Marcus.

"You mean, we need to keep Crookshollow safe from you?" Ryan grinned.

Clara clapped him around the ears. "I mean, if you'll take an old witch with a gammy hip in your pack, I'd love to help in any way I can."

Caleb was beaming. He turned to me, as though he was expecting me to add my voice to the mix. *I'm in, Caleb. I'll be your mate.* I opened my mouth, but I couldn't make the words come out.

It felt too much like commitment – saying I was willing to be something to him, and he was something to me, and I just couldn't do it. The words didn't exist yet. They had burned up in the fire with Lennox, carried away by the winds with the ashes of my life.

I bent my head, chewing on a loose piece of bacon, feeling Caleb's eyes burning into my skull. *I'm sorry. I wish I could be with you, but I'm too scared.*

An uncomfortable silence descended, which everyone tried to fill with chewing. I jiggled my foot nervously, wishing I could make a run for it and not have to sit here being the only one who wasn't in it.

"You boys look awful," Clara scolded, grabbing Luke's arm and indicating a long cut along his bicep. *Nice one, Clara.*

"Way to stroke a man's ego," Luke shot back.

"Ryan, get my first aid kit." The red-haired man got up, and rummaged through the kitchen cupboards, before planting a large wooden box down on the table. Clara opened it and I peered inside, expecting to see bandages, saline, and paracetamol. Instead, rows of glass vials stood in perfect rows, and a small mortar and pestle were nestled into the corner.

Clara selected several vials, dumping the contents into the mortar. She mumbled to herself as she worked, though I wasn't sure if I recognised any words. She pulled an oil decanter off the shelf above the stove, added a couple of drops, and then proceeded to crush the herbs together with short, deft twists. She smeared the resulting paste on Luke's cuts.

"Thanks a lot." Luke wrinkled his nose. "Now I smell like a stew."

"Stop your complaining." Clara moved around the table. "It's your cousin's turn."

Caleb leaned back and tugged down the collar of his shirt so Clara could apply the cream to the cuts across his chest. His eyes met mine, and I caught a flash of pain. I knew I was the cause of that pain.

I'm sorry, Caleb. I really am.

The pain was gone in a flash, replaced by Caleb's wicked smile and sparkling gaze. He looked down at the cuts on his shoulder, the lines crisscrossing the nearly healed bite marks from his first altercation with Angus. "Don't look so worried, Rosa. Werewolves heal quickly, especially if they're covered with Clara's special *bouquet garni*. Trust me, Angus looks way worse."

"You mean they're gone for good?" The text message flashed before my eyes again.

"I wouldn't be so sure about that," Caleb said. "But they won't be back any time soon, and it will take them some days to return to Aberdeen with additional muscle."

I reached into my pocket and closed my fingers around my phone, the message burning in my eyes. I opened my mouth to tell him about the text, but something stopped me. I glanced around the table at this happy family of shifters, and I realised that I didn't want them all to know. I didn't want to say the words "black bitch" in front of Clara and Ryan and have them believe it. Besides, it was just Angus, trying to get to me since Caleb sent him packing. I resolved to tell Caleb as soon as we were alone, but for now, there wasn't any reason to draw attention to it. I dropped the phone back into my pocket, and reached for my lukewarm tea.

I realised Caleb was talking "—in the meantime, I think we should try to find out exactly why the Bairds want me."

"How do we do that?" I asked, trying to bring myself back into the conversation.

"*You* don't do anything," Caleb said. "You go to your cabin, and work on your book. You've already been inconvenienced enough with all this drama. Let me and the pack handle it." There was a hardness in his voice that hadn't been there earlier.

"You mean, my cabin is safe now? I don't have to share it with everyone?"

Caleb nodded. "Luke and I even checked it out on the way over here, just in case they'd left some kind of trap. But it's fine. We'll keep an eye on you from a distance. You should be able to get a ton of work done."

"Thank you. Thank you, all of you." I looked around the table, at all these people who hardly knew me, yet who had risked their lives and their home to keep me safe. A lump rose in my throat. What I would've given to have people like this in my life back in Old Garsmouth.

And Caleb ... what if I had met him last year, before Sam walked into the office, before my life got completely messed up. I shook off the thought. *You didn't meet him then, you met him now. And you have to deal with what that means.*

"You're welcome." Ryan beamed.

"Yeah," Caleb said, an edge on his voice. I glanced up at him, but he looked away.

WE STAYED at Clara's house for another couple of hours, chatting around the table like old friends. Well, the boys chatted, and Clara bustled around with yet more food. I mostly sipped tea and listened. I didn't feel much like talking.

Caleb walked me back to the car. My stomach knotted. I felt his disappointment seeping off him, dissipating the special energy that usually sizzled between us. He opened the door, and as I turned to get in, he wrapped his arms around me, pulling me close.

"Hey." He wiped away a strand of hair that had escaped from my bun. His eyes were kind again, but sad.

"I'm sorry," I said. "I know what you were asking back there, but I just can't—"

"It's okay, Rosa."

"It's not, though. You've been so kind to me, Caleb. You only met me four days ago, and you've turned your whole life upside down to protect me. And all the others ... they don't even ... they can't ... and yet they're ..." The lump rose higher. I gulped, dangerously close to losing it. "I don't feel like I deserve it."

"Dear Rosa." Caleb kissed my eyelids. "Of course you deserve it. Everyone deserves to feel safe, to live a peaceful life without a crazy wolf trying to kidnap them. Even if I didn't feel for you ... what I feel, I would still be protecting you, because what my stepbrothers are trying to do is wrong."

I gulped again. A tear escaped the corner of my eye and slid down my cheek. Caleb kissed it away. The gesture was so simple, but the power of it made my whole chest ache.

"Come here." He rested my head on his shoulder, his fingers playing in my hair. "One day, I hope you'll trust me enough to tell me what has hurt you so bad, but in the meantime, don't worry about me. Yes, I'm hurt you don't want to be my mate, but—"

"It's not that." I sniffed, tears coming thick and fast now, staining the collar of Caleb's shirt.

"It is that. You're not ready. I'll wait for you, Rosa. I'll wait as long as you need. But sometimes, I'm allowed to be a little gutted you're not ready now, okay? I'm not exactly known for my patience."

I laughed, hiccuping into Caleb's shoulder. God, I was a total mess.

"There's that laugh I love so much." Caleb's arms slid away, and he studied my face with concern. "You gonna be okay up there on your own?"

I thought about the text message in my pocket, but decided not to bother him about it. "Yeah." I smiled. "I'll be fine. I'll see you tonight."

"Yeah. Maybe I'll take you out to dinner. We could have an actual date, no homicidal werewolves or meddling pack-mates allowed."

"I'd like that." A date with Caleb. It sounded like such a wonderfully normal thing, and yet, totally and utterly magical.

I drove back to Margaret's place. It felt odd to be stepping out of the car on my own, without my handsome wolfish escort. But this was exactly as it should be. Caleb had got rid of the threat, so I could be alone again.

Alone.

I stepped onto the path leading out to my cabin, glancing around the trees. My stomach tightened in knots. I started moving forward, at any moment expecting the wolves to jump out and attack me.

But none did.

Ahead of me, the familiar slope of my cabin's roof became visible through the trees. The chairs were still set out on the porch, just as we'd left them. The beer bottles Luke and I (mostly Luke) had emptied stood in a row along the centre of the small table. I took out the key from my pocket and held it up. Dappled sunlight streaked through the trees and glinted off the metal. My cabin, the freedom I had bought from the evil that had been done to me.

Suddenly, I couldn't wait to get back to my book.

I leapt up the steps, and thrust my key into the lock. I pushed the door open and scanned the room, checking for anyone – or anything – hiding inside. That SMS from this morning still had me a little freaked out, even though I knew it was just Angus, lashing out even as he was forced to retreat.

Satisfied my cabin was absolutely empty, I strolled in, slamming the door behind me. My laptop sat on the desk by the window, begging me for attention. I made a pot of tea, and sat down to write.

Today, the words flowed as they never had before. Armed with the knowledge that my wolfish pursuers were, for now, neutralised, and that Caleb was trying to be patient with me, I could slip back into the world of Old Garsmouth, and the person I was when I first encountered Sam Seymour.

The person I wished I could be with Caleb.

I wrote a flashback chapter, from Sam's point of view, to the day he first saw me ... er, Nellie ... sitting at my desk in the accounting firm. How Nell had rebutted each of his lines with a witty retort, then lowered her eyes and smiled shyly when he'd finally asked her out. How he told his wife he had a business meeting in Leeds, and he would stay overnight in the city so as not to wake her and the kids. How he'd gone to pick up the young black girl and they gone out to an amazing Chinese restaurant, then fucked in a hotel room until the wee hours of the morning.

My fingers slammed against the keys, pounding them down harder and harder as the words came out, as I slipped right into Sam's head and saw myself as he saw me – this exotic, flirtatious creature who made him feel young and intelligent and interesting. How he didn't even think about his wife at home when he was with me.

I typed the final line of the scene:

Nellie fell asleep, her head resting against his white shoulder. Peace descended upon her, the last moment of peace she would ever feel.

I leaned back, stretching out my arms. It felt good to be making progress on this book. Maybe I did have what it took to be a writer. Maybe, if I told this story, I could help another young black girl who had fallen into the same trap that had captured me. Maybe if just one white person read it and rethought the things they said and did ...

Could my book make a difference? Was that my future, to use words to fight for equality? I thought about what Ryan and Marcus had said, about the discrimination within the shifter community, about how they had to hide what they were, lest they became yet another minority fighting for justice ...

Lest they become like me ...

My tea had gone cold, so I made myself another cup. As I stood by the oven, trying to decide if it was an Earl Grey or English Breakfast moment, I heard an odd sound from outside. Sort of a whoosh, like air being let out of a tire.

I set down the tea box as silently as possible, and moved toward the door. My heart pounded. Blood roared in my ears, almost drowning out the *whooshing* sound that was absolutely, definitely coming from outside.

It's just an animal. It's some kind of bird call, or it could be a tree branch scraping against the side of the cabin—

The more I thought of logical explanations, the more I was certain the sound did not fit them at all. My stomach churned, and a familiar sick sensation rose through my chest. My hands started to shake uncontrollably.

No. This can't be happening. Not here. Not in my beautiful cabin.

"Hello?" I croaked out, trying to push through the panic attack. "Is anyone there?"

The noise stopped. My heart was pounding so hard I thought for sure it would burst from my chest. Through the haze of my panic, I registered that if it was an intruder, I needed some kind of weapon. As silently as I could, I slid a knife from the chopping block, and held it in front of me. I grabbed the door handle.

One, two, three ...

I yanked the door open, and rushed to the edge of the porch, looking both ways. I heard a crunch. Something raced from the corner of the cabin into the trees. I whirled around, catching a glimpse of a man in black cargo shorts and a black t-shirt racing into the trees.

Oh shit, oh shit.

"Hey," I called out, with more bravado than I felt. My hand was shaking so hard, I nearly dropped the knife. "Who are you? What are you doing here?" I staggered down the steps, heading toward the trees where he'd disappeared. But it was no good. He had too much of a head start, and the trees were too thick. I'd already lost him, and I was never going to catch him in my current state.

But who was it? I hadn't been able to get a good look at his face. It could've been Angus or Robbie, but the guy didn't look big enough or muscled enough to be either of them. It had been hard to see, though – he'd moved so fast.

I turned back to the cabin, my heart racing. *I'll have to call Caleb, and see—*

I let out a cry of surprise. The knife clattered from my hand, lost in the leaves.

There, scrawled across the side of my beautiful cabin in big, ugly letters the colour of blood, someone had spray-painted the message:

DIE, BLACK BITCH.

10

CALEB

"This was not exactly how I pictured bonding with my pack-mates." Marcus tossed a large amethyst wand into the air, catching it and twirling it between his fingers like it was a marching baton or a cuban cigar. "There's no alcohol, or naked chicks. No one even brought snacks."

The four of us were crowded into the back room of *Astarte*, Clara's occult shop on the high street. Ryan and Luke had their noses in some of Clara's shapeshifter mythology books, looking for clues that might somehow link my family to the Bairds. Marcus and I were huddled in one corner, a laptop screen between us, scanning recent issues of "Shift in Focus," a membership-only news site that curated content relating to the worldwide shifter community. Apart from some recent articles about the discovery of the caves, and one with a shot of my back and the headline, *Lowe Pack Re-Established*?, we'd found nothing.

"Shut up and keep looking," Ryan said, without even looking up from a thick volume of English folklore.

"There *has* to be a connection." Luke mumbled as he tossed a book called *American Werewolves in Europe* against the wall, and picked up another from the stack.

"No matter how many times you say it, doesn't make it come true," Marcus muttered, pretending to stab the cover of the book with the tip of the wand.

Clara popped her head around the corner, and wrenched the wand from Marcus' hand. "Can you boys keep it down in here? I've got customers out here, and it's hard for them to feel the spiritual connection to my overpriced crystals if all they hear is you lot cursing at each other."

"Sorry, Mother." Marcus tried to grab the laptop off me, but I held it out of reach. "The new alpha won't let his minions help."

"I *did* let you help," I shot back. "But all you wanted to do was look up videos of tractor accidents on YouTube."

"Why not? That shit is hilarious. Did you see that one in Russia when the tractor ran over that bicycle—"

Clara rolled her eyes at me, and I stifled a snort. "Marcus, dear. Why don't you pop down to the bakery and get us all some lunch?"

Marcus grumbled as he got to his feet.

Ryan grabbed the waistband of his brother's jeans. "Get me a piece of that Heaven & Hell cake, would you?"

"Hang on." Luke leaned forward, a thick volume open on his knees. "I might have something."

I slid the laptop off my knees and scooted over, peering at the page upside down and trying to make sense of the strange diagrams.

Luke jabbed his finger at the page. "This says that the Lowe pack was once in possession of a powerful artefact, an ancient ring called the Benedict ring. It's quite a unique design – two snakes curled around a bloodstone."

"They sell those at every goth store at Camden Market," Marcus growled.

Luke ignored him, which I was beginning to understand was the best way to deal with Marcus. "Apparently, the Benedict ring had been passed down through one of the most powerful witch families since the time of the Great Plague. The last descendant of that line lived here in Crookshollow. When the witch hunters came, she knew she would soon be burned, and the ring would fall into their hands. So she gave it to the Lowe alpha, who was her lover, for him to hide away. Apparently, it was never heard from again."

"What's this ring supposed to do?"

Luke consulted the book. "Apparently its original owner, a Lord Benedict, was a powerful magical worker. He would suck out the magic of other witches, and store all that power inside the ring. It enabled him to have many times the power of any equivalent witch. Apparently, he could even use it to fly. With that power he controlled a vast kingdom, until he was killed by his own daughter. Here's a picture of him with the ring, see?" He jabbed his finger at a woodcut of a cold-looking dude in an elaborate coat. His right hand clasped the hilt of his sword, and his left hand rested against his breast, over his heart. The ring was on his left index finger, drawn large, to emphasise the detail of the coiled snakes circling the stone.

"How come we never heard of this before?"

Luke shrugged. "Maybe our parents and grandparents didn't know about it. If the artefact was lost in the eighteenth century, perhaps it passed out of all knowledge, the way the one ring in Lord of the Rings came to be lost until Bilbo Baggins—"

"That's enough of that, Gandalf."

"Right, sorry."

Ryan said. "Are we assuming the Bairds know about this artefact?"

"It's definitely plausible."

"Could there be any reason why they'd believe Caleb has it?"

"Of course, the caves!" I grabbed the computer and navigated back to the article with the grainy picture of me near the

Crookshollow caves. I turned the screen around to show Ryan and Luke. "Shift in Focus were speculating that Luke and I were re-establishing the Lowe pack in Crookshollow, which I guess isn't really speculation anymore."

"Guess not." Luke grinned back at me.

"The fact that we've marked out new boundaries for our pack around the forest probably solidified the rumour," I continued. "If the Bairds saw this article, and they knew about the ring, they might theorise that the artefact would be hidden in our ancestral caves. They'd assume that I was staying in Crookshollow in order to obtain it and use it."

"They could believe Caleb would use this ring to gain control over all the wolf clans," Luke said, his voice tight with excitement. Ancient rings of power were just his kind of thing.

"And they want it for themselves," Ryan said. "That, or they want Caleb as an ally while he builds up his power."

"This whole thing sounds insane," Marcus snorted. "Rings of power, bloodstones, seriously? This isn't Harry fucking Potter."

"I agree, but it's no more insane than some of the other stuff that's gone on in Crookshollow over the last year." Luke looked over at Ryan. "Do you agree?"

"Fair enough." Ryan grinned. After all, he was the centre of much of the drama that had put Crookshollow front-of-mind for shifters in the last couple of years ...

"So does this mean we have to go hunt out an ancient ring?" Marcus asked, sighing.

"We don't have to actually have the artefact," I said. "We just have convince them we have it, which should be pretty easy. Like you said, there are dozens of rings that look like this in every goth store in the country. Clara might even have one."

Ryan ducked his head out the door and explained what we wanted.

"Hold on." Clara returned a moment later with a small black

tray displaying several garish rings. "I think this one would be perfect." She plucked one from the tray and handed it to me.

It was perfect. A huge, chunky band decorated with elaborate filigree, with two snakes coiled around a glittering red stone.

"That's not a real bloodstone, of course," Clara said, as I slipped the ring on my finger. It looked ridiculous. "It's glass. But it is silver-plated."

"Well, isn't that fancy?" I grinned.

"Right, we've got our fake magical ring," Marcus said. "Now what do we do?"

"I think we're going to have to go see my friend Irvine Baird," I growled, flashing my finger at him. "He needs to know that he can't mess with the Lowe clan."

11

ROSA

*A*s soon as my limbs could move again, I raced back inside the cabin and slammed and locked the door. I grabbed all the knives from the block and lined them up in front of the door. Then I wrapped my hands around my knees and rocked back and forth, trying to stop myself from throwing up.

My phone vibrated in my pocket. I grabbed it, nearly dropping it through my fingers. I checked the number. It was Caleb.

"Hello?" I whispered.

"Rosa, you won't believe what we've discovered." Caleb sounded so excited. "Apparently, the Lowe pack was in possession of an ancient ring—"

"Someone was here, at the cabin." My voice trembled. Relief flooded me, just from hearing his voice.

"What?"

The lump rose up in my throat. Now that I had said it out loud, I was dangerously close to losing control. "I just saw someone outside. They spray-painted DIE, BLACK BITCH on the side of my cabin."

"Wolf or human?"

"Human. He ran into the bushes. I–I–I didn't get a good look at him."

"Stay inside. Lock all the doors. We're coming for you now."

He didn't have to tell me twice. I moved around the cabin on shaking legs, and gathered up some of my things – my laptop, a couple of books, some clothing and underwear. I crouched with my bag on the centre of the rug, the knives spread out around me like a rainbow of stabbing. My gaze flicked between the kitchen window and the window above the desk. Every hair on my body stood on end, every muscle tensed, ready to strike.

My cabin looked different now, all gloomy corners and no escape route. My space had been violated, tainted. I knew I could never write in peace here again.

It seemed like a whole day passed in strained silence while I waited. When the knock sounded, I was so wound up, I nearly jumped out of my skin. My heart hammered against my chest.

"Rosa, it's me," Caleb shouted through the door. "Open the door."

I scrambled across the floor and unlocked the door. Caleb threw it open, and picked me off the floor, cradling me in his arms like a frightened child. I rested my head on his shoulder, and all the tension in my body poured out of my eyes. Great sobs wrenched from deep in my stomach, my whole body shaking as I poured it all out, all the fear and panic.

I felt strangely detached from the whole experience, as though I were standing behind myself, watching my breakdown. *This isn't you. This isn't who you are.* But it was. I *was* this hopeless, distraught human. I was losing it. The sting of the words against my cabin of freedom had cut too deep.

Caleb's arms tightened around me. His hand cupped the back of my head. His voice cooed in my ear, a deep rumble that resonated right through my body.

"I'm sorry," I sniffed, looking up at him. "I didn't mean to ..."

The words failed me, so I just gestured to my tear-stained face. I'd smeared snot all over the other side of his collar now, but if he noticed, he didn't seem to care.

"You have nothing to be sorry about." His voice shook, and for the first time, I saw the raw fury in his eyes. "My stepbrother is the one who is going to be very, very sorry."

"I thought you said he left Crookshollow."

"He must've doubled back to do this."

"I could deal with it when it was just text messages, but this is on my wall—"

"What text messages? Have you had more like that one from the other night?"

My face flushed. "Yeah, a couple more. He said he was watching me."

Caleb growled. "He's signed his own death warrant."

"I don't want you to—"

"Crossing a shifter's territory after being forbidden is a declaration of war. I won't tolerate this, Rosa. You deserve to live without this fear in your life."

I snorted. "Caleb, I'm a black woman. As long as I live, I will live with fear in my life."

"It shouldn't be that way. I won't let it."

"I don't even know if it was Angus. I didn't get a good look at the guy, but he didn't seem as big or brawny as I remember." The more I thought about the blur I'd seen darting into the bushes, the more I was certain it wasn't Angus.

"Who else could it be? Who else knows about your cabin?"

"My parents, my lawyer, and my therapist. That's it."

"And presumably none of them want to frighten you out of your wits. We'll call them as soon as we get back to the village; check that they're all right."

A chill ran down my spine. "You don't think they could've hurt my parents?"

"I fucking hope not. But if what we found out today is true, there might be more going on here than we think. You can show me where he ran off, and I'll try and find the trail. That'll tell us quickly if it's my stepbrothers, or if they had someone do it for them. I didn't think they have many allies down here."

"Could they still be here, watching us?"

"The two of them had some serious wounds, and they know better now than to go up directly against Luke and I. I think they'll go back to Aberdeen, if they aren't there already. But when they return to Crookshollow, they'll have reinforcements. Unfortunately, I think we might have made the situation worse. My brother Angus doesn't like to lose."

"What do we do?"

"I don't think you should stay here," Caleb said. "It's too isolated, and harder to protect. Ryan's in the car. He says we can stay at his place—"

I looked down at my packed bag on the rug, and a wave of anger shot through my whole body. I shook my head. "I don't want to sleep on some guy's couch I hardly even know, even if he is a member of your pack. I'm not giving up my cabin. This was my dream. I'm not calling it quits after only a few days. That means they've won."

"If you die, they also win." Luke's voice cut in. I jumped. I hadn't even seen him standing there. "I agree with Caleb. It will be much easier to protect Rosa from the hall."

Caleb's eyes focused on mine. He leaned forward, lowering his voice, so we were the only two people who could hear. He stroked my cheek with his thumb, and a wave of desire shot through me. "I don't want you to feel as though you've giving up anything," he said. "But for a few days, would you consider being a guest at our new friend's house? I think you might like it."

"I don't know, Cale—"

"Did I mention that Ryan's a billionaire?"

"Um ... no." Ryan, with the paint-splattered skin? "Doesn't he paint houses?"

Caleb laughed. "He's Ryan Raynard."

Holy shit. I knew nothing about art, but even I'd heard of Ryan Raynard, the reclusive artist who had practically founded the modern impressionist movement.

"He owns Reynard Hall on the edge of the village. There's a spa pool and a fully-stocked bar and a butler and some big comfy beds. Besides." Caleb's eyes twinkled mischievously. "It's going to be hard to give you your reward for what you did to me the other day, with all these guys looking on."

His other hand rested on my thigh, his fingers snaking closer, closer ... he brushed a finger over the crotch of my jeans, and the ache sprung up inside me, as if he'd flicked a switch. I bit my lip to stop myself moaning out aloud. It *would* be much ... *nicer* ... to have a room all of my own. And if it's only a few days until Caleb can sort things out with his father, then what's the harm?

"All right," I said, picking up my bag. "Take me to the fox's mansion."

REYNARD HALL WASN'T JUST opulent, it was *palatial*. The gothic manor sprawled in all directions, as far as the eye could see. It had clearly been neglected for several years, as there were cracks along several walls, overgrown flower beds filled with weeds as high as the first floor balcony, and dirt and grime encrusting everything. But I could see work was being done to bring it back to its former splendour. There was scaffolding around the far end of the western wing, and some stone-mason's tools lined up beside the front steps, with fresh paint along half the front wall. The hedges were freshly trimmed, and the garden beds around the steps were brimming with white and yellow flowers.

A beautiful blonde woman greeted us at the door, wearing a floaty maxi dress covered in baroque flowers. A paintbrush was tucked behind her ear. She introduced herself as Alex, Ryan's fiancee.

"Welcome." Alex embraced me. "Ryan's filled me in on everything that's happened. You'll be perfectly safe here. This place is protected from all manner of supernatural creatures by some of Clara's strongest charms."

"That's ... that's great." As if werewolves weren't enough, I was now hanging out with a billionaire vulpine in an enchanted manor. What was next, a vampire butler?

As if on cue, a willowy man with beady eyes and thick, demonic-looking eyebrows emerged from the shadows and held his arms out for my coat. "This way, ma'am," he said.

I couldn't help it. I burst out laughing.

Alex grinned, as if she knew exactly what I was thinking. "It takes a little getting used to," she whispered, so the butler wouldn't hear. "The first month I was living here, I was sure at any minute I'd stumble into some dark corner and find Simon's sleeping figure peering out at me from an upright coffin."

I grinned back at her. *I think I'll like this girl.*

"I've had Simon prepare rooms for you in the guest wing." Alex started up the grand staircase. "I'll let you get settled. You look like you've had a pretty rough day. Ryan and I are going to have supper in the green drawing room in a couple of hours. Feel free to join us, but I thought you'd like some time to shower and freshen up."

"You must be a mindreader," I said, twisting a frizzy lock of hair in my finger. I wondered if psychics were another made-up phenomenon I was going to have to get used to being real.

"Close," she grinned. "I'm a woman. I know these things. Good to have you here, Rosa."

"Nice digs." Caleb's gravelly voice penetrated my thoughts. He stood in the doorway, staring around the room the vampire butler had "prepared" for me.

I couldn't help but agree. Unlike other stately homes that were decorated with heavy antiques and stuffy drapes, this room was light and airy. I'd dumped my bag on a creamy Scandinavian-style recliner by the floor-to-ceiling windows overlooking the back garden and the forest. I was now sitting on the edge of the bed, running my fingers over the smooth sheets and soft, downy duvet. Weariness washed over me, and I lay back, letting the soft bed float around me while I stared up at the industrial-style chandelier above my head.

Are these four-hundred count sheets? I bet they are. In a house like this, of course they are. They feel like butter. I've never slept in a bed made of butter before.

I thought of the hard, lumpy bed back in the cabin. *I should get some nice sheets, and a decent mattress. Hell, I've got three-hundred thousand pounds in the bank. I could buy four-hundred count sheets if I wanted to.*

I was debating whether it would be appropriate to ask Alex where she shopped, when Caleb stepped inside the room, casting a looming shadow over the edge of the bed.

Reluctantly, I dragged my body up into a sitting position, and was rewarded with a view of shirtless Caleb, the dim light in the hall throwing a shadow across the dark stubble running along his chin. He surveyed my bed with a satisfied smirk

"Where's your room?" I asked.

"Just down the hall, but I don't intend to spend much time

there." In a moment, Caleb was on the bed beside me. Two strong arms wrapped around my torso, rolling me over so I faced away from him. Caleb's teeth grazed my earlobe.

Yes. All weariness forgotten, my body sizzled with desire once again.

"I missed you last night," Caleb whispered into my ear, as his hands explored my body, cupping my breasts, skimming my sides, squeezing my ass. His touch left trails of fire across my skin.

The words hummed against my brain. *Why does knowing he missed me make me feel so good?*

It was probably that damn Scottish accent. It made everything he said sound like sex.

"Oh, yes?" My voice came out low, almost like a growl. "Why don't you show me just how much you missed me?"

In response, Caleb growled low in his throat. His hands tightened around my thighs, and he shunted me further onto the bed. I turned around to face him, but he used his arms to stop me.

"Stop trying to take charge, woman." He stroked a finger along my chin. "Let me drive you crazy first."

"If you insist." I sank back into the bed-cloud, as Caleb continued to stroke and kiss my body, his fingers everywhere at once – running down my back, curling around my thighs. He undid the buttons between my breasts and slid my shirt over my shoulders. My skin tingled with heat as he placed his lips on the back of my neck, kissing a line down my shoulders and pulling down the strap of my bra with his teeth.

My breasts weren't even naked yet, and already the ache inside me was desperate for him.

Caleb wrapped his arms under my body, and flipped me over, so I was on top. I leaned back, straddling him, my whole body aching with need. He was still wearing pants, so I reached down and tugged at his belt. Caleb grabbed me around the wrist, holding my arm away.

"Not yet, wench."

"Then what?"

"Sit on my face." He grinned. "I want to watch you enjoying this."

My face flushed with heat. I'd never done that before. But if Caleb asked ... I would obey. I wriggled forward, planting my thighs on either side of his head, so that he was between my legs. He reached up and tweaked one of my nipples, and I gave a little moan.

"Keep your eyes locked on mine," he said, his mouth so close to me that every word sent a waft of wind across me, teasing the ache growing inside me. I nodded.

Caleb reached behind me and grabbed hold of my ass with both hands, holding me in place. His tongue connected with my clit, and oh, the sensation of it nearly sent me over the edge.

He started slow, moving with deliberate care, dragging his tongue across all of me. The torture of waiting while his eyes danced over mine drove me wild. I growled low in my throat, begging him for more.

While he worked me, his eyes drank in my reactions. Watching him as he watched me made the whole experience more intimate than anything I'd ever experienced. I dug my fingers into his shoulders as the ache inside of me grew stronger, spreading out through my limbs, ready to take me over completely.

Caleb increased his speed, focusing all his attention on my clit, pounding it over and over with his tongue. My legs started to clench as I grew closer and closer. He took one hand from my ass and worked it between my legs, pushing a finger inside of me as his tongue licked and swirled.

My legs turned to jelly, and I collapsed as the orgasm

claimed me. My legs convulsed, tightening around him, driving myself further against his face. He responded by sucking me into his mouth, sending another wave of pleasure through my body even before the first had abated. His eyes never left my face as the second orgasm tore through me. I lost sight of him as red welts appeared in my eyes, and the room swirled in a maelstrom of ecstasy.

I woke in a stupor of pleasure to find myself flat on my back against the sheets, Caleb leaning over me, now completely naked, his fingers trailing across my skin. My whole body tingled.

"So that was ... good?" He lifted one eyebrow.

"That was ... the most intense orgasm I've ever ... I mean, wow."

"I loved watching you," he said, running his hands over my stomach.

"I loved watching you watch me. I loved everything about it. What do we do now? I don't think I can even move."

"I'll take things from here." Caleb rolled me over, so that once again I was facing away from him, his arms around me, with ample access to my body. His lips grazed my neck, and the arm under my shoulder bent at the elbow to play with my nipple, while his other hand fumbled for something in his discarded pants.

I heard the rustle of a foil package, and then Caleb had both hands on me, stroking my skin. His cock pressed against my ass crack, before working his way between my thighs and slowly, achingly, beautifully slowly, entered me.

I was so tight from the two orgasms that it took a few strokes for his whole length to be inside me. All the while, he continued to stroke my skin, his lips warm against the nape of my neck. A hand snaked down my body and pressed between my legs.

The ache inside me flared up again. My clit burned with all

the attention it had received, but Caleb took it carefully, just brushing his fingers over the little bud, barely touching it at all. But the sensation coupled with his length sliding inside me grew the pleasure inside me once more.

This felt so different from the sex we had the other night. That was primal, animalian. This was intimate. It wasn't really sex. It was more ...

... making love.

Did I just think that? Did I just think the word love? *Am I really starting to fall for this guy?*

The thought didn't fill me with dread, the way it usually did. Instead, it made a new warmth spread through my body. The ache rose higher, pressing against my skin. Caleb's hand trailed over my stomach, while the other brushed me faster, working in time with his strokes.

"That's it," he whispered in my ear as the ache spread further. "Come again for me, you gorgeous woman."

The ache burst forth, flooding my body with heat and light. My walls tightened around his shaft, and he started to thrust faster as he approached his own orgasm.

Caleb's teeth sank into my shoulder, a sharp pain that only heightened the sensation of him hardening, shuddering inside me. His body tensed, then relaxed, collapsing against mine. One last, final thrust, and he too was spent.

I couldn't move, didn't want to move. His body against mine felt whole, complete, like we were two lost puzzle pieces that slotted together perfectly.

Finally, my limbs woke up enough that I thought I could move. I rolled over, so that I was facing Caleb. My hands cupped his cheeks. His stubble grazed my palms.

"That was pretty intense."

"Yeah." His heavy lidded eyes smiled back at me. "The intensist."

I laughed. "That's not a word."

"You'd know better than me, Miss Writer."

"Yes, I would. Hey, Caleb?"

"Mmmmhmm?"

"About this mate business ... what exactly happens when a woman becomes your mate?"

His eyes bore into mine. "Why are you asking? Are you—"

"No, I'm not ready for that. But I have a right to know, don't I?"

"Sure." He trailed a finger over my shoulder blade. "Well, when I take a mate, I would place a bite on her to mark her as my own."

"A bite? Does it hurt?"

"Yeah, but I'd be very gentle. Any woman who is strong enough to be the mate of a werewolf wouldn't have a problem with the pain."

"That's ... not very reassuring."

"When I bite, my saliva mixes with her blood. Other wolves can smell that, even after the wound heals. They would always know that this woman belonged to me and my pack, that she was protected. The bite is a symbol of a pair, like a wedding ring in shifter society, but it's also a form of protection. Any wolf who attacked a mate would bring the full fury of the pack down upon themselves. Is this scaring you?"

"Oh, no. Biting and wounds and werewolf wedding vows are perfectly normal, non-scary things. Is there anything else I should be aware of?"

He squeezed my arm. "No. I mean, there's probably a bunch of stuff about pregnancy that's a little odd, but you'd have to ask Anna about that. She'd know more than me. The only other thing I would say is that if you did become my mate, I would be the luckiest guy in the whole entire world."

"Caleb?"

"Yes, Rosa."

"I had an affair with the mayor."

The words were out of my mouth before I knew it. Once they were out, I wished like hell I could take them back.

Caleb blinked. "Of your old town? So?"

I'd dreaded the words he might say, but his reaction did nothing to loosen the heavy stone that now pressed against my chest. This was exactly how I'd felt when I'd started seeing Nancy, like I was walking around with a boulder on my chest, weighing me down. The only thing that made it better was talking. And I didn't want the boulder between Caleb and I any longer. So I talked.

"He was a white man."

"So? I'm a white man."

"That's not a *so*. You can't understand what it's like for me."

"I know what it's like to be different, yeah. To feel like an outcast in your own family." Caleb patted his chest.

"I guess, but it's not really the same. You can blend in. When you walk down the street, people don't stare at you like you're an alien. When you're good at your job, people don't make comments about how you're stealing work from true British citizens. When you go to buy toilet paper and are made to feel like your money isn't as good as anyone else's. It's not the same," I repeated.

"Okay." Caleb kissed my nose. "It's not the same. Keep going."

"I was the other woman. He was married to a woman who was best friends with my boss at the accounting firm I worked for. His wife was white too, and my boss. In fact, pretty much everyone in the village was white. They could be rude sometimes; muttered comments behind me in line at the post office, overlooking me for projects at work even though I had the most experience, the usual kind of thing. Most racism is just that –

thoughtless comments made by normal people. But it was my first job after university, and I wanted to make a success of it. I saved a lot of money – I didn't exactly have friends to go out with – so I bought my little Tudor cottage and I was going to stay until I paid the mortgage down, then move on and keep it as a rental."

"Sensible," Caleb murmured.

"When it comes to money, yes. But that's where my common sense ends, trust me. I got sucked in by Sam's charisma. He was handsome in that old-fashioned, upper-class, Mr.-Darcy kind of way."

"I wouldn't know." Caleb's eyes glinted.

"He owned an estate and wore these snappy suits and was in line for a title and his eyes crinkled in the corners. He would come into the office and flirt with me, and it made me so happy. One day he asked me out, and things just spiralled out of control from there. He was easy to talk to. I told him everything about my life. He was such a great listener.

"When the affair started, I didn't know Sam was married. I didn't even know he was the mayor. Who really knows who their mayor is? One morning I was reading the paper and there he was on the front page at a ribbon-cutting ceremony for the new statue on the village green. His tall, blonde wife smiling beside him."

Caleb looked appalled.

"I swear my heart fell into my shoes. I felt so betrayed. I hadn't realised how much I'd opened myself up and let myself be vulnerable to him. And all this time, he was ... he was ..." I gulped, forcing back the tears that were threatening to spill over. "I confronted Sam with it that night. His whole composed façade broke down. He begged me to stay with him. He had tears in his eyes as he gave me all the usual sob stories – he was unhappy, his wife was a cold, heartless bitch, he loved me, and he was going to leave her for me as soon as he was re-elected.

Like a fool, I believed him. That night, we went to a hotel together, and many nights afterwards."

"I was so happy. Nothing could touch me, not even the stupid village and their increasingly racist interactions with me, fuelled by Brexit and all the political bullshit that's been going on. My boss, Susan, was becoming an even bigger bitch, and she started palming Sam's work off to other juniors, when she used to do it all herself. I should have been suspicious, but all I could think was that soon Sam would leave his wife and then we could escape together to his estate and I could tell Susan where to shove her job. But of course that never happened. It all fell apart."

"The story came out." Caleb squeezed my hand.

"Of course it did. They always do, don't they? Susan told the wife her suspicions, and she went snooping, and found a dirty text I'd written Sam on his phone. She confronted Sam, and he stormed out, so she called another of her blonde friends at the local newspaper, and went public with the affair. They found an unflattering picture of me at a nightclub in London that a friend had tagged me in on Facebook from my university days, and that was the image they ran in the paper opposite Sam's official mayoral photo and an portrait of his sobbing wife. A bunch of other papers picked it up. Why not, right? The upright English public servant led astray by the wanton black harlot? It fit perfectly with what everyone in the country already wanted to believe."

"I'm so sorry." Caleb's hand cupped my cheek.

"Don't be. I was an idiot. I should have seen it coming, how it would end. My therapist said that I stayed in Old Garsmouth for so long afterward because I was punishing myself, and there's probably some truth in it. The town was stony toward me before, but now they were outright hostile. I couldn't go out on the street without people calling me names or throwing things at me. My car got trashed three times, and the garage in the village refused to fix it for me. The wife's blonde friends would follow me around the shops yelling at me to go back to Africa. People threw rocks through my windows and left cruel notes in my letterbox. But Susan was the worst. She made my life an absolute hell. She downgraded my job from accountant to secretary, cut my pay in half, dumped three people's worth of work on me, and threatened to fire me for negligence if I didn't step up. I should have quit, but I felt like I had to prove I wasn't what they said I was."

"But you *did* leave. Why?"

I sucked in a breath. Here it was. "One night, I came home from visiting my parents in Leeds. I rounded the corner of the street, and noticed a strange, flickering orange light. It was a house on fire. It was *my* house on fire."

The words sounded hollow, like they weren't coming from my mouth, like I was listening to someone else telling their story. But it was my story, and it really happened.

"Fuck." Caleb's fingers clenched on my shoulder.

"The firefighters were there when I pulled up, but they could only do so much. My beautiful little cottage burned to the ground that night, with my beloved cat and all my worldly possessions inside it."

"Those bastards," Caleb hissed, his embrace so tight it crushed my bones.

"Tell me about it." My voice cracked. A single tear escaped from my eye and trickled down my cheek. I hope Caleb hadn't seen it, but he reached up with a hand and wiped it away. The gesture made my eyes spill over, and more tears fell. "I get panic attacks about it."

"Panic attacks?"

"Yeah. One minute I'll be fine, and the next I'll suddenly realise everyone around me is white, and my brain thinks they're all closing in on me, like a mob ready to pounce. I get this over-whelming, paralysing fear, and my whole body shuts down. My head spins. I get dizzy and my brain turns to mush. Sometimes, I'll even faint. My therapist said it would take awhile for them to stop, and maybe they never would."

"That's terrible. But what about the people who torched your house? Are they in jail?"

"They got away with it. The police investigated, of course, but the investigating officer is Susan's husband's friend. Draw your own conclusions. I have."

"And the guy? What happened to him?"

"Sam? Oh, he's still the mayor. His wife publicly forgave him. He made this really heart-wrenching speech about mistakes and re-dedicating himself to looking after the good of the town, and they re-elected him." I laughed woodenly, remembering how remorseful Sam sounded, how his voice cracked when he talked about how he was going to turn over a new leaf. "His approval ratings shot through the roof. He's still lording it over the whole county, with his forgiving wife by his side. The perfect family."

"Fuck. No wonder you don't want to be with a white guy. I don't blame you."

Caleb's jaw was clenched, his expression stony. He looked furious on my behalf. I hadn't realised how much tension I'd been carrying around about it, until I'd started talking. Seeing that Caleb wasn't on their side sent all the tension away. My limbs slackened, the knot in my stomach starting to unfurl.

"I'm sorry, Caleb," I sobbed with relief. It was out now. He knew everything.

"Why are you sorry? They're the ones who—"

"I didn't mean to paint you in the same brush as them. You're *not*. You're so nice to me, and I don't understand why."

"Hey, you're pretty damn nice to me, too." Caleb loosened his grip and resettled himself, laying flat on his back, his arm wrapped around me, stroking my shoulder. "You shouldn't say things like that about yourself. You know why I'm nice to you. I like you. *More* than like you, in fact. And I know it's only been a few days, but I can't imagine my life without you now."

"Caleb ..." My voice croaked and my chest tightened again.

"It's okay, Rosa. I know you need time. After what happened, I don't blame you. I'm here for you whenever you're ready. And in the meantime ..." He raised an eyebrow suggestively. "We can always do more of what we just did."

"I like the sound of that." I nestled into Caleb's shoulder. "Have you ever been with a black woman before?"

"Once." He grinned. "We fucked in the bathroom at a shitty club in Aberdeen. She called out some other guy's name. Her hair wasn't nearly as cool as yours."

I laughed.

"I don't care what colour your skin is, Rosa. I think you're beautiful, and clever, and funny, and amazing. And I wouldn't have you any other way. If you can handle being with a werewolf—"

"I can."

"—then I can take anything you got, you gorgeous woman."

I couldn't think of anything to say after that. The words *I love you* were dangerously close to escaping my lips, but I couldn't say them. I couldn't take that risk now, and potentially spoil the hard-won peace I could feel settling over me. Caleb was right, I needed time to figure things out between us before I made any kind of commitment.

Instead, I snuggled deeper into his embrace, breathed in his intoxicating scent, and fell into a vivid daydream about what it would be like to be married to a werewolf.

12

CALEB

*R*osa's eyes closed, and her breathing became steady. She'd fallen asleep on my shoulder.

My stomach rumbled. I desperately wanted to head down to the drawing room and partake of that supper Alex had talked about, but there was no way in hell I was going to wake Rosa up, not after everything she'd been through over the last few days, over the last year.

The woman deserved a little bit of peace.

Rosa's words swirled around in my mind, and all the pain that soaked through them swelled inside me. I'd been part of a pack where I had no allies except my mother, but I couldn't imagine living in a village where everyone hated me. I couldn't even *fathom* how anyone could look at her and see anything other than a smart, fun, gorgeous woman. To burn down her *house*? Because she made a mistake? It just seemed out of proportion.

You can't understand what it's like for me, she'd said to me. From everything she'd just said, that was true. I *couldn't* understand how anyone could hate another person so much that they would consider committing an indictable crime just to drive them away. I'd always cared much more about who a person was or what they did than their skin colour, but I was beginning to realise that was because I had the luxury *not* to care.

Rosa didn't have that luxury. Life had been cruel to her. But that ended, right now. She needed protecting, and I was the one who would protect her. No racist bastard was ever going to hurt her like that again.

NEEDLESS TO SAY, with Rosa sound asleep on my shoulder, I didn't make it to supper that evening. I woke up in darkness with the worst hunger imaginable. Moonlight streamed in the window, and my wolf strained against my skin, desperate for release. I lifted my hand above my head, and noticed to my horror a line of fine grey fur running down my forearm. It was only a couple of days until the full moon, when my wolf would take over. At least now I knew that I could leave Rosa here with Ryan and Alex and Marcus when Luke and I went feral.

My stomach rumbled. I had to get something to eat, or the wolf was going to win this battle, and I didn't think Rosa would appreciate waking up next to a drooling beast.

Rosa was still sound asleep. I lifted her arm and slid out from beneath her, replacing my body with a pillow. She mumbled something and squeezed her arms around the pillow, lifting up her knees and giving me a delicious view of her gorgeous rear.

I padded through the silent house, and found my way to the enormous kitchen. I was surprised to find it already occupied. Ryan's butler Simon stood at the stove, stirring something in a large bowl.

"Good morning, sir," he said pleasantly.

"Hey, Simon. You cooking breakfast already?"

"Master Ryan requested everyone congregate in the green

drawing room at seven sharp. I will make sure you're all properly fed."

"Seven?" I yawned. "That sounds early. What's the time now?"

"A quarter past five."

Yikes. "I missed supper last night, and I've woken up starving. Is there anything I can munch on to tide me over until seven?"

Simon walked to the freezer and inspected the contents. "I have raw leg of pork, if that pleases you?"

It took me a few moments to realise the butler was making a joke. "Ha ha."

"Sorry, sir. Sometimes one must give into temptation. If you can wait for ten minutes, I will make you something hot. Should I prepare something for Miss Rosa, as well?"

"Yes please, and I'll take a pot of tea up to her, as well."

True to his word, Simon bustled around the kitchen, opening packets and popping bread in the toaster. Less than eight minutes later, he handed me a tray of scrambled eggs, homemade grainy bread, lightly toasted and slathered with butter and jam, and a pot of hot tea.

"Anything else I can help you with, sir?"

"Yes." I fiddled with the fake Benedict ring on my finger. "Could you bring me a really strong piece of twine?"

Simon nodded, and disappeared into the depths of the house. A few moments later he turned, carrying a thick strand of leather cord. I took the ring off my finger, threaded it on the cord, and knotted it around my neck. Now, even if I shifted, the ring would always stay with me.

I took the tray gratefully and went back up to Rosa's room. Having a butler was pretty damn awesome.

Rosa sat up when I entered the room, her bright eyes meeting mine. "I woke up and you were gone."

She sounded kind of grumpy.

"I only went for food and coffee." I pulled a small table over to the edge of the bed and perched the tray on top. "I brought you back some tea, but it takes so long to find my way through the labyrinth of this house that it's probably cold by now."

She laughed her big, happy laugh. "It's true. This place is *insane*. I can't believe someone as normal as Ryan lives in a house like this."

"I'm not sure I'd classify Ryan as *normal*. Despite the way it looks on the outside, he loves this place like it was his child. Raynard Hall has been in his family for centuries. I bet it makes your old boyfriend's estate look like a kid's dollhouse."

Rosa's face darkened. "Sam wasn't my boyfriend."

I filled a cup with tea and held it to her. "Hey, no worries. I shouldn't have joked about it."

"No. I'd prefer that you didn't."

Her tone was so strong, I almost dropped the mug I was holding.

"I won't, ever again." I ventured a tiny smile, which she didn't return. She did take the tea though, giving the hot liquid a tentative sip. I studied her face. Was I imagining it, or did she seem a bit off, like she was trying desperately to hold back a great well of rage bubbling up inside her.

No. I must be imagining it. There was no reason for her to feel upset, not after everything we shared last night. She was probably just grumpy from a lack of sleep.

"I spoke to Simon in the kitchen. Everyone's going to meet in the drawing room at seven, and we'll come up with a plan." ...

Rosa yawned. "I guess I'd better get into the shower then, to make myself presentable."

My cock hardened at the thought of warm, soapy water cascading down her body. "Do you want me to join you?"

She shook her head, setting down her cup. "I've been

successfully cleaning myself for twenty-three years. I think I can manage."

Okay, something was definitely up. Rosa never missed an opportunity to flirt. She was already scrambling off the bed, the food untouched. "Rosa, you're okay, right?"

"Yeah." She grabbed her overnight bag and dashed toward the bathroom without looking at me. "I'm fine."

"Are you sure—" The door slammed behind her, and I heard her slide the lock into place.

You're not fine. I stared at the locked bathroom door. *But I don't know why.*

EVERY MEMBER of my pack sat around the drawing room, their eyes on me. *My pack.* I still couldn't believe I had a pack. Luke, as the older wolf and the only one currently mated, was the de-facto alpha, but the first thing he'd done when Rosa and I entered the room was officially sign over that duty to me. The pack voted and agreed.

I, Caleb Lowe, the adopted, forgotten, neglected child of Amos Lowe, was now the alpha.

Granted, my pack was probably the most motley collection of individuals ever to be assembled under one shifter banner. We had Luke and I, cousins who only found out each other existed less than a year ago. Then there was Luke's wife Anna, who was joining us via a video call on Ryan's laptop. There was Ryan Raynard himself – the reclusive artist with the impossibly enormous home – and his brother Marcus, a brutish, lad's lad who seemed to have only football and girls on his mind at any one time. Standing by the espresso machine in the corner, expertly making coffee to everyone's exacting specifications, was Alex, who'd already informed me she had some other friends who might be interested in joining the pack should we need their expertise.

We weren't exactly a match for the Macleans, but it was definitely a start.

As soon as everyone was seated, coffee in hand, and Simon had arranged trays of pulled pork sliders and tiny eggs benedict bites on the coffee table, I filled everyone in on what had happened at Rosa's cabin, and what Luke had discovered about the Benedict ring. I showed them the fake ring I had around my neck.

Everyone's eyes locked on me as I spoke, a strange sensation after years of carrying out barked orders from my stepfather and the other Maclean pack alphas. I'd never had a chance to lead, and I wanted to be good. But now wasn't the time to second-guess myself – I had to be strong and decisive in order to keep Rosa safe.

Speaking of Rosa, she hadn't cheered up much since her shower. She was now the only one not looking at me. Instead, she toyed with the spoon in her coffee, staring at her knees. I still had no idea what was bothering her, and I hoped she'd tell me soon.

"What do we think Angus and Robbie were up to with this attack?" Ryan asked. "Are they trying to send us a message?"

I shrugged. "Honestly, I think it was Angus' attempt to ensure he had the last word. It's a classic Maclean move, to terrorise intended victims with attacks like this, to make them feel unsafe. Rosa's been receiving a few SMS messages with similar types of juvenile insults. Perhaps my brothers know about what happened to her back in Old Garsmouth and are attempting to use that against Rosa."

"What happened in Old Garsmouth?" Alex asked.

I glanced over at Rosa. Her jaw was set hard, her fingers clenching the handle of her cup so tight, her knuckles were white. I knew everyone in this room would 100% want to kill the bastards in that village, but Rosa didn't know that. And it wasn't my story to tell, so I changed the subject.

"That's not important now. What's important is that we need to secure Rosa's safety as soon as possible. I think Angus and Robbie are probably on their way back to Aberdeen right now, to return with reinforcements, but I won't feel certain until we've checked over the whole area. We'll split into two teams, one fox and one wolf to each team. Rosa will stay here, at Raynard Hall, where it's safest. Luke, you and Marcus go back to the cabin, see if you can find any clues as to who put the graffiti there, and follow any scent trails. Ryan and I will go—"

"I don't think it was them," Rosa said, her voice shaking.

I stared at her. She was folded and refolding her hands in her lap.

"I keep going over and over what I saw," she said. "The man running into the trees was shorter and skinnier than Caleb's stepbrothers. Also, he was a human. If it was Angus or Robbie, wouldn't they have changed into their wolf form so they could escape faster?"

"Maybe not. Perhaps they were wearing clothes and didn't want to leave them behind," I said.

"No one in your family seems particularly fond of clothes," she snot back, her face sneering as she regarded my naked torso.

"Are you sure about this? Because the way you described it to me yesterday, he was quite far away by the time you saw him, and sometimes tall trees can distort perspective—"

"I know what I saw," Rosa insisted. "Are you doubting me?"

Her words came out as a harsh rasp. A shudder ran through me.

"I'm not doubting you," I said. "I'm just making sure we have the exact information and we don't jump to conclusions. If the guy you saw isn't one of my stepbrothers, that means we have a different problem – they've left someone here in Crookshollow to keep an eye on us."

"Is there anything I can do?" Alex asked.

"Sure. Keep Rosa company."

"I don't need babysitting," Rosa snapped.

"I'm not saying that. I'm just saying that you and Alex should hang out here, where it's safe."

Rosa's face was a perfect storm of emotion. Her hands were clenched in fists. She looked like she wanted to say more, but she didn't. Instead, she flattened her back against the couch, and drew her knees up to her chest.

Ryan shot me a concerned look. So it wasn't just me.

What's up with Rosa? After the conversation we'd had last night, when she'd opened up to me, I thought we'd finally moved onto a new stage. I'd hoped she'd tell me more about living in Old Garsmouth, and how I could help stop the bullying and racism that followed her around like a bad smell.

Instead, she was the opposite. She looked like she wanted to punch me in the face. And every word that came out of my mouth seemed to make it worse.

I'm trying to keep you safe. Why are you suddenly so cold and uncaring? What did I do?

13

ROSA

*Y*ou shouldn't have told him.

I sat like a statue, listening with building rage while Caleb and his friends made their plans. The anger bubbled under my skin, like a pot about to boil over.

Last night I'd gone to sleep with calm in my heart and a satisfied weariness in my body, knowing that Caleb knew about everything that had happened, and that he seemed to understand why it made me react the way I did. I'd fallen asleep on his shoulder, tempted by the thought that maybe this guy was different.

Then I woke up, and he wasn't there.

And I stared at the ceiling and thought over everything that had happened since I met him. Caleb had stormed into my life under the guise of protecting me, taken over my little cabin, and moved me into his friend's house. There was this constant, over-riding assumption from everyone around us that I'd become his mate, like it was just inevitable, like I didn't have a choice.

Did I really need all this protecting? Was I so hopeless that he thought I needed to be watched every minute like a naughty child? If I did become his mate, did I really want a relationship that was based on me being a damsel in distress? Sure, it was nice to think of him out there, looking out for me. He was the first person in my life who'd ever done that. Thinking of it made a lump rise in my throat.

But was that what I wanted? Caleb had distracted me from my real reason for coming to Crookshollow. I had a book to write. Every minute I spent with him made the horror of Old Garsmouth fade a little. It felt so good, but it wasn't right. I needed that pain. I needed those memories – for my book, and because they were a part of me.

I was still thinking about it all now, while they were sitting around deciding my fate. If I wasn't Rosa, the oppressed, the girl whose house got burned down, then who was I?

The discussion petered out as everyone settled on tasks to do. I was the only one who didn't have a task. This was my story, and yet I was the only one without any agency. The lump of anger in my stomach flared higher, mixing with a horrible, sickening churn when I thought of walking away from Caleb and all this.

I stood silently as all the boys left, my whole body all twisted in knots. Caleb came over to me. "You okay?"

No. "Yeah, I'm fine."

"Sure. But you don't need anything else from me?"

I need to be more than just a girl who needs saving. "No. I'm fine."

Caleb brushed his lips across mine, and I longed to wrap my arms around him and pull him closer, to lose myself in his kiss. Instead, I stepped back, and said in a flat voice, "Good luck."

His blue eyes flickered over me, then looked away. "Yeah, sure."

He shuffled off down the hall, glancing over his shoulder at me as he followed Ryan and Marcus around a corner. His face looked drawn, full of hurt. *I did that. I hurt him.*

I wish my stomach would stop churning so much.

The front door slammed, and they were gone. I felt like I might throw up at any moment.

Alex set me up in Ryan's office with a shiny laptop and a cup of fresh tea. "Just ring the bell over there if you need anything, and Simon will come running," she said. "I'll be in the studio, and I'm in the middle of a huge installation, so you might not see me for a few hours."

I opened the laptop and found my file on my cloud backup. I reread over my last couple of paragraphs. The protagonist was at the police station, giving her statement. But the police officers kept twisting her words and making horrible lewd and racist comments about her.

My fingers poised over the keyboard. The scene floated in front of my eyes, the memories as fresh and visceral as they were the day it happened. All it would take is a little twist here, a tweak there, and my life became a fiction.

I started to type, but the words felt wrong. Everything sounded clunky, stilted. I couldn't get the pacing of the scene right. There were too many heads talking without any sense of real tension. I couldn't convey the sheer panic of it – the feeling of terror when you realised the people who were supposed to be protecting were on the side of the criminals who'd just burned down your house. And there were four of them and one of you and they were staring at your chest with a glint in their eyes—

I shuddered. *Focus, Rosa. Get it on the page.*

This is what Caleb is doing to me.He's robbing me of all my creative expression. And I have to get this book written. I have to tell this story.

Rage bubbled up inside me. I deleted everything I'd written, and started typing again. But it was no good. If anything, it all sounded worse.

What I needed was inspiration. I needed to read the words of another great writer, words rich with pain and desperation. But I only had a couple of my books with me, and I'd foolishly grabbed ones I'd already read. I hadn't had time to replace my ereader. Some lover of literature I was.

I scanned the bookshelves in Ryan's office, hoping for something that would suffice, but they contained volumes of art history and natural science, and all of Dan Brown's paperbacks. *Ick.* There was nothing with a Man Booker Prize sticker on it.

I thought of the stacks of beautiful books beside my bed at the cabin, all those pages of strong, heart-wrenching prose, stories of black lives in tatters. Words carved from the ashes of pain and horror. The images on the spines of strong black women telling their stories, staring out from the paper, just daring the reader to cross them, to deny them.

I wanted so badly to be one of them, but with Caleb in my life, I felt like I was failing them all.

It was foolish to even think about going back to my cabin. Caleb said it wasn't safe. Just the thought of running into his stepbrothers again made my stomach churn. But what was the alternative? Sitting in this opulent house, writing my book thanks to the benevolence of white men?

That wasn't my story.

I *needed* my books. They were *my* books. And I wasn't going to wait around for permission to go get them.

Be bold, Rosa. Be bold.

I rang the bell. A few moments later, Simon materialised in the doorway. How had he got there so fast? Did he have a transporter, like on Star Trek? Hell, I was hanging out with shapeshifters; nothing was off-limits now.

"I want to go to the bookstore in the village," I said. "Will you drive me?"

"Master Ryan said you were not to leave the house."

"Master Ryan isn't the boss of me. And he actually said I wasn't to go anywhere *alone*. I won't be alone. You'll be with me."

"I should have Lady Alex accompany you—"

I shook my head. "She's working, and I don't want to disturb her. We'll go there and come straight back, I swear. It'll take twenty minutes at the most. And it's not as though anything can happen. Even if those werewolves are back, they're not going to be able to do anything in the middle of the village, with all the people about. And if you're so worried, we'll even take one of Clara's anti-bad-wolf charms in the car with us."

Simon looked dubious, but he was a man who spent his entire life obeying orders. "As you wish, ma'am."

I was already slinging my coat over my shoulder. "Let's go."

BOOKSTORES ARE the happiest places on earth.

As soon as I walked through the door of *Spellbinding Books*, I felt instantly at home. The store was housed in a narrow terrace between a chemist and a tarot reader. Crooked bookshelves lined every wall and stuck out at odd angles into the tiny room. Haphazard stacks of books stretched as high as the ceiling, and handwritten signs made a poor effort to differentiate the chaos into genres and sections. Another sign on the narrow staircase indicated further treasures could be found upstairs.

I picked my way around two teenage goths fawning over a hardcover copy of *Interview with a Vampire*, and headed up to the second level. In a small alcove off the main room, I found just what I was looking for – literary fiction, with a single shelf dedicated to "POC fiction."

I scanned the titles and authors with reverence, pulling out several books to buy. I didn't know how long I'd be stuck at Raynard Hall for – not that I was complaining – but if I had lots to read, maybe I'd start to feel more as if I were working toward something.

My arms full of books, I moved away from the alcove, checking out the other fiction titles for sale. They had a beautiful hardback copy of Colson Whitehead's *The Intuitionist*. I wondered if Luke might enjoy it. I added it to my stack.

As I was moving through the displays, a man and woman – white and in their fifties, judging by their greying hair and conservative clothing – entered the room, and went to the alcove. The man jabbed his finger at the "POC authors" shelf. "What a load of PC nonsense," he scoffed.

My chest tightened. *Here we go.*

"Why do *they* need a whole bloody section? You don't see us asking for a white authors' shelf," the woman said. "It's bloody racism, is what it is."

You don't get a shelf because you have the whole bloody store, I fumed silently. This is exactly why I have to write my book, exactly why I can't let Susan and Sam and everything get away with it—

Caleb's kind face flashed before my eyes, reminding me that not all white people were out to get me. I took a deep breath, and decided to approach them.

"I mean, look at this one." She yanked a copy of Diana Evans' *26a* off the shelf and waved it around. "What a load of rubbish. The only reason this stuff gets published is to fill up some quota—"

"Excuse me," I said, pointing to the book she was holding up. "I think you'd really like that, if you liked *The Sparrow Sisters*. It's about these twin girls who—"

"Like you would know." Her eyes flashed back at me. "You don't read Ellen Herrick. She's not black."

"I have, actually, and—"

The woman tossed *26a* onto the floor with disgust. "This

shouldn't even be in here. You should get your own bookshop if you're so desperate to read this dreck; leave the rest of us to enjoy real literature."

"Explain to me how that book isn't real literature—"

"You bloody immigrants," the man swore. "This isn't your country. Why are you always trying to take our jobs and force your culture on us?"

My blood boiled. "Excuse *me,* not that it's any of your business, but I was born in Leeds. And so what if I was an immigrant? People have been moving around on Earth for millions of years. It's pretty rich being lectured by a white guy about forcing culture."

"Colonialism is what made this country great. We had a responsibility to stop you blackies worshipping devils and spreading disease—"

"It destroyed hundreds of indigenous cultures, and most of the time it was the English who brought disease." My face felt hot. The ball of rage that had been sitting in my stomach ever since I'd woken up swelled to double its size. I couldn't *believe* these people.

The woman touched his elbow. "Don't engage her, Robert. She's just trying to make you feel guilty that you're successful and she's probably on the benefit. Britain isn't Britiain anymore with all these goddamn foreigners running the place."

"I'm not on the benefit! I have all the money I could ever want because some racist bastards like you burned down my house and murdered my cat!" I screamed at them.

"Ma'am." A hand waved in my face. It was the elderly proprietor. He looked deeply apologetic. "I'm going to have to ask you to leave."

"Me? But they're the ones who—"

"All the same. I'd like you to leave the shop."

I looked around, and realised there were three other white

customers in the room, all staring at me with a mixture of curiosity and revulsion. "Fine." I dumped my stack of books on the floor, wincing as the beautiful covers thwacked against the carpet. "I was going to buy all those, and all *she's* going to get is another copy of Dan Brown's latest blockbuster. But fine."

My hands shaking with anger and fear, I clattered down the stairs, the woman's laughter echoing in my ears. Hot, angry tears stained my cheeks. I'd made a fool out of myself, for no reason. I was never going to change those people. It was pointless even trying.

I stepped out onto the street, and fumbled for my phone to call Simon to come pick me up. A hand grabbed me from nowhere.

"What the hell do you think you're doing?" A familiar voice growled in my ear.

"Caleb?" I whirled around, ready to wrap my arms around him and calm myself from the altercation. "I'm so glad to see you. How did you know where I—"

"We got back to the manor, and you weren't there. Alex had no idea where you were, but Simon was gone, so we followed the GPS in the car using Ryan's security system. Rosa, this is *insane*. Why did you leave the house? I told you not to leave the house."

His face was a raging storm. Behind him, Luke, Ryan and Marcus were standing with their arms folded, looking either worried or annoyed. The four strong, white faces staring back at me suddenly became threatening. They weren't the faces of friends, but of people who would hurt me.

Panic rose in my chest. My throat started to close. *No, not now. Please not now.*

"I needed books," I said quietly, trying to force back the emerging panic attack. I took a step back, but Caleb only charged forward, his face inches from mine.

"Ryan has a whole library in his house. One of those wouldn't do?"

"It's filled with rich, white guy books."

"Fucking hell, not this again." Caleb threw up his hands in exasperation. His gaze fell on my hands. "You don't even have any books, Rosa. This is bullshit. Just tell me the real reason you came here."

"I ..." My hands started shaking again. "There were these people, a man and a woman, they were horrible to me. They said these awful things about me being black and an immigrant and that black writers don't deserve to be in the bookshop at all and I kind of snapped and yelled and dropped all my books everywhere and—"

My hands were shaking really bad now, and the words dried on my lips. My head spun, and I grabbed his arm to steady myself, my nails digging into his flesh. Behind him, Luke was saying something, but his words sounded far away, as though I was hearing them underwater.

Caleb must've read my grip on him as an indication to leave, because he started to drag me toward Ryan's car. He said something, his eyes blazing, but my ears were roaring with the sound of my own heartbeat, and I couldn't hear him.

Caleb shoved me into the passenger seat. I clutched my stomach with shaking hands, hoping to keep my breakfast down. *Please, please, don't throw up.*

As Caleb pulled the car away from the curb, and I watched the *Spellbinding Books* sign fade into the distance, the panic attack subsided, leaving me shaken.

"You look agitated," he said, gripping the wheel tight. His voice sounded strained.

"I am. I—"

"Rosa, you can't let what people say get to you. People say a lot of dumb stuff, and most of it, they don't really mean. Getting upset does not help matters."

His words stung. "So that's it? I'm just supposed to let white people say shit to me and it's my fault that I'm upset?"

"That's not what I meant at all. I think you're being way too sensitive, because Angus and Robbie are after you and you're scared, and because of what happened to you in Old Garsmouth—"

"Throw it back in my face, why don't you?" I was trembling again, but this time it was from anger. How *dare* he? How dare he try to put this all on me. Some white people are openly horrible to me, the woman he supposedly loves, the woman who's supposed to be his mate, and he's blaming me for my reaction. "Oh, no, they couldn't *possibly* be the ones in the wrong, because they're white. It must be the black girl who just misunderstood."

"This isn't the time to be worrying about this shit, not with my stepbrothers on our tail. You were right, whoever graffitied your cabin was human, but his trail went down to the stream, and then we lost it. We're going to try and follow my stepbrothers' scent trials from where they left Crookshollow, but they're nearly two days old now, so they're going to be faint—"

"How can you say this isn't the time for this? When is it ever a good time for racism? But it happens, Caleb, and I have to—"

"Dammit, Rosa—argh!" A car pulled out in front of us. Caleb slammed on the brakes, and we jerked to a halt with only a millimetre to spare. The car sped away, and Caleb leaned over the steering wheel and yelled out the window. "Learn to drive, you fucking black bastard!"

Shock reverberated through my whole system. He didn't just say that. He *did not* just stay that.

But he did. The words hung in the air, turning everything wonderful between us into dust. Caleb stared at me, and his whole face sagged. He opened his mouth, as if he might be able to swallow the words again. But he couldn't. It was too late.

The truth hit me like a freight train, the pain of it tearing through my whole body. I knew who he was. He was exactly the same as all the rest of them.

"Stop the car," I said, my voice steady, firm.

"Rosa," he said, his whole face dropping.

"Caleb, stop this car right now."

He must have heard the finality in my voice, because he pulled over to the side of the road, and parked. His hands on the wheel appeared white, and they twitched as he put the hand-brake on. "I'm sorry. I'm so sorry. I didn't mean it. I was just worried about you, and I—"

"Goodbye, Caleb." I grabbed the door handle, my fingers fumbling for the seatbelt. I won't cry. I was so past crying now. Everything felt oddly calm, serene. I was doing what I had to do, what I should have done four days ago.

"Rosa, please—"

I flung the door open, and a gust of cold air caressed my face. I pulled myself to my feet, the movement visceral, like tearing off one of my own limbs. "I never want to talk to you, ever again."

I slammed the door, and sprinted away from him, not daring to look back.

You're such a fool. You thought you'd finally found someone who understood you, who was ready to love you for who you were but it was all a lie.

Now that I'd left Caleb behind me, the rage I'd felt toward him slipped away, replaced by pure, horrific sadness. I wanted nothing more than to head back to my beautiful cabin and have a good cry, but that wouldn't work. Caleb would think to follow me there, and the words DIE, BLACK BITCH were still scrawled across the wall. I don't think I could bear to see them again right now.

I need a drink.

I remembered Caleb mentioning a local pub, so I wandered aimlessly around the high street, searching for it through tear-stained eyes. Not far from *Bewitching Bites*, I found it, down the end of a tiny alley. It was past 2 p.m., and the place was nearly deserted. My stomach rumbled. I hadn't eaten anything since breakfast.

I hovered in the doorway, afraid. Should I really go in there, looking like hell? I'd just broken up with Caleb, was this really what I wanted to do?

You can't break up with him. You were never going out in the first place. You were shagging him and he was trying to control you.

I don't need Caleb to protect me. I can do it just fine on my own, the way I'd been doing for twenty-two years before I met him.

Be bold, Rosa. Be bold. Go and get yourself a drink.

I walked up to the bar and slid into one of the stools, staring at the rows of spirits stacked behind the counter, their labels blurring through my wet eyes. The thought occurred to me that I'd have to start looking for a new cabin in another forest. There is nothing else to do now. I couldn't stay in Crookshollow, not with all these memories.

At least I still had my money. It couldn't buy me the respect and kindness of other humans, but it could damn well buy me some peace. *I'll go to London, get on the first plane to somewhere. Anywhere. Maybe I'll do what they all want me to do, and fuck off to Africa.*

My stomach rumbled. I picked up the enormous plastic menu and hunted through my options, fighting to keep my tears at bay as a young publican hovered in front of me.

"Hi, I'd like to order your full English breakfast, with a side of extra hash browns. And a glass of merlot ... no, better make it a bottle."

He gave me a sideways look as he scribbled down my order. "Sure. Are you waiting for someone? Do you want me to get you a second glass?"

"No. I do not want a second glass." I turned the menu over. "Is this true? All your desserts come from the *Bewitching Bites* bakery?"

"Yeah. We used to make 'em ourselves, but Belinda at the bakery is too damn good."

"Then I'll have a slice of the Heaven & Hell cake, as well." I patted my pockets. I had my wallet with me, but I'd left my mobile phone back at the manor. "And could you call me a taxi, please? I need to get to the train station after I've finished eating."

My car was also still at Raynard Hall, and I wasn't about to go back to get it. I'd take the train into London, then get on a plane from there.

"Sure thing." He darted away, and came back a few minutes later with my bottle and a wine glass. "Have a seat anywhere. I'll bring your food over."

I slipped into an empty booth in the darkest corner of the pub. From there, I had a view of the front door, so I could see if anyone who I didn't want to talk to chanced to come in. I poured myself a glass and gulped it down, then poured another. The wine tasted like vinegar. I wondered if anything would ever taste good again.

Ten minutes later, my new best friend the publican delivered a tray of sorrow-drowning food. "I've booked your taxi for half an hour's time," he told me, handing me a card with the details. "I'll give you a wave when he arrives."

"Cheers." I lifted my glass to him in a limp gesture of thanks, then proceeded to angrily eat my way through an enormous plate of sausages, baked beans, bacon, mushroom, black pudding, and eggs.

The food sat in my stomach like a huge, undigested lump. Every time I pictured Caleb, all red in the face, those angry, hateful words falling out of his mouth, I wanted to throw it all up again.

It's your own fault. You fell for his whole protective schtick. You believed he could be different.

But he wasn't different at all. Now you're alone again, and broken, and stuffing your face with cake. At least he can't burn your house down this time.

I stared at the ceiling, wishing like hell that things could be different, that I could rewind and freeze time to this morning, when I was falling for a hot, sweet, funny guy who totally wasn't a dick.

I feel a presence over my shoulder. I whirl around, ready to tell Caleb to fuck right off. Bu it was only my bartender, looking almost apologetic. "Your taxi's arrived. He's up on the high street. The driver's name is Barry."

"Thanks." I shovelled the last mouthful of cake into my mouth, grabbed my coat, and headed for the door.

A chill ran down my spine as I stepped out into the alley. I whirled around, but there was no one behind me. No one else was in the alley, either. I took a deep breath, trying to calm myself. *You're just paranoid because of all the running and hiding you've been doing over the last couple of days. Caleb's made you like this. It's time to be bold and stop being afraid.*

There's no one here with you, except possibly ghosts. Crook-shollow probably has a lot of ghosts.

I put my head down and set off in a brisk walk. At the top of the alley, I caught sight of the taxi. It was parked across a disabled space and a yellow line, with all the audacity only a cabbie could muster. The driver was hunched forward over the wheel, a wool cap pulled low over his face. He didn't look up as I sank into the backseat.

"Barry, was it?" The driver nodded, still not looking at me. "I'd like to go to the train station."

He grunted a reply, and pulled out into the street.

While we weaved through traffic, I pulled out my wallet and inspected its contents. I had my passport, fifty quid in cash, and all my cards. I would be able to buy a cheap phone at the airport, so I could at least call my parents and tell them what happened. Everything I needed to start a new life was right here with me. I was going to be okay.

I don't feel okay. I don't think I'll ever feel okay again.

I looked out the window, and spotted the end of the train platform zooming past. *Bloody useless cabbie.*

"Um ... Barry. We've gone past the station. Could you turn around up here, please?"

From the boot behind me, I heard a scraping sound. As I turned around to see, a shadow loomed out of the boot and lunged at me. Something cold and metallic pressed against my throat. "Move, and you're a dead woman," a voice hissed in my ear. A voice with a very familiar Scottish accent.

It was Angus.

14

CALEB

*Y*ou're an Idiot.

I slammed my head against the steering wheel, as if the pain might somehow undo all the shitty things I'd said and bring Rosa back.

I can't believe I said those things. I can't believe I yelled at that guy in the traffic (he did cut me off, but it was no excuse). Why did I have to do that right at that exact moment? My whole body was wound up with tension from not knowing where Rosa was. I was half-expecting to find her torn to pieces on the street, or whisked away to Aberdeen where the Macleads could do anything to her they liked.

When I'd seen she was just at a bookstore, acting like nothing was wrong, I was *so* goddamn angry. I was trying to save her life and she was just taking it for granted. And then we'd started fighting, and all my fear and anger came out as harsh, insensitive words. I knew what she'd been through, and yet I'd acted like a complete insensitive idiot.

And I lost her.

Someone banged on the car window. I yanked my hands

from my face, my whole body surging with hope. But it wasn't Rosa at the window, it was Luke.

"What happened? You just drove away in Ryan's car. Where's Rosa?"

"She ran away."

"Why did she do that?"

"I fucked up." I slammed my head into the wheel again. The horn honked, making both of us jump. "Dammit! She's out there on her own, Luke. She doesn't want to speak to me ever again."

"Okay." Luke crossed his arms. "What did you do?"

"I yelled at her." My hand clasped around the ring against my chest. It felt heavy, unwieldy. "Then I yelled at a random black guy who cut me off."

"Shit, dude. That's ... not good."

"No, it's fucking not good. And now Rosa has run away and I have no idea where she's gone and—" I glanced at the seat, where her phone was lying on the leather. "She doesn't even have her phone with her. How am I going to find her?"

Luke pulled open the door and slid into Rosa's seat. He patted me on the shoulder. "You can fix this. She can't have got too far away. We just have to find her, and then you'll apologise. And you'll grovel. Women love a good grovel."

"I don't know if that will fix this."

"You've got to try. She's worth trying, trust me."

"Yeah," I thought of Rosa's wonderful laugh, the laugh that could cure all the world's problems. "Yeah, she is."

I dragged myself out of the car, and locked it behind me. Ryan and Marcus were jogging up the street towards us. Luke filled them in on what had happened, while I frantically cast my eyes around in search of her. Which way had she ran? I couldn't even remember, I'd been so upset.

"It'll be okay, cousin," Luke was saying, patting my shoulder again. "All we have to do is find her, and you'll get her back. You guys are destined to be together, remember? It'll all be fine."

"I hope so," Ryan said, his face grim. "We'd better hurry. I just caught a whiff of Angus' scent. Your stepbrothers are back, and they're close by."

15

ROSA

y blood turned as cold as the blade against my jugular. My heart pounded in my ears. How could this happen? How did Angus get into the taxi? Why didn't the driver ...

The driver pulled off his cap and tossed it on the seat beside him. "I head straight down the M1, right, Angus?" It was Robbie. Of course it was. How did I not see that? How could I be so *stupid?*

"Get that knife away from me," I said through gritted teeth. My fear came out as anger. I'd been on my own for less than an hour, and I'd managed to get myself kidnapped.

"And give you the perfect opportunity to escape?" Angus sneered in my ear. "I don't think so, lassie."

"We're in a moving car. What am I going to do? Leap out onto the highway and get myself crushed under a lorry?"

"She's right, Angus," Robbie said. "We've got her now. Let's not draw attention to ourselves." I noticed his hands gripped the wheel so hard his knuckles had turned white. He was scared, too. I guess he would be. This *was* a kidnapping, after all. From everything Caleb had told me, he didn't seem the kidnapping type.

Angus lowered the weapon. "Don't try anything stupid," he hissed against my ear. His hot breath made my stomach turn. I couldn't believe this guy was Caleb's brother.

Caleb.

His horrible words flashed before my memory again. In the cold reality of the taxi, surrounded by deadly wolves, they didn't actually sound that bad. If Caleb had grown up with these two charming characters as role models, it was no wonder he said those things. His words had been awful, sure, but his actions over the last few days had been nothing but heroic.

He lashed out in anger because he was worried about you. Because you'd been cold to him all morning without explanation, and you foolishly ran off without telling him. And look how that ended up for you?

Nothing like a crazy werewolf holding a knife at your throat to make you reexamine your priorities.

It's too late now. I'd told Caleb I never wanted to see him again. Now that he didn't have to worry about protecting me anymore, he could focus on establishing his pack. I hoped one day he'd become the most powerful pack in all the United Kingdom, and he'd decimate the Macleans once and for all.

And I hoped he'd find someone to be his mate, someone who didn't refuse his kindness because she was scared. Maybe he'd even find his fated mate one day.

I closed my eyes as Angus clambered out of the boot over the seat and slid down beside me, the knife still pressed against my skin. I had to stop thinking about Caleb. After the way I'd spoken to him, a guy who was only trying to protect me, Caleb wasn't going to come after me.

Which meant that Angus was going to tear me to pieces. If I was lucky, that was all he'd do. I had to stay alert, in case there was a way out of this. Maybe I could convince them I was now useless to them ...

"This is a waste of time," I snapped at Angus, who's settling into the seat beside me and leering at me with a disgusting grin, as though we're just three good chums on a road trip. "Caleb and I are no longer together. In fact, he hates me. He's not coming after me. I told him I never wanted to see him again."

The words were like poison on my tongue.

"Aye, do y'hear that, Robbie? They had a lovers tiff. Tell me, lass, have you ever known Caleb to listen to anyone?"

I didn't reply.

"I thought so," he smirked. "Caleb will be on our tails in a matter of hours. But don't worry, we've no intention of letting him catch up."

"If he knows where you're going, aren't you afraid he'll just take a flight and beat you there?"

Angus shrugged. "Unlikely. He's on the no-fly list."

"Why?"

"Because I put him there. Come on, Robbo. We need a little music, eh?"

Robbie fiddled with the radio dials, until he go to one of the local college stations. Jidenna's "Long Live the Chief" boomed through the taxi. Under normal circumstances, I loved this song, but now the lyrics seemed ominous.

I stared out the window, watching the rolling countryside, gas stations, and villages speed by. *Please Caleb,* I pressed the thoughts against my skull, hoping like hell that by some miracle, he'd be able to hear me. *I know I blew our fight out of proportion. I know I took everything you said too personally, because I was scared, and I was looking for any excuse to push you away. I have no right to ask you to put yourself in danger to save me. But please ... please hear this. I might never see you again, and I want you to know*
...

I love you. And I wish ... I wish I wasn't going to die, so I could tell you to your face.

I love you.

16

CALEB

"No one's seen her on this side of the street, but I got us some supplies," Luke panted as he ran up to me. He looked stricken, or perhaps his face was just reflecting my own distress. He pressed a small jar of lycan pills from Clara's shop into my hand. Both of us were feeling the tug of our wolves, and the full moon was only hours away.

I scanned the street again, but no answers came. We'd been searching for two hours, but I had no idea where she'd gone.

I'm such an idiot. How could I let this happen?

With every minute that went by, and every whiff of Angus' scent on the breeze, I grew more and more concerned, my stomach twisting up in knots at the thought of what might've happened to her.

As angry as Rosa was at me, I still had a duty to protect her. After hunting around the high street with no success, and making the trip out to the forest to check the cabin, Ryan and I drove back to the manor to see if she'd taken a taxi back there to collect her car, but no luck. We dragged Alex from the studio, and quizzed her and Simon on everything Rosa had said and done that morning.

Now we were back in the streets looking for her. Alex had a picture of Rosa she'd taken on her phone, and she was showing that to anyone who would stop. I was just coming out of *Spellbinding Books* after giving the owner an earful about his treatment of her, when I heard someone shouting my name.

"Caleb!"

I whirled around. Ryan was running up the alley from *Tir Na Nog,* his face flushed. "We have a sighting! The bartender in the pub said she came in about two hours ago, ordered a full-English and a bottle of red, and asked him to call her a taxi." Ryan pulled out a bar napkin. "I've got the taxi company number here—"

"Give me that," Alex snatched the napkin from his hand and started dialling the number.

My heart pounded. With her free hand, Alex reached out and squeezed my shoulder. My mind whirled with possibilities. If Rosa got into a taxi two hours ago, she could be anywhere by now ...

"Hi," Alex said. "I was supposed to meet a friend at the *Tir Na Nog,* and I've just arrived and the bar staff said they called her a cab. She doesn't have her phone on her and I'm wondering if you could tell me where she is—"

Alex will sort it out. She got in a taxi. That means she's still around her someplace. Perhaps she's gone back to the cabin. They'll be able to tell us. It's going to be okay. It's going to be—

This is all your fault. Guilt surged through me, guilt at the awful things I'd said during the fight. I'd been so agitated with worry, I hadn't been thinking. But that was the point, wasn't it? Rosa said the racism she experienced every day came from thoughtless comments made by normal people. I'd just proved her right.

"Oh, really? ... That's right, that is strange ... Thanks so much." Alex frowned as she hung up the phone. "You're not going to like this, Caleb. This dispatcher said that a driver named Barry Einhorn did pick Rosa up from the pub, about ninety minutes ago. She asked him to take her to the train station, which is only ten minutes drive away. But Barry has gone completely silent. He won't answer his phone or pick up his radio, and he seems to have disabled the GPS in his car."

My blood froze in my veins. "Angus."

"That's what I'm thinking, although we should go to the station and check she isn't there, just in case." Alex took one look at my face, and squeezed my arm even tighter. "We'll find her, don't you worry."

Alex offered to go to the station and check with all the ticketing officers to see if Rosa got on a train. She took Ryan's car. Luke, Ryan and I continued to prowl along high street, trying to sniff out Angus' trail amongst the hundreds of criss-crossing paths. We finally caught the tail of it, stopping on a disabled parking spot at the top of the alley leading down to the pub.

"The taxi would've pulled in here to pick her up," I said, my stomach churning. "There aren't that many people around today. Angus and Robbie could've knocked the driver out, and somehow convinced Rosa to get in the car."

"Where's the driver now?" Alex asked. "Would they bring him with them?"

"He's not our concern right now," I said, to try and deflect her question. I knew my stepbrothers well enough to know the driver was probably dead in the boot.

"It's isn't good. They could have gone anywhere, and we have no way of tracking them," Ryan said.

I shook my head. "Their plan hasn't changed. They're taking her to Aberdeen."

"It's good news, though." Ryan said. "We know where she's going, and we know she'll be alive when they get there. They're expecting you to follow her, right? That's the whole point of this exercise, to get you to go back to your father's clan?"

"Yes, but it's vital that he gets there first. Angus wants Rosa for himself. He wants to make her his mate. He's afraid of all of us, now that we're a pack and he knows we'll fight him for her. I think he's counting on the rest of the Maclean clan to back up his claim to her when he arrives. He'll tell them that she was his mate, and that I tried to take her from him. Douglas will believe him, unless we can get there first and he can smell the fated connection between us. If we get there too late, we'll be walking into an ambush."

"So we have to get to him before he arrives in Aberdeen, or else we're hopelessly outnumbered?"

"That's pretty much the situation. And we can't fly. Angus has connections in British Air. He'll have already made a call to ensure I can't get on a plane."

"Okay." Ryan doubled back down the street, heading for *Bewitching Bites*. He grabbed the handle of the bakery door. "Come on."

"How can you think of your stomach at a time like this?" I growled. "We don't have any time to waste if we're gonna—"

"I know," Ryan grinned. "Just trust me."

The bakery was pretty busy. Every table was occupied, and a line snaked between them from the counter all the way to the door. Behind the counter, a tiny, gorgeous Asian girl darted every which way, serving coffees and cutting cakes.

Ryan barged right past the line, ignoring the cries of indignation that followed in our wake. If there's one thing an upstanding British citizen cannot stand, it's people who cut into lines.

He marched up to the woman behind the counter. "Belinda, where's Cole today? I need to talk to him urgently."

"Oh, hey Ryan." The pretty Asian girl's face lit up in a bright smile. "He's upstairs, actually. He wanted to get some of the paperwork done for the bird sanctuary. He's trying to get it registered as an official charity. Go on back."

Bird sanctuary? Charity? This whole conversation was really bizarre. I didn't have time to ask questions or protest, as I followed Ryan through the kitchen and up a narrow flight of stairs into a tiny flat at the top.

A small kitchenette beside the door held a coffee machine and a kettle and several dirty teacups. Every available inch of wall space was covered with posters of brightly-coloured birds, native bird species charts, migration patterns, newspaper clippings, and the odd scone recipe.

The only other furniture in the room was a lumpy-looking couch under the window, a tiny desk in the centre of the room, under the light, and a man with long, black hair, a thin, hawk-like nose, and beautiful dark eyes. He was hunched over a laptop, his muscled thighs barely fitting under the desk. He wasn't wearing a shirt.

What was going on here? Who was this guy? Live-in toy boy for the bakery lady? Hell, anything's possible in Crookshollow.

The man stood. "Oh, hey Ryan. Do you like what we've done with this place? Belinda and I got our own apartment a couple of months back, so I've been using this as an office for the sanctuary—"

"I need your help, Cole." Ryan introduced me and started to explain the situation.

"Hey." I jabbed him in the arm. "Who is this guy? Can I trust him?"

"This is Cole. If I trust him, you trust him. That's how this whole pack thing works."

I nodded. Ryan was right. Just because I was the pack alpha, doesn't mean I had to be like Douglas. Ryan knew what he was doing.

"Any idea what the taxi looked like?" Cole moved over to the wall, and flung upon the window.

"Yeah, it's one of the yellow ones. Licence number BD17 SKR. The girl is black, with super frizzy hair. She was wearing a red sweater. The other two guys have short hair and Maclean tattooed on their arms, but they might be in disguise."

"Maclean tattoos?" The man scrunched up his nose.

I rolled up my sleeve and showed him the large castle. Cole nodded.

"I'm on it. Tell Belinda I'm running an errand for you." Cole faced the window, and flapped his arms. I stepped forward, certain he was having some kind of fit. Then I saw the change in his face, the way his bones cracked and rearranged themselves, the way his nose elongated, extending out from his face and hooking over at the end. He let out a croak as his knees bent backward, and he jerked to the ground. Black feathers poked from his skin, extending down his spine. His jeans and shoes dropped to the floor as his legs shrunk and his toes grew into talons. With a final cry, the man's outstretched arms unfurled into enormous wings, and a black raven flew out the window, swooping into the alley below and disappearing over the village.

"A Bran?" I turned to Ryan in surprise. I hadn't seen a raven shapeshifter in years. Usually, they were hidden away behind the walls of rich estates, slaves to the bidding of their masters. "Is he yours?"

Ryan shook his head. "And if you want him to do you any favours, don't *ever* let him hear you say that. Cole was granted his freedom. It's kind of a long story, another of Crookshollow's secret supernatural affairs. Suffice it to say, if anyone can get to Rosa before they reach Aberdeen, it'll be him."

"And then what?" I growled. Watching Cole shift had yanked my wolf even closer to the surface. At any moment now, I could be overcome, and that could get very, very bad.

"Cole's resourceful. He'll figure something out."

"I hate this." I glared at the window, wishing I was flying alongside Cole, ready to tear Angus to pieces with my talons. I touched the ring around my neck. "I need to find her, Ryan."

"I know you do." Ryan patted my shoulder. "We will. In the meantime, we'll go grab some road-trip sustenance from Belinda, and wait until Alex gets back with the car."

ALEX RETURNED JUST as we were stumbling out of the bakery, laden down with boxes of goodies. She shook her head as she got out of the driver's seat. "She definitely didn't make it to the train station. You said in your text that Cole was following the taxi."

"He left ten minutes ago. We'll head up the M1 and wait for his call." Ryan kissed her on the cheek. "This is going to get dangerous. I'd really prefer it if you didn't come with us."

"This is the 21st century, Ryan. Girls can be heroes, too."

"I don't doubt it. I'd just prefer if *my* girl wasn't the hero in this particular instance."

"Fine." Alex rolled her eyes. "I guess I've already saved your arse more times than I can count. I will take one of those boxes, though."

"That's my girl." Ryan handed her the Heaven & Hell cake.

"You boys stay safe now." Alex bent up and kissed Ryan on the cheek, then dropped the keys into his hand.

The four of us piled into the car. Ryan behind the wheel, me in the passenger seat, and Luke and Marcus in the back. Ryan tossed me his mobile phone. "Cole will send an SMS when he's located them," he said. "If we're lucky, we'll be able to gain some time."

"How?"

"He carries his phone on a pouch under his chest. He's never without it."

Ryan sped out into the street, careening around the corner and heading for the M1. I gripped the dashboard. "Jesus, man. You're a worse driver than Luke."

"I resent that," Luke said, his mouth full of cake. Loose crumbs splattered over the seat.

"I'll drive," Marcus piped up.

"This is the latest model BMW," Ryan growled. "I'm not trusting a mutt with it."

"I resent *that*," Marcus growled back.

"Caleb?" Luke asked. "Do you have those lycan pills on you?"

I pulled the tiny bottle from the pocket of my jeans and tossed it to him. "Save half for me. We're gonna need them."

"What's going on?"

"It's nearly the full moon," Luke said. "In a matter of hours, Caleb and I could go full werewolf on your asses."

"Shit." Ryan slammed his foot on the accelerator. "We'd better start moving faster. The last thing I want is claw marks in the leather seats."

I stared into the mirror as the Crookshollow village faded into a blur behind us. My wolf clawed at my skin, begging to be released and tear Angus to pieces for hurting my mate. I popped another pill under my tongue, hoping like hell I'd be able to hold off the change until after I found Rosa. If Luke and I went 'full werewolf,' there's no telling what we'd do.

We're coming, Rosa. We're coming.

17

ROSA

*T*he minutes dragged on like hours. Long, terrifying hours filled by my overactive imagination conceiving of a hundred equally horrifying ways this scenario might play out. Most of them ended in me being torn apart by a pack of rabid wolves, or with having Angus' thin, ugly lips pressed against my own.

Robbie sang along on the radio, and Angus tried to engage me in conversation. But I wasn't in the habit of engaging with men pointing knives at my spleen. He'd stopped pointing it at my throat, in case someone saw it through the window, but he was making it damn clear he could still do some serious damage if I tried something foolish.

"We're getting low on gas, Angus," Robbie said.

"Pull over, then, wankstain."

We turned into a gas station just off the M1. It was busy, with a line of cars waiting for the pumps. Angus fidgeted for a bit, tapping the knife impatiently against the seat, while Robbie manoeuvred the car into the line. Finally, he announced, "I have to piss. Take this and watch her, would you?"

He shoved the knife at Robbie, who paled. "Angus, you said I wouldn't have to—"

"It's just for a fucking minute. Don't be such a feardie." Angus swung his body out of the car. "I'll even get us some snasters. You want anything, princess?" He leered at me through the window.

"I want you to drop dead, but I'm guessing this isn't my lucky day."

Angus laughed cruelly, then slammed the door shut behind him.

"I'm sorry about Angus," Robbie said. "He ain't as bad as he seems, honest."

"You mean this whole kidnapping thing is just a big misunderstanding?" Sarcasm dripped from every word. I sensed that Robbie wasn't really as into this plan as Angus thought he was. If I kept reminding him of the severity of the crime, perhaps I could get him to crack. It was a stupid, hopeless plan, but right now it was the only one I had.

"He's just not used to hearing no, and he ain't never liked losing out to Caleb. The way he figures, anyone wanting to be Caleb's mate must not have had all their options presented, know what I mean?"

"No, I don't know what you mean." My heart pounded against my chest.

"Well, you being Caleb's mate and all."

"What are you talking about? I'm not Caleb's mate. I never agreed to it. He never marked me."

"Yes you are, and he didn't have to mark you. We can smell it all over you. Caleb and you are fated mates. You're destined to be together. It's sort of rare to find that these days."

"So Caleb and I ..." I couldn't believe it. Caleb had told me about fated mates, but he'd never even suggested the possibility that that's what we were. He must've known right from the moment he met me. But he hadn't pushed it. He hadn't forced it on me. He was taking it slow, just the way I'd asked him to. *Oh god, and I let him go.* "... and you're telling me Angus is *jealous?*"

Robbie shrugged. "Probably. He was always jealous of Caleb not having to live up to Dad's legacy. Caleb has his mum, but our mum was killed and Dad only looked at Angus as the next in line for his job. He had to be tough all the time, even if he scraped his knee or broke his tooth."

"You want me to feel sorry for Angus? That's no excuse for kidnapping me or betraying Caleb."

Robbie sighed. "I know, but I think it will be okay. Angus is thinking that if we get to Aberdeen first, he can convince Dad that you were his mate first, and then Dad will back him against Caleb. But I bet Dad will see though the whole thing, and he'll straighten Angus out. You don't just take another wolf's fated mate. It would be very bad for the clan to support Angus. It would make Dad look weak, and he won't like that."

Angus is jealous of Caleb, so jealous that he was willing to break this huge werewolf lore just to deprive Caleb of his mate. *That's me, I'm his mate.* I couldn't believe it.

Wait until Caleb hears about this. He won't believe that his step-brother—

But he won't hear about it. Because as soon as they realise Caleb isn't coming, I'll be dead.

"Why didn't you try to talk Angus out of this stupid plan? You don't seem as though you approve of the way he's handling things."

Robbie shrugged again. "The Bairds have Maria, and I love her like my own mother. If Angus thinks this is the way to get her back, I'm just gonna do what I'm told."

"Why, though? You can't be scared of your brother the rest of your life," I said. "If you don't take a risk every now and then, speak up for what you really believe is right, then everything stays the same."

"What do you know about it?" He looked miserable, playing with the knife against the dashboard.

"Look at my skin. Do you think I've had it easy?" My voice choked up. "All my life, I've had to stand up for myself. It's hard, but if you don't do it, no one else will. There was only one time when someone ever tried to look out for me, and—" My voice completely choked. Instead, I snorted, and gestured to the car. "And look how that turned out."

"You'll be fine. Caleb will come for you."

"He won't. I messed it up. Don't mess up, Robbie. Don't say or do something you can't go back on. Caleb would have been a brother to you, the kind of brother you always wanted, if you'd let him."

Robbie snorted. A van in the queue pulled out, and we inched up another place. A giant raven fluttered down and landed on the bonnet of the car. It peered in the window at me, its dark eyes looking me over thoughtfully.

"Look at that!" Robbie shuffled forward, sticking his head out the window. "That's the biggest bird I've ever seen, And look, it's got a pouch around its—"

The raven glared at me, nodded its head, then darted forward through the open driver's side window and poked Robbie in the eye.

"Argh!" Robbie screamed. He slapped his hand over his eye. Blood poured between his fingers. People at the pumps turned to stare.

"Croooak!" The raven hopped up and down. It was almost as if it was signalling me—

Shit. Of course. Robbie was distracted. Angus was still inside. This was my chance!

I reached past Robbie and flicked the lock for my door. He shoved out a hand to try and stop me, but the raven appeared at the window again, flapping its wings in Robbie's face and letting out loud, excited croaks. I flung open the door and bolted across the forecourt, heading for the cafe on the other side of the petrol station.

"Help!" I cried out, sprinting toward the door. People looked up from their lunches in confusion. Behind me, the raven swooped overhead, croaking excitedly.

"Help me! These two men have kidnapped me and—"

Something slammed into me. I sprawled across the ground, my face slamming hard against the concrete. Pain lashed behind my eyes, and I gasped for breath as the wind was driven out of me.

"Crooak!"

"Get away, you stupid bird!" Angus' voice tore through me. He was holding me down with his knee in my back, and fighting off the raven with his hands. After one particularly terrified croak, the raven gave up, and swooped away.

"What's going on here?" People began to crowd around, staring down at us in confusion. I tried to speak, but I still couldn't get enough air.

"Oops, didn't mean to knock you right over, honey." It was Angus' voice, speaking loudly for the benefit of the people in the cafe. He grabbed my arm roughly and hauled me to my feet. "You'll have to excuse my wife here," he said to the staring people, squeezing my arm so hard I winced. "She has these horrible fits. I know it can be quite scary to see." To me, he said, "Don't worry love, I've got your medication in the car." His voice was low, kind, but his eyes blazed with rage.

As he helped me back toward the car, he whispered in my ear, "Try that one more time, Princess, and I will hurt you somewhere no one can see."

My heart hammered against my chest. Tears sprung in the corners of my eyes. The car loomed in front of me like an electric chair. My feet dragged on the concrete. I didn't want to get back in and spend any more time with these two. All the tension had wound my body up in a knot.

The raven circled overhead, letting off a constant stream of croaks.

Angus held the door open for me like a gentleman. My hands shook as I got inside. What choice did I have? Robbie was still in the front seat, wailing about his eye.

"You have to get him to a doctor," I said, staring out the window at the raven as it flew toward the nearest copse of trees.

"Shut the fuck up," Angus growled. "Robbie's fine, aye Robbie?"

"It fucking *hurts*."

"Stop your bellyaching, and get out." Angus yanked open his door. "I'll drive."

Angus gunned the engine, and we screamed out of the petrol station. As we hit the ramp to head back onto the M1, and Angus sped up, the taxi shuddered violently. Angus growled and put his foot down, but that only made the shuddering worse.

"What's wrong, Angus?" Robbie asked, dabbing his eye. I was surprised that I felt pleased to see he only had a long, deep cut over his eye, and that the raven hadn't pecked his eyeball out.

"Fuck!" Angus pounded the wheel. "It slashed the tires. That fucking no-good flea-ridden bird slashed our fucking tires."

It did? I couldn't help but smile as the cars behind us honked with impatience. *Thanks, raven.*

"Wow. I didn't know birds could do that."

"That's no bird. That's a fucking bran."

I had no idea what that word meant, but Robbie clearly did,

because his face paled. "Caleb has a bran? What does this mean for us, Angus?"

"It means our dear stepbrother is right on our tail." Angus' limped the car along in the slow lane, indicating to turn out at the next exit. "But the joke will be on him. If he makes it to Aberdeen before we do, we kill the girl."

18

CALEB

"Why does this SMS say, 'I might have made things worse?'" I asked, holding the phone up for Ryan to see. A sinking feeling settled in the pit of my stomach.

"Call Cole," Ryan said, his eyes never leaving the road as he yanked the car around a caravan puttering along the fast lane. "Do it quickly, before he transforms back into raven form."

I rang Cole's number. He picked up on the first ring.

"Talk quick," Cole whispered. "I'm currently perched on a very precarious gutter."

"What happened? How did you make it worse?"

"They stopped for gas just outside of Leicester. I jabbed the driver in the eye and she managed to get away. But the mean one grabbed her again. He's pretty angry."

"Dammit." Not only was Angus likely to take that setback out on Rosa, but if they were outside Leicester, then they were still a good fifty minutes ahead of us.

"I did slash one of their tires. They're getting it fixed right now, but the place is pretty quick. They never got gas at the station, either, so that'll take some more time."

"That's good. If you get the chance again—"

"Yeah, I know. They're getting back in the car now. I can keep following if I get off the phone." He sounded irritated.

"Yeah, do that." I snapped the phone off, trying to calm the rage circling through my veins. The guy was trying to help, but I hated this. Hated that it was him out there and not me. My inner wolf felt slighted by someone else doing the tracking. He wanted to tear something apart, and sooner or later, it was going to be one of my friends.

I gripped the door handle. This was no way for the pack alpha to behave. I had to gain control. *Please, just hold on a little longer.*

"Um, Caleb ..." Ryan looked down at me with a concerned expression. "If you could refrain from destroying my car, I'd be grateful."

I glanced down at my arm. It had transformed into a paw, my fingers curled over into toes, with sharp claws digging into Ryan's very expensive door upholstery.

"Argh, shit." I dropped the handle, the upholstery now hanging in tattered ribbons.

"See, this is why I make it a rule never to go on road trips with werewolves." Ryan grabbed the bottle from my hands. "Tip your head back."

I obeyed, and after fumbling one-handed to open the jar, Ryan dropped a pill on my tongue. I wasn't really supposed to eat these things like candy, but if Luke or I changed in the car, we might run Ryan off the road.

We're coming, Rosa. I know you hate me and never want to see me again. But I swear I won't let them hurt you. I'll protect you even if you never want to see me again.

19

ROSA

*E*vening fell, and we passed Hadrian's Wall and on into Scotland. A sickly smell rose from the boot of the car, but I was too afraid to ask what it might be.

The towns and cities blurred together. The fear ate away at my composure, and I stopped staring out the window, instead focusing on the back of Angus' head.

The city lights of Aberdeen spread out before us, a blanket of twinkling comfort. We were heading toward civilisation, people, perhaps another chance of escape ...

But no. Angus yanked the wheel hard around, and drove the taxi down a forested road. After a few minutes, the asphalt gave way to a single-lane dirt track. The taxi bounced over the uneven ground, and my head smashed against the roof after one particularly large bump.

This continued for what seemed like hours. Outside the car, all was dark. I noticed a few paths diverging from this main road. Apart from the trees, there were no other landmarks or signs. Even if I managed to escape, I'd never find my way back to the main road.

Angus pulled over and stopped the car, grabbing his knife and directing it at my throat while Robbie got out.

"Where are we?"

Robbie opened my door, and Angus handed him the knife, which he held with a shaking hand beside my throat.

"Home sweet home, Princess." Angus got out and grabbed me under the arms, lifting me out of the vehicle. "And it looks like we're the first ones here."

His grin sent a shiver of terror down my spine.

I shuffled to my feet, grabbing the car door for balance as I looked around. Angus shoved me down a narrow path, and I stumbled around in the dark for several minutes before we emerged in a clearing in the middle of a forest. Moonlight shone from above, illuminating piles of twisted shadows. The place was a dump, littered with broken cars, piles of rubbish, and huge metal drums. Here and there were crude lean-tos – shelters of corrugated iron propped up against stacks of tires. The place looked like something out of Mad Max.

"What is this?" I asked. Angus didn't reply. Instead, he told Robbie to hold me, and keep his human form. Robbie wrapped his arms around me, pressing the knife to my throat again.

"I'm sorry," Robbie whispered into my ear. All my good thoughts about him faded away as that cool blade touched my skin.

"Ah, it feels good to be back." Angus stretched out his arms and transformed. His face elongated and sank into itself, the eyes growing large as his cheeks and nose knitted together to form a snout. His ears grew into points and shifted to the back of his skull. He fell to his knees, his fingers gripping the dirt as his bones snapped and rearranged themselves into a new shape, a terrifying shape.

A huge, snarling wolf.

Angus threw his head back, and howled.

An echo of howls rose up from the trees, answering his call. The sound chilled me to the core. I froze in place, cold in Robbie's embrace. There was nowhere to run, no way to hide. I was completely surrounded.

"Angus," Robbie moaned from behind me. Prickly hair sprouted along his arms. "I don't know how much longer I can—"

His voice cut off with a high-pitch squeal. The knife clattered from his hand, and his arms slipped from around me. I whirled around. Robbie backed away from me, his arms in the air. "Stay away from me," he groaned. "I can't—"

I glanced up. Of course, the moon was full. That meant neither Angus nor Robbie could control their shift, nor anything they did in their wolf form. They were acting on instinct alone.

That meant things had just got a hundred times worse for me.

Robbie's face contorted, his snout extending and his lips curling back into a snarl. He toppled onto his hands and knees, his eyes wide as they stared back at me. "Get away," he croaked out, before his words turned into a low, mournful howl.

Angus was over at the edge of the clearing, howling into the trees. I raced toward the pile of Angus' torn clothes, and fished through the remains of his jeans until my hands closed over the taxi's car keys. I whirled around, and raced for the trail.

A wolf stepped in front of me. Its teeth curled back into a snarl. I stopped short, my heart in my throat. I ducked to the side, but another wolf leapt into my path.

Wolves began to emerge from the trees, their eyes glowing in the moonlight. They circled me, moving in closer, closing all the gaps. Saliva dripped from their teeth, and their mouths pulled back into cruel grins.

There were hundreds of them, all creeping toward me.

Everywhere I looked, all I could see were glowing eyes and sharp, pointed teeth.

A huge wolf stepped forward, and the howling suddenly stopped, like someone had flipped a switch.

This wolf was at least twice the size of the others. His coat was a light grey colour, with a black band running along his spine, and black curlicues around his eyes. In any other circumstance, I might have considered him beautiful.

But since he was rising up on his hind legs, row after row of sharp teeth gleaming in the moonlight, *beautiful* was definitely not the adjective he was going to get.

Before my eyes, the giant wolf began to change. Its paws elongated, the sharp claws on each finger contracting, becoming nails. Its bones cracked, jerking as they broke and repaired themselves in new configurations. In the moonlight, it appeared as though its fur melted away, leaving behind a towering, muscled and very naked man, who glared it me with cold, ruthless eyes.

How can he control his shift under the full moon? That must be one powerful werewolf.

"Who the fook is this?" the man boomed. "I told you to bring me Caleb, or is he so afeared of our enemies that he's turned into a lass?"

Angus stepped forward, between me and the man. He lay down on his stomach, his tail thumping against the dirt. For a few moments, there was no sound. I remembered Caleb telling me wolves communicated telepathically. Great, now I wouldn't even be able to hear them decide how they were going to kill me.

Several of the wolves turned their heads to each other, panting heavily. It almost looked as though they were discussing Angus' thoughts. The tall man strode over to Angus, his eyes blazing. I noticed tattoos running down his arms. On his shoulder was a crest depicting a tower, similar to Caleb's but much more elaborate. The slogan *Virtue Mine Honour* wrapped around the crest, and across his chest in dark gothic script was the phrase, "Bàs no Beatha."

It could only be one man – Douglas, Caleb's stepfather. I stared at the bulging veins in his neck, the arms like tree trunks, the battle-scarred, humourless face. *Imagine growing up with that creature as your father.*

Douglas strode forward, walking around his son. But he didn't stop. Instead, he leaned over me, his face inches from mine. I wanted to shy away, but there was nowhere to run, so I stood my ground, glaring back at him with all the ferocity I could muster. He studied my features intently, his dark eyes darting all over my body. I longed to turn away from his scrutiny, but I didn't dare. He sniffed the air around me, then stuck out his tongue. He licked my cheek, his tongue scraping across my skin. I screwed up my face in disgust, but I didn't dare pull away. This guy could snap me in half like a twig.

Douglas turned to Angus. He reached up a thick arm. I thought he was going to embrace his son, congratulate him on a good day's work, but instead he grabbed the wolf by the neck, lifting him off the ground. Angus whimpered as his feet dangled below him. His paws swung in the air, useless.

"You stole his mate from him?" Douglas growled, his face inches from his son's. Angus' eyes bugged out, and his tongue loped to the side. "We don't do that. This woman has already been fated to Caleb. Don't you ken she ain't yours to take."

Angus' teeth snapped and snarled. He glared at me, but there wasn't much he could do with Douglas gripping his throat. No other wolf stepped forward to help him, but they all watched the scene with wide, beady eyes.

I could feel the panic rising up within me. The sickening feeling spreading out from my stomach, the uncontrollable shaking starting in my hands. I kept my eyes focused on Angus and Douglas, trying to will away the rising terror. But after a whole day of being in the car with Angus, my nerves were totally shot. I knew any minute now, the panic would overrun me, and then I'd be completely at their mercy.

Angus choked out some whimpers. A couple of wolves in the circle nodded their heads in agreement.

"I don't care how much you want her. She don't want you," Douglas snarled. "Else she wouldn't be shaking like a fucking leaf."

Angus whimpered again.

"You can't have her." Douglas released his neck. Angus dropped to the ground, letting out a loud whine as he fell hard on his side. He let out a squeak, and lay on his side, licking his paw and rubbing it against his neck where Douglas had held him.

From behind me, I heard another wolf bark. A small wolf darted through the trees, pawing at the ground as it let off a series of low growls. Robbie went over to the wolf and licked his cheek, then barked three times, and the sound was taken up by other wolves in the circle. My blood chilled.

"What's going on?" I stammered at Douglas. "What are you planning to do to me?"

Douglas rushed forward and grabbed my collar, yanking me toward him. "They tell me your mate is nearly upon us," he growled.

Caleb.

My whole heart soared. He had come after all, even after everything I'd said to him.

Douglas' head tilted to the side, as though he were listening to another telepathic message. "He's brought with him a whole pack. Another wolf, two vulpines, and a bran. A fucking *bran*. Is that the filthy bird that attacked my Robbie?"

"Your sons kidnapped me against my will. Any damage done is justified."

"That true?" Douglas' eyes bore into mine. "Angus says they took you because Caleb wouldn't come. His own *mother* has been taken by our enemies, probably tortured, and he *wouldn't come*. But now we have you, and here he is with a whole bloody pack ready to fight the family that raised him—"

"*Raised* him?" I snorted. "Your sons were cruel to him, and you encouraged their cruelty. Yet you seem surprised he left your clan? He has a new family now, one who respects him and cares for him. He doesn't *need* you anymore."

Douglas' eyes darkened. My stomach twisted. Perhaps that had been the wrong thing to say.

"If my adopted son no longer considers himself part of our clan," he snarled, directing his words not to me, but to the sky above, "and he condemns his mother to death in the hands of our enemies, then before you all I disown him, and I declare him an enemy of our family. As for his mate, I will support my son's claim to her."

I gasped. From his position kneeling at his father's feet, Angus let out a satisfied howl.

Douglas' lip curled back. "I'm sure she will, my son, but she's black. Can't you find one of your own kind for a mate?"

"What do you think I am, a walrus?" The words were out of my mouth before I could stop them.

Douglas laughed. The wolves in the circle tossed back their heads and barked.

"Aye, she's a feisty one, alright. She'll bring a little colour to our clan." He slapped his son on the shoulder. "Very well. She is yours, son. No wolf who calls himself a Maclean will desert us for a fucking *bran* and git away with it."

The wolves howled their approval. The sound echoed around the clearing, rising like a cone through the trees.

Oh, well that's just swell.

Douglas' face contorted, his nose growing long, before shrinking back to normal again. I noticed a layer of fine grey fur had sprouted down his arms. He was now struggling to hold his human form.

"Mark her," he barked at his son. "Before the traitor arrives."

Angus rose to his feet, bounding toward me. Robbie leapt in front of him, his teeth bared, but Angus shoved him away. Robbie went sprawling across the clearing, his back slamming into a pile of old tires.

I raised my hands to ward off the blow, but I was too late. Angus' paws hit my chest, sending me hurtling backwards into the dirt. I scrambled backward, trying to get to my feet, but Angus was too fast. He pinned my shoulders to the ground, his claws digging into my skin. His eyes bore into mine, sparkling with triumph as a thin trail of his spittle dribbled down my cheek.

Angus bent his head. I screamed as he sank his teeth into my shoulder. Searing pain pulsed through my body. Red welts appeared in my eyes.

His teeth tore away my skin, and he tossed his head back and howled. The wolf pack matched his cry, every Maclean howling in unison. It was their howl of triumph. They had me now.

The howls pounded in my ears, a wild, unhinged sound that paralysed me with fear. The pain blotted my vision, and my whole body sank into a black pit. Angus' howl rose above the rest of his kind, high and triumphant. It was the last sound I heard before my body went numb and the darkness swallowed me up.

CALEB

"Up here!" I jabbed my finger at the dirt road leading into the forest. Luke yanked the wheel hard around. The car bounced up the path, the headlights illuminating dense bush and towering larch and Scots pine.

I hated being back here. Seeing the forest after nearly nine months away, after everything Angus and Robbie had put me through, made me feel like a failure. The scent of my former clan clung to the whole area like after hours at a Cross-fit gym. They had all come to witness Angus' return.

Here I was, crawling back to the Macleans with my tail between my legs. At any moment, I expected a wolf to leap from the bushes, or a bullet to blast my brains out.

But if Rosa was here, then I was damn well going to march right in and take her back.

My inner wolf clawed at my skin, begging for release. At any moment, I would lose my battle against him. I barked directions at Ryan, who yanked the car so fast around the dirt road I thought for sure we'd come off in the ditch. As we neared the meeting place, the scents grew stronger. The whole forest stunk of rotten, despicable wolves. Ryan had the windows down, and the wind roared around us, blowing the scents of my clan all over me, until they invaded my whole body.

"What's that noise?" Marcus yelled over the roar of the wind.

I strained to hear. He was right; there was a low humming sound carried on the wind.

Hang on, that's not humming.

"It's howling," I cried, straining to hear what they were saying. "The Macleans have called the whole clan together. They know we're on our way. They're waiting for us, and they have Rosa."

"Are you going to go postal?" Ryan yelled, indicating with his chin the moon poking between the branches.

"Not yet," I growled, tipping the rest of the pills between my teeth. "We still have to—"

"Pull over," Luke yelled. "I can't hold on."

"What?"

"I said, pull over!"

Ryan slammed on the brakes. I pitched forward, my head slamming against the windscreen, before being flung back against my seat. I glanced Luke in the rearview mirror as he swung the door open. His face had already contorted into a wolfish snout. As his hand shoved the door, it transformed into a paw, the long claws scratching against the glass. Just as I turned around to help him with the door, he threw his weight against it, and toppled out of his belt, landing on all fours and dashing to the trees, a bushy tail flapping wildly behind him.

"That's one down," Ryan said wryly, frowning at the damage to the door. "You boys owe me a new interior."

"We'd better keep driving," I said, gritting my teeth as my wolf clambered to follow Luke into the forest.

"No need. I think we're here."

He pointed up ahead, and I realised he was right. The taxi my stepbrothers stole was parked just up ahead. I recognised the bent trees, the cairns of rubbish scattered at intervals along the road. We were here, at the main meeting place of the pack, our centre of operations.

"How do we approach this?" Ryan asked, as the three of us got out of the car. "They're all going to be in their wolf forms, and they know we're here. They'll overpower us in a heartbeat."

"I know." I gritted my teeth.

"The Maclean's aren't the only ones here. I can smell Bairds all through these woods. They must've heard I was coming, too. They're here to make the exchange – my mother, for me."

"That's just wonderful," Marcus grumbled. "We're like foxes to the bloody slaughter."

I raised my gaze to the moon. The light hit me square in the eyes, and my face exploded with fur. My skin felt as if it were crawling with insects, so insistent was my wolf to be unleashed. Soon, soon, I'd be able to resist no longer. But first, I needed to make sure my pack was safe.

A bird flew across the face of the moon. A black raven. It swooped down and landed on the boot of the taxi, transforming into the same black-haired, tattooed man I'd met on top of the bakery.

"They're in a clearing just up ahead," he said. "The wolf Angus has claimed Rosa as his own."

"That's impossible. Douglas would never agree—"

Cole leapt off the boot and flipped it open, revealing a man stuffed inside, dried blood caked to a wound on his head. Barry the taxi driver, I guessed. From the smell of him, I guessed he'd been dead some hours.

"He *has* agreed to support Angus' claim. It seems he hasn't taken kindly to you establishing a new pack, and abandoning your mother to her fate. Angus has given Rosa his mark."

Rage shuddered through my body. How dare they touch Rosa like that? How dare they try to mate her without her consent? My hands shook violently. I tried to curl them into fists, but my fingers had become short toes with long claws.

"It's no good." I gritted my teeth. "I can't hold it any longer. Listen, I'm going to the Bairds. It's my only hope. Follow me in your animal forms, but stick together and don't go near the clearing—"

My words turned into barks as my mouth transformed. I pitched forward as my knees snapped back, landing with my paws in the dirt. Seams tore as my body transformed, my clothes no longer fitting. Luckily, though the leather cord tightened around my thick neck, it stayed on.

Instantly, my wolfish senses kicked in. The scent trails through the forest lit up like a carefully constructed map, new smells and sensations assailing my body. My mind reeled, drinking it all in.

The man who was Caleb faded from my mind. I no longer had any sense of my human identity. Now, my veins thrummed with raw energy ready to be unleashed on my enemies.

I whirled around to face my pack. They had transformed, too. Cole sat on the bonnet, his black feathers resplendent in the moonlight. Where Cole and Marcus had stood were two large foxes, one a deep reddish brown, the other a lighter tan colour. Their bushy tails thumped against the fallen leaves as they waited for directions. From the edge of the forest emerged Luke, his head bent down as he trotted toward me.

I stared back at the two foxes and the raven. Instinct told me they would be an easy meal, and my stomach growled with hunger. But they carried my smell, the scent markers I had placed on them to identify them as friends. They were my pack. I wouldn't eat them.

Rosa. You have to save your mate.

I sniffed the dirt, seeking out the trail I wanted. I led the way into the forest, Luke close at my heels, and the foxes following some distance behind. Cole darted from branch to branch, keeping an eye on things from above.

I could tell from the way the paths crisscrossed that Bairds had been here several times in the past month, although they hadn't clashed with the Macleans. I guessed they'd been monitoring the area, figuring out when the best time to strike would be. Another strong smell wafted across my nostrils, a familiar scent that brought up the few good memories I had from this place.

Mother.

She'd been here recently, with the last few hours. That meant that, for now, at least, she was still safe.

The Baird smell grew stronger, overpowering the other scents of the forest. I followed the main scent trail until it emerged into a clearing right on the edge of the Maclean territory. The smell of the Bairds swirled all around it, and there were fresh tracks heading off in all directions. But I couldn't see any wolves in the trees.

They should be here, I said to my pack as I paced around the outside of the clearing. *Stay back, it could be a trap—*

A wolf stepped out of the darkness, directly into my path. His eyes glowed, his front legs spread apart, ready to pounce. He pulled his lips back revealing rows of long, sharp teeth.

Caleb Lowe, the wolf growled. *I've been waiting for you.*

21

ROSA

*M*y eyes fluttered open. *I'm awake. I'm—*

Pain seared through my body, and a terrifying coldness spread through my arms and legs. I tried to raise my head, to move my limbs, but I seemed frozen in place. I opened one eye, and stared up into tree branches and the moon glowing directly above. Everything came flooding back to me; the car ride, the clearing, the wolves, Angus' bite—

I must've passed out after he bit me.

No wonder, the pain coursing through my body was unbearable. I gritted my teeth and raised my head, trying to see what was going on.

Wolves danced around me, teeth bared, tails beating furiously. They leapt over each other, howling and barking as they celebrated their victory. Angus' leering face loomed over me, his teeth pulled back into a vicious grin. Blood dripped from his gums.

My blood.

Behind Angus, Douglas' wolf looked on, a satisfied expression on his face. It being the full moon, none of the wolves could change back, which meant I couldn't hear what they said to each other. But I knew enough to know what would happen next: Caleb would come, and they would fight him, and overpower him, and then I'd become Angus' mate and Caleb would be lost to me forever.

I had to find a way ... but I could barely move. My shoulder throbbed with pain where Angus had bitten me. I'd managed to turn my head to see the wound, but the sight of it made my head spin. He'd torn a whole chunk of skin away. My body was frozen with shock. I was helpless to save myself.

Caleb, if you're out there, if you can hear me, don't come here. It's too late. You can't save me. Don't come, please. Don't get yourself killed for me. Please, Caleb.

22

CALEB

I bowed my head and sat down, leaning my chest into the dirt in a sign of respect. Behind me, Luke did the same.

You have a pack of your own now. Irvine's thought landed in my head. t wasn't a question. Irvine Baird didn't ask questions, he knew everything that was going on in shifter circles. I wondered how long the Bairds had been watching me.

Irvine was the Baird alpha. He'd come into the job quite young, being only a year or two older than me. His father was quite unexpectedly shot by a local poacher, who then had to be silenced so he wouldn't reveal the existence of wolves in the forest. I remember Irvine going to take care of the poacher himself, then coming back and telling his pack that they would no longer kill without good reason. I'd dealt with Irvine on some occasions, running errands for Douglas. I always found him to be level-headed and fair, and he would never hurt or kill unless there was a direct danger to his pack. Which was why the kidnapping of my mother was so odd.

The Lowe territories are mine now, I answered. *I control them, and I needed a pack to help me defend them.*

And the Lowe treasures, what of those?

Bingo. So our suspicions were correct. Irvine *did* think I had the Benedict Ring. I decided to feign innocence. *I'm not sure what you're talking about.*

This isn't a time for lies, Irvine growled. *I can see the ring around your neck.*

Right. I'd forgotten about the leather cord hanging there.

I understand the Macleans have your fated mate. We must stop them before they do something they'll regret.

Why the 'we'? You have my mother.

She is unharmed. You're the one we want.

Now we were getting somewhere. I stood up, showing him I was his equal. *What do you want with me? You can't just take the ring, you know. Only members of my pack can use it.*

I know. We want your pack to join with us.

Excuse me?

Irvine tilted his head to the side. His eyes deadly serious. *Let the Bairds and the Lowes become allies. You will keep your alpha status. You will retain your ancestral lands in the Crookshollow Forest. But you will have the full power and protection of the Bairds behind you.*

His words threw me. What he was offering was completely unprecedented. Wolf packs were highly territorial and rarely made alliances, unless there was some huge local threat to overcome.

A wolf darted up beside me. It was Luke. He thought, *Why are you offering this? You're infinitely more powerful than us.*

Because, as Caleb has pointed out, both the Lowe territory and the Lowe treasure are useless without a Lowe, Baird thought. My jaw dropped open as the wolf sat down across from us, his stomach touching the ground in the ultimate sign of respect.

This is for real, I thought. *He wants an alliance. But why? What does he want to do with all the power of the ring?*

If you want an alliance, why take my mother? Why did you not just ask me?

Irvine turned around and beckoned into the forest.

"Hello, my son." A warm voice echoed from behind the trees.

My mother stepped out from the forest, her red hair bouncing around her shoulders in loose waves. She wore her city clothes – a narrow pencil skirt and long-sleeve blouse. Dead leaves crunched as her heels sank into the soft earth. Her smell overpowered me, and I rested my head on the ground.

She patted my head. "I know you think it's dangerous for me to be here with the Bairds during the full moon, but don't fear. I've been meeting with Irvine in secret for months, ever since I discovered the existence of the Benedict Ring."

She discovered it? Of course. My mother was a librarian at the University of Aberdeen. She was responsible for the medieval collection. If anyone would stumble across our name in some long-forgotten tome, it was her.

"I went to Douglas first, of course," she explained, still stroking my head. "But the stubborn old git wouldn't have anything to do with the Lowe family. So I came to the Bairds for help." She took a step back, so she was standing beside Irvine, and placed her hand on his shoulder. "Luckily, Irvine has the same vision as me."

What vision? Why didn't you talk to me before coming to your enemy? I pawed the ground. I wished I could transform into a human and talk to her, but I hoped she knew me well enough to answer most of my questions without me needing to ask. Above all, I wanted to ask her why she hadn't told me, but I suspected I knew the answer already.

She confirmed it. "I am sorry I kept you in the dark. I couldn't tell you, my son, because you weren't powerful enough. If we're going to put my plan into motion, we need the loudest, youngest, toughest voices in the shifter world to get onside. Of course, I was going to bring you in once I had all the pieces in place, but then the old Lowe caves were discovered and you ran away before I got the chance."

She smiled. "When I heard you had reunited with your cousin and reclaimed your territory, I was so proud. I've wanted so badly to see you for months and months, but I couldn't risk going down to Crookshollow without Douglas finding out. Instead, I had the Bairds 'kidnap' me, in the hopes it would bring you up here, and the final stage of the plan could come together."

What is this plan? Why do you want the ring? I asked the wolf.

Because it is time, Irvine hissed. *It is time the shifters of the world stopped hiding in the shadows. With the ring, we will be able to reveal ourselves at last. We need the ring to act as leverage for when we establish ourselves within the human world.*

Whoah. That was their plan all along, to use the ring's power to reveal the existence of shifters and gain a voice.

You can't be serious, Luke said.

We are very serious, Irvine said. *Shifters should not be hiding, living as criminals because that's the only avenue open to us. I want a better life for my pack, and my children. I want a voice in government, and I want our rights recognised, and our culture celebrated. Don't you want this for your people, too?*

I thought of Rosa, of what she'd said about not being able to hide the way we did. Every day she walked down the street, knowing she was different, and that people hated her because of that difference, but she lived her life anyway. I thought of how brave she, and others, were to stand up for their rights in big and small ways, to be the trailblazers who would make life better for countless future generations.

For all our talk of bravado, shifters had chosen to hide because we were afraid of what would happen if humans learned we lived amongst them. It had never worked so well in the past. But we'd just given up, retreated back to the shadows, while people like Rosa blazed on. The world was different now. There was a culture of tolerance and understanding, even though it wasn't always perfect.

I wanted to be brave, like Rosa. I wanted to show her that I was proud of who I was, as she was proud. I wanted to stand beside her and know I had done the best for my kind.

I glanced from Luke to my mother, before turning back to Irvine. *Yes. I want this. I agree with you. It is time.*

What? Luke cried. I ignored him.

Then let us unite, and take the ring to our government, Irvine said. *We have no time to waste. We—*

I don't have it.

What's that around your neck, then?

I broke the cord with my claw, and the ring toppled into the dirt. *It's a cheap goth trinket. We don't have the Benedict ring. We only learned about it a few days ago. But we will make it our mission to find it.*

But-but I don't understand, Irvine spluttered. *Without the ring, how did you make your claim on the Crookshollow forest? How did you dispel Angus and Robbie over your border?*

I gave him a grin. *Sheer brute force. There was no one down there except for a few vulpines and a couple of rogue wolves, who were easy to send packing. Then we just re-established the old boundaries and let the rumour mill do the rest.* Shift in Focus *really blew things out of proportion.*

"What's going on?" My mother tapped Irvine on the ear. "I hate not being able to hear what you're all saying."

Irvine snorted, shaking his head furiously. My mother's brow furrowed. "He doesn't have the ring?" She bent down and picked up the ring, frowning as she realised it was hollow pewter and a cheap glass crystal. She tossed it away and frowned at me. "Then why did you come here? How were you intending to set me free?"

At that point, I called my pack forward. Ryan and Marcus dashed into the clearing. Cole swooped down from the tree above and landed on my shoulder, his talons digging into my flesh.

My mother gave me a sad smile. "Oh, Caleb. That's not a pack. It's a joke."

This is what the great Lowe family have sent to fight the toughest wolf gang in Scotland? Irvine growled.

They have my fated mate, I growled back. *I can't not fight, even if fighting is hopeless.*

We stand by him, Luke added. *What Angus and Douglas have done is inexcusable.*

Irvine's eyes blazed with anger. *I agree. It is not honourable.*

I pawed the ground. *They are waiting for me, and they know I am outnumbered. I am willing to be allies, to return to Crookshollow and find the ring. Will you help me save my mate?*

Irvine glanced at Ryan and Marcus, and his face twitched. His gaze fell on Cole, and his lips curled back in an expression of utter disgust.

I should never have showed him my pack, I thought. *He's an old-school wolf. The idea of aligning with other shifters, especially Bran, is abhorrent to him. The fact I even asked him means he'll rip my throat out any second now.*

But I had to try. For Rosa.

I poised, ready to fight Irvine off should he lunge at me.

Instead, the wolf lifted his head, and let out a mighty howl. I joined in, tossing my head back and lending my voice to the night. Irvine's howl was answered from deep in the woods, and I heard the footsteps of several wolves running to meet us.

The Lowes and the Bairds were going to war.

23

ROSA

I gritted my teeth as a fresh wave of pain rocketed through my body. No one ever told me that when I was badly injured and bleeding out all over the ground, that once the initial shock wore off, the pain came not all at once but in volleys, as though it were sending wave after wave of pain soldiers to battle over possession of my body.

Something was supposed to happen, but it hadn't happened yet. The wolves were getting agitated, but the delay had given me time to collect myself. The panic had subsided a little. I was no longer going to throw up. My hands were still shaking, but that might have also been from the blood loss. I had no desire to pass out again. Instead, I felt a determined survival instinct click in. I'd been living with Angus' terror for nearly a week now, and I hadn't died yet. I could find a way out of this.

It took me three tries, but I managed to rip off the torn sleeve of my shirt. Pain stabbed down my arm every time I moved it, and watching my blood trickle out of the wound was starting to make me feel dizzy. I'd planned to tie the material around my shoulder to staunch the bleeding, but I now realised I couldn't physically do it, and I couldn't exactly ask Robbie to do it for me.

The wolves had ceased their dancing, and now stood around in a circle, facing the trees and occasionally letting out low, menacing growls. Two of the smaller wolves had disappeared into the forest some minutes ago, presumably to act as scouts. Angus stood on top of one of the shelters, staring into the trees. Every few minutes he circled around impatiently, snapping at the other wolves crowding his feet.

There was no sign of Caleb, or anyone else. Maybe he heard my pleas. Maybe he was staying away. Which meant that any moment now, they would figure out Caleb was no longer in the forest, and they'd kill me.

Damn them if they thought I was going to go down on my back in the middle of a wolf pack, without even putting up a fight. I placed my good hand on the ground and tried to heave myself up. Pain shot down my arm as soon as it moved. I kept pushing, trying to force myself through it. Tears streamed down my face.

You have to do this. You have to get to your feet and run for the trees—

It seemed impossible. But so did carrying on after my house was burned down, and I did that anyway. I could do this too. I dug my fingers into the earth, and pushed with all my might.

As I raised my back off the ground, a long, low howl echoed through the trees. The wolves turned to each other, their eyes wide. Hope surged in my chest, mingling with fresh fear. I'd recognise that howl anywhere.

It's Caleb!

Before I had time to think, hundreds of wolves tore from the trees, barrelling down toward the circle that surrounded me. Angus leapt back in surprise, his feet toppling off the back of the lean-to. He scrabbled for a foothold as the wolves bore down on him.

At the front of the approaching pack, I saw two foxes

ducking and weaving between the wolves. Above them, a black raven swooped low, its wings spread wide and its talons pointed directly at Angus. Beside them, a great grey wolf with a red streak down his back tossed his head back, and howled.

Caleb.

My heart soared to see him, majestic in his fury as he bore down upon his foes. As more wolves poured out of the trees and fell into line behind him, I realised he hadn't just come to rescue me, he'd brought a whole damn *army*.

Where did they all come from?

I had no time to ponder it, for the wolves crashed into each other. Limbs and fur flew everywhere. Claws sliced through the air, jaws snapped, teeth tore at flesh and bone. The world around me became a surging ocean of snarling wolves piling on top of each other in a desperate attempt to gain control of the clearing. They moved so fast, I couldn't even tell who was winning.

An acrid smell filled my nostrils. *Blood. Werewolf blood.*

I heaved my torso into an upright position, tears streaming down my face as I jerked my torn shoulder. I slid backwards, so I was leaning against a stack of tires, pulling my legs up to hide in its shadow. My eyes swept back and forth, searching for one wolf.

Caleb, where are you?

The fighting started to thin out as several of Douglas' wolves ran for the trees, chased by Caleb's recruits. The black raven soared down, waving its wings at one of Douglas' wolves as it tried to approach me, and it turned away, yelping as the raven pecked at its back. I cried out in triumph, until I saw the scene they left behind. Wolves lay dead in dark puddles, their necks torn open, limbs bent at impossible angles. Beautiful, powerful creatures reduced to meat and bone.

No. This isn't what I wanted. I couldn't bear the idea of Caleb in the midst of that fray, dishing out death and destruction, or worse, having his throat ripped out by his own jealous step-brother.

"Stop," I tried to yell over the din, but all that came out was a croak. I cleared my throat and tried again. "Stop right now!"

If they heard me, they didn't care.

A voice rose over the din. A human voice, sharp and piercing. A voice that wasn't my own.

"Douglas Maclean, what do ye think you're doing? Stop this madness right now!"

24

CALEB

*M*y mother strode across the clearing, her fiery hair a halo around her face. She picked up a younger Maclean wolf by the scruff of its neck and tossed it aside like an out-of-season purse.

Douglas' teeth were buried in my shoulder. I was trying to ignore the burning pain as I tried to hook my back leg around him and slam him against the ground. As soon as he heard my mother's voice, his whole body stiffened, and his teeth loosened from my skin. I dropped to the ground, too shocked to move. Douglas Maclean didn't just let his enemies go free.

All around me, wolves were losing their fighting spirit. That my mother had such an incredible power over both clans was evident in the authority in her voice as she told them again to stop. I scanned the clearing for Angus, and just caught sight of his tail dragging something large behind one of the rubbish piles.

Rosa!

He had her by her bun, strands of her hair sticking out from either side of his mouth. She held her scalp, her legs kicking frantically, searching for purchase on the slippery earth. She sobbed quietly, her face twisted in pain.

Oh, no, you don't.

I leapt up and bounded toward her. Pain seared down my arm as soon as my paw hit the ground. My whole front leg collapsed, dragging me down with it. Douglas had really done a number on me.

From my prone position, I noticed several wolves also on their sides in the dirt, blood dribbling from deep wounds. Irvine was on his back, trying to fend off a young Maclean wolf who'd torn a deep cut down his stomach. The air stank of blood and death.

No, this can't be happening. I felt sick. Even though I hated what Angus and Douglas had done to me, I never wished for wolves to die. But here they were, bodies littered across the clearing, the victims of my rage.

I turned toward Douglas. He was standing on his hind legs, his head level with my mother's face. He tried to lick her cheek, but she slapped him right across the face.

"That's our boy right there." She jabbed a finger at me. "That's my son, who you promised to raise as your own. Why are you fighting one of our own?"

Douglas turned his snout toward her, and let up a keening howl. *He ain't no son of mine,* he snarled, even though she wouldn't hear him. *He deserted us for a clan of fucking circus animals.*

SMACK. She slapped his other cheek. "I know what you're thinking, and you can stop it right now. Of course Caleb deserted us to claim his birthright. What's he got here for himself? An' what's this I hear about Angus stealing his mate?"

Douglas tried to rise up again, but she slapped him down once more. His wolves cringed away, and even Angus stopped pulling at Rosa and stared at his father in dumb shock. Even though my body ached from his bite, I couldn't help but smile to see my mighty stepfather being chastised in front of his own clan.

He howled with rage. *Angus wants the girl for himself—*

"He can't 'ave her, can he?" Mum dropped Douglas' throat, and slapped her hands against her hips. "He can't go around trying to take another shifter's mate, that ain't right. That ain't the Maclean way. You should be ashamed of yourself, Douglas Maclean, giving permission for such an abomination. That's why I've come to put things right."

Douglas bared his teeth at her. *You sought an alliance with my enemy,* he growled.

Even though Mother couldn't understand Douglas' wolven words, his message was crystal clear. But she didn't even looked phased. "You can stop that nonsense right now. There ain't no sense being mad at me for bringing the Bairds into this. They're only here because you're too stupid to listen to me, and if they *weren't* here, your son would've killed our Caleb by now. I brought them because someone had to knock some sense into that thick skull of yours. Is that the way the great Maclean clan behaves?"

By now, every wolf had gone silent, listening to the exchange. Mum had been with Douglas through so many full moons, she knew him so well that it was practically as though they were holding a conversation.

Douglas reared up to his full height, tossed his head back, and let out a mighty howl. For a moment, I thought I'd have to leap in to stop him from attacking her. But then his body sagged, and he lay down on the ground, showing the whole pack that he submitted to her. *Aye, you're right, my dear. This is madness.*

She patted his head. "Thank you, my love."

Douglas barked at Angus. *You let her go now. She don't belong to you.*

She don't belong to no one, I thought. I watched with pounding heart as Angus dropped Rosa's hair, and backed a few steps away. She held her head between her hands, her eyes filled with pain. I noticed blood splattered down her shirt from a nasty bite on her shoulder where Angus had marked her. *Please let her be okay.*

I took a step toward Rosa, but my leg caved again, and I fell heavily on my shoulder. Angus' eyes caught mine, a blaze of anger and humiliation.

I didn't have time to think about him. I needed to get to her. I picked myself up on my three remaining useful legs, and dragged my throbbing body toward her. With every step, my shoulder screamed in protest. But I had to see her; I had to know she was all right.

"Caleb," she squeaked out, her eyes flooded with tears. "I can't believe—"

A hundred wolf eyes watched me as I made my slow journey across the clearing, toward my mate.

As I got closer, I could see she was in bad shape. Her skin was deathly pale, and slick with sweat. Her head lolled on her shoulders. There was a lot of blood on her clothing, and she couldn't seem to move her arm. When she saw me, the corners of her mouth turned up in a beautiful, dazzling smile.

"I knew you'd rescue me," she said, reaching up with her good hand to stroke my fur.

The words were like a knife through my heart. I didn't rescue her. I was the one who dragged her into this mess in the first place. I was the reason she was lying there with a wolf's bite marring her beautiful neck, with another man's scent all over her.

She'd been through so much already. All I'd done was put her through more trauma. Looking down at her, so happy to see me amidst all the horror she'd endured, my heart tore apart. I knew what I had to do, but it would take every bit of control I had to do it, and in my wolf form, I didn't have a lot of that to spare.

I bent down and licked at the wound. My saliva mingled with her blood, helping to staunch the bleeding, and working over Angus' scent. As my tongue met her skin, a surge of power rocketed through my body. Rosa's eyes fluttered shut, and her body shuddered as it went through her, too. We were mated. Our connection had been forged.

I'm sorry, Rosa. This wasn't how I wanted it to be.

I called Ryan and Marcus forward to collect her. They transformed into their human forms. All around the circle, wolves growled as two men materialised in their midst. But a barked command from Douglas held them at bay. They wouldn't dare disobey their alpha.

"Here, sweetheart. We've got you." Ryan picked Rosa up in his arms. She rested her cheek on his shoulder, but her eyes remained glued to mine.

Ryan carried her through the circle, to the edge of the clearing. He turned, smiling, and waited for me.

Irvine pulled himself along the ground, and placed his paw on mine. His eyes were filled with pain as he looked up at me. *You did it, Caleb. You won the battle, and the girl. I'm proud to call you my ally.*

At the sight of Irvine, Douglas growled, but my mother clamped her hand over his arm.

"You let him go, Douglas Maclean. You let our son go off and find his own way, or so help me god, you'll be sorry."

I glared at Douglas. *Well?*

Douglas' face clouded over. My stomach tightened. The blood pounded in my ears. I didn't know how much longer I'd be able to last against him if he decided to have another go—

He waved a hand at me. *Go on, git out o' here, and take your mate and your pack with you, before I change my mind.*

All Douglas' wolves took a step back, a clear sign they had surrendered. Rosa sobbed with relief. Luke bounded toward me, licking my face in a gesture of fealty. *Help Irvine,* I said to him. *I'll be fine.*

I got to my feet, balancing on my three good legs, and started to make my way toward the edge of the circle.

"Caleb, watch out!" Rosa screamed.

Something slammed against my side. My bad leg collapsed from under me, sending me sprawling across the dirt. The momentum carried me into a scrap heap. Empty cans and bottles toppled down on my head as I struggled to turn my body to see what had hit me.

Angus' teeth scraped my neck. I yanked my head away just in time, and his jaws snapped around thin air. I slashed at his face with my claws, tearing a shallow cut across his cheek. Angus growled, and his claws tightened around my neck. I tried to lift my arm to slice him again, but he clamped it under his paw, and bit into my neck.

Pain seared through me, a kind of cold burning in my veins, like plunging naked into icy water. My vision blurred, and red welts floated in front of my eyes. Angus' raging eyes burned themselves into my brain, the last image I would ever see.

I'm gonna enjoy tasting your blood, Angus rasped in my ear. Warm saliva dripped from his mouth and ran down the side of my cheek. *But not as much as I'll enjoy taking your mate for my own.*

Some mate you are, I snapped back, trying to keep myself alive through my anger. *You attacked her, kidnapped her, sent her threatening text messages, wrote horrible things on her cabin walls—*

That wasn't me, he hissed inside my head. *I never had her*

*number, and I didn't write anything on her wall. I would have no
need to do those things.*

Then who—

I don't know, and I don't care. And neither will you in a minute—
his teeth dug deeper, and I faded, the fight within me dwindling
away as the world exploded in a supernova of pain.

Angus, stop. I heard Robbie's voice, but he sounded far away,
like he was calling to me underwater. *Angus, no. He's our brother.
You can't do it to your own brother.*

He was never our brother.

Angus, this isn't you. This isn't right and you know it. Damn you,
Robbie's voice wavered. *Don't make me into the brother of a killer.
Don't make me hate you.*

Angus' head snapped up.

What? Seriously? I thought. *Does he actually care about what
Robbie thinks of him?*

Through the fog of the pain, a memory surfaced. When we
were cubs, we were playing at the edge of the forest, when we
happened upon a tiny cub shivering in a tree stump. It was a
runt of a thing, likely abandoned by its mother to either die
from the elements or torn apart by one of our pack.

Angus bared his teeth and growled at the cub. It froze with
fear, trembling so hard it pissed all over itself. Angus had
laughed as he dragged the squealing cub out of the bush by the
tail. "I'm going to crunch all his bones," he laughed cruelly.
"Damn little thing will barely be enough for lunch."

"Don't do it," I'd said. "He's only little. We should take him to
Mother, and—"

"Shut up, or I'll cut you again." Angus lifted a claw in warning. I winced. I already had a deep cut over my eye from the last
time I disagreed with him. I backed away, not wanting to watch
him do the grisly act.

Robbie stayed where he was, his eyes locked on his brother.

"Come on," I called to him, knowing how seeing something like that would upset him.

"No," Robbie had said. "I'm not going anywhere. And Angus is going to let the cub go."

"Why?" Angus growled.

"Because my brother is not a killer. My brother is honourable and wise."

I laughed. Angus was neither of those things. But Robbie said those things with such a wide, earnest look, I could tell he really, truly believed that Angus was an honourable wolf.

Angus had the wolf clamped between his paws, but he didn't bite down on its neck. Instead, he stared at Robbie, his mouth frozen in an open-mouthed grin.

"My brother is not a killer," Robbie insisted.

Finally, Angus sighed, and lifted his paws. The tiny cub, once presented with the possibility of freedom, didn't hesitate. With a final, piercing squeal, it rolled onto its feet and barrelled away into the forest.

Angus, Robbie's voice carried that same earnestness as he begged for my life. *Please don't do this. You can't never, ever take it back. And I will never forgive you for it.*

Angus glared at me, his jaw quivering.

He sighed.

The anger in his eyes faded, replaced by ... something that might've approached sadness if Angus were capable of such an emotion. The weight on my chest lifted. Angus backed away.

I groaned as I tried to roll over, and fresh pain flared through my shoulder. I gritted my teeth and tried again. This time, I managed to get my feet underneath me, but my leg collapsed again.

Angus reached down. I shrunk away, but his paw hooked around mine, and he hauled me to my feet.

His breath hissed against my ear. *This isn't the end of it. I'll have her one day, Lowe.*

You're not having her. The thought hit me with the force of a freight train. *She's mine, and I'm hers. I love her.*

I swung my arm up, wrapping my hands around his neck, and with a surge of strength that I didn't know I possessed, I threw Angus aside. He rolled in the dirt, and I scrambled up and threw myself at him.

My teeth clamped around his neck. I bit down, tasting blood. Angus went limp in my arms. The fight fled me, and I dropped him, collapsing back on my hind legs. I was too tired to fight any longer.

I just bit my brother, I thought. *I wanted to kill him. He was going to let me go, and I would've taken his life.*

Angus lay in a pool of his own blood. He glanced up at me with wide, pain-filled eyes. Guilt rocketed through me. He may have been horrible to me, but he was still the only family I'd ever known. Even now, I was that little boy from my memory, just wanting approval from his bigger brother.

You win, he gasped, holding his hand over the wound in his neck. *She's yours.*

She was never yours to give away, I shot back, backing away from him and the smell of his blood, before my instincts got the better of me.

I took a shaking step toward Douglas, and gave him a lick across his cheek. *Virtue mine honour,* I said.

Douglas' lip curled up, the way it always did when he was secretly pleased. He leaned forward. I froze, waiting for his response, fully expecting him to rip my throat out. Instead, he dragged his long, wet tongue over my cheek, a gesture of respect, an alpha addressing his equal.

Virtue mine honour, he said to me. *Now get the fook out of here.*

I stepped away, hardly daring to believe that we'd done it. We were going to walk out of here.

My mother stepped forward, and threw her arms around my neck. "You make me proud, my son," she whispered in my ear. "Keep my secret from Douglas, and I will come to you soon. We'll find the ring together, and bring the truth to the world."

I licked her ear, and she laughed. "That's my boy."

I looked into her eyes one more time, and saw my own eyes reflected back at me. We were alike in more than just genes – I too was willing to sacrifice a lot for what I believed to be the greater good.

Speaking of sacrifice ...

I turned away, and addressed the rest of the clan. *Bàs no Beatha*. I gave a little bow to the rest of the clan, the pack that had called me a brother, albeit an unwanted one, for so many years. The wolves watched in silence, acknowledging my goodbye with their eyes.

I signalled to Irvine that it was over. He nodded, and silently, his wolves surrounded him, and helped him on his feet. They disappeared into the trees, a few remaining behind to carry off their dead.

Ryan was still standing at the edge of the clearing, Rosa slumped in his arms. Marcus was there too. He'd torn away a piece of her shirt and was using it to bandage the wound on her shoulder. Her eyes met mine, filled with pain and joy.

Everything else faded into the background. All that existed was her and me, the connection that had been ignited between us, and the freedom I had won. I hobbled toward her, standing on my hind legs so I could reach her face. I licked her cheek, the taste of her exploding across my senses. I could drown in the joy of her.

"Caleb." Rosa's voice rasped with pain. She raised a hand, and stroked the side of my face. "My beautiful wolf. You saved me, again."

Her touch was like a burst of energy, shooting bright sunlight into my veins. Her smile drew me in, until I was drowning in her scent.

"I can't say I understand everything that's just happened," she said, stroking behind my ears. "But I can't believe you did this for me. You stood up to all these wolves to save me. I'm so sorry for doubting you, Caleb. Please, I don't want to be apart from you ever again. I want to be your mate."

This was all I ever wanted, all I'd dreamed about, to hear those words.

But now they were cold against my guilt. We weren't right, Rosa and I. Not anymore.

I stared down into her eyes. She'd never looked more beautiful to me.

I have to go, I said, the words almost breaking me. She couldn't hear them, of course, but she felt me pull away from her.

Her smile froze. "Caleb ... Caleb? Where are you going?"

I backed further, heading toward the tree line, my eyes drinking in her pain, the pain I had caused. Every muscle in my body begged me to go back to her, to wrap her in my arms and never let her go. But I had to resist. Rosa didn't need a guy like me.

I'm sorry. I'm so sorry, for everything I've done to you.

I tore my gaze from hers and darted into the trees, pumping my legs as hard as I could with my wounds. I needed to put as much distance between us, before I succumbed to the tug of my heart, and returned to her. I had to do what was right, what she deserved.

I had to set her free.

Goodbye Rosa. I never dreamed I could love someone the way I love you. That's why I'm doing this. That's why I'm giving you your freedom back.

25

ROSA

"Caleb!"

I cried his name over and over, but he didn't come back. I tried to climb down from Ryan's arms, but my legs were like jelly. My whole body felt numb, as though I were no longer inhabiting it.

"Caleb, come back!"

Ryan gripped me tight against his chest. "Shhh," he said, stroking my hair. "It's okay."

"It's not okay. Caleb's gone. He's left me here. Why did he leave me?"

Ryan's face looked stricken. He knew, of course. Caleb had said something, and Ryan had heard it with his shifter telepathy.

"Where is he?" I pounded my fists against Ryan's bare chest, but he only shook his head, his eyes sad.

"He's gone."

It was the woman. She stood next to Ryan, gazing down at me with familiar blue eyes, Caleb's eyes. I knew I was looking at Maria, Caleb's mother.

She stroked my cheek, and the gesture made me so sick for

my own family, for unconditional love, for the love I thought I could get from Caleb. Hot tears streaked down my cheeks.

"Why did he leave me?"

"Oh, honey." She swept her arm around the clearing. "Can you blame him?"

"I don't understand."

"He's a wolf. His first instinct is always to protect the people he loves. That puts you at the number one spot. Right now, he's a newly crowned alpha who just had to fight his way to dominance." She gestured to the carnage strewn across the clearing. "He's left a trail of destruction in his wake. If he thinks that is the only life he can give you, then he believes you deserve something more, more than him."

"I don't want more than him, whatever that means. I just want him."

"He'll figure that out, love. But he has to do that in his own time, in his own way. He's just won the right to his freedom. I think he wants the same for you."

Freedom. Caleb had spoken about it before, how he'd never felt as though he had it under the reign of his stepfather, how he admired me for renting my little cabin and forging my own freedom from the ashes of my tragedy. Why, then, did he not feel we could be free together? I just couldn't understand.

"We have to go after him," I said to Ryan.

"Rosa." Ryan's arms tightened around me. "Come on now. We'll take you home."

"But Caleb—"

Ryan shook his head. "He doesn't want to be found. He wants you to go back to Crookshollow and write your book and live your life and forget you ever met him."

"But how? How can I just pretend he never existed? All my life, I'd had to be my own hero, until I met him. Caleb saved me. He saved me from everything, especially from myself. I was going to drown in anger and revenge, but he stopped me. He made me see that I could do more."

"He feels like he let you down," Ryan said, as he started to walk back through the forest, Marcus and another tall, naked guy with long black hair followed behind him. "He needs to find a way to make it up to you."

"But I forgive him, I forgive you, Caleb!" I wailed as they opened a car door and bundled me inside.

There was no answer from the forest. Ryan shut the door. Marcus slid into the seat next to me and buckled my seatbelt. The engine roared to life. I sat, numb with pain as we pulled away and bumped along the forest road, staring out the window at the trees rolling away into the distance, leaving my heart behind me.

EVERYTHING WAS fine after that night, except that it wasn't.

Ryan took me straight to a hospital in Aberdeen, and had my wounds dressed. Caleb's saliva must have done wonders for my healing abilities, because by the time the doctors got to me, the wound barely even needed stitches.

We made it back to Crookshollow without incident. I can't even recall the drive back. I spent the entire trip thinking about Caleb, begging the universe to send him back to me. I didn't care anymore about what he'd said. People said stupid stuff all the time they don't mean. I weighed him by his actions. He'd waded into hell to save me. He'd defeated his powerful family to secure my freedom. That was what really mattered. Why couldn't he see that?

Back in Crookshollow, I returned to my cabin. Margaret had already hired someone to scrub off the graffiti. All my stuff was there, exactly as I'd left it. I stared at a blob of dried egg stuck to the wall, a remnant of one of Caleb's breakfast disasters, and cried for hours.

Ryan went back to his big house, and Marcus went back to his flat. I didn't seek them out, and they didn't try to stay in touch. I don't think they knew what to say to me.

Alex came to check on me every other day, her clothes stained with bright paint splotches. We sipped tea on the porch while she kept up a steady stream of chatter about all sorts of things. I barely said a word to her, and she didn't ask me to. I appreciated that, and came to look forward to her visits – the one bright spot in the black hole of my pain.

Every day, my laptop stared at me from the desk under the window, but I ignored it. Instead, I read book after depressing, heartbreaking book, watched reality TV shows on the tiny screen of my phone, and cried my way through fifty-one boxes of Coles tissues.

A week after we returned to Crookshollow, there was a knock on my cabin door. I wasn't expecting Alex, so I peered cautiously out the window. Luke stood on the porch, his face impassive, his hands jammed into his pockets. For the first time ever, he looked uncomfortable.

I threw opened the door. "Have you seen him?" I demanded.

Luke shook his head. "Is that any way to greet your second-favourite werewolf? How's the book going?"

"It's not, and you know that it's not. Answer my question, have you seen Caleb?"

Luke looked even more uncomfortable. "He doesn't want to be found right now. He said there was something he had to do. Can I come in?"

I held open the door for him. Luke slumped down in the chintz chair, and I put on the kettle for both of us.

"I thought you might like to know that the Macleans have

agreed to leave you alone," he said. "Maria got Douglas and Irvine to sit down and make a truce. Douglas has even agreed to support us when we reveal the existence of shifters to the world."

"So he knows about the ring?"

Luke nodded. "Maria explained it to him again, and he agrees that a lot of good could come from having the shifter society out in the open. He's a changed man since the battle. He can't abide what Angus did, what he nearly supported. I think Douglas sees that his legacy will be one of cruelty and cowardice, and he can't abide that."

"Good for him," I said flatly, pouring out the tea and handling Luke his cup. Without Caleb, all of this seemed pointless.

Luke beamed as he took a sip. "And there's more. Robbie has asked to join our pack."

Now that was a surprise. "And you let him?"

Luke nodded. "He showed he can stand up for what is right, that when the time comes, we can count on him. He wants to help us find the ring, and honestly, with Caleb gone, I could really use the help."

"Could you track Caleb down, if you had to?" I tried to keep my tone casual, but my voice was thick with hope.

Luke looked away, as though he didn't want to answer. He was silent for several moments, before saying, "If it was life or death, yeah. I could find him."

"This *is* life or death, Luke. I need him."

"You don't, though." Luke looked around the cabin. "A couple of weeks ago, all this was enough for you."

"That was before I knew him." My throat closed. "We had a fight, before I was kidnapped. It was a shitty fight, but I don't understand why we can't just sit down and talk about it."

"From what he told me, you can't do that because he knows

he was wrong. And he's not very good at saying sorry. He has to find a way to show you."

"Can't you do something? You're the closest family he's got."

Luke shook his head. "This is Caleb's thing. You know as well as I do that he's a stubborn git. Nothing I could say will convince him of something if he doesn't believe it himself."

I stared at the laptop, lying untouched on my desk, a layer of dust across the lid. "I don't know how to go on without him."

"You do what you have to do, Rosa. You use the freedom he won for you, and you do the thing you're supposed to do – you write your book, and tell your story."

I wiped a tear from my eye. "Before I met Caleb, I never thought I'd get the chance for a happy ending. I was positive my life was just going to be one struggle to be accepted after the next. But he showed me that I had so much more to live for than that. He made me feel like I could do anything. He could've been my happy ending, if I hadn't messed it all up."

Luke shrugged. "You didn't mess up, he did, and that's what he's trying to fix. Maybe there's no happy ending because it isn't time for the ending yet."

How I wished that was the truth. But I had to face facts. Caleb had run away. He didn't want me to contact him. He was gone from my life for good. I had to find a way to get over him and move on with my life.

26

ROSA

TWO MONTHS LATER

*M*argaret had been visiting my cabin a lot more since I'd got back from Aberdeen. She told me that Caleb had moved out a couple of weeks after he'd left me. So he'd been back in Crookshollow, but hadn't come to see me.

She didn't know where he'd gone. Which was good, because if she did, I might be tempted to find him. And he clearly wanted nothing to do with me.

Luke stayed in Crookshollow for a few weeks to help Robbie settle into his new Crookshollow flat. The two of them would disappear into the forest for days at a time, but when I asked Luke what they were doing, he just said they were on "pack business." I knew they were meeting Caleb.

Again and again, I begged Luke to tell me where he was, but he wouldn't budge. He also wouldn't deliver a message for me, nor even tell me what he and Caleb and Robbie were plotting together. "It's Lowe family business," he said. "This isn't something you should get involved in."

I didn't blame him for the secrecy. I wasn't a member of the pack. I wasn't anyone's mate.

I was rejected, again.

Being alone in the cabin gave me so much time to think, but all my thoughts were about Caleb. I thought it would be more than enough time to get over him. After all, we'd really only known each other for a couple of months. But every grain of wood in the place made me think of him.

I hated him for leaving me, for building up all that love and hope inside me and then crushing it under his paw. I hated him for proving me right, for becoming just another white guy who had screwed me over. I hated him for how weak I felt whenever I thought of him. And yet ... I missed him terribly. I missed him so bad, my chest hurt to think about it.

I forced myself to write, to mask the pain with words. The story morphed – almost without me realising it – into something dark and twisted. Nellie systematically worked her way through the people who had wronged her, enacting increasingly more violent revenge upon them. At first it was fun, dreaming up the ways I'd like to hurt everyone, how Susan would be choked by her own Chanel scarf, how Sam would have his penis cut off and fed to him. But the more I wrote, the deeper I sank into Nellie's vengeance, the more I realised how much I didn't want to be like her.

Caleb had shown me I had so much more to live for, to look forward to. I didn't want to be consumed by the trauma of my past. Nancy was wrong, the book was a *great* idea, just not in the way I'd envisioned. It wasn't going to win me the Man Booker prize, but it was helping me to move on.

One day, about two months after we got back from Aberdeen, I sat down at the computer, opened the revenge novel, selected all the words, and hit the delete button. As soon as the screen went blank, a wave of relief washed over me. I smiled my first genuine smile in two months.

And then immediately thought of Caleb, and burst into tears again.

During one of my many calls to her, Nancy said that time would heal me, but time didn't do jack shit to dull the pain of Caleb's absence. His presence followed me wherever I went. Every time I went out to the bathroom, I remembered the first night we met – the fun, easy flirting, the way our skin sizzled when we touched. He haunted my dreams, his hands all over my body, his breath hot against my ear. I'd wake up with a start, certain I could still taste the ghost of him on my lips.

I started working on a mystery book, where a plucky black detective solved puzzling murders in a small town filled with quirky characters. The town, of course, had a history of supernatural occurrences. It was a fun book, but I wasn't sure I really got the character. She felt flat.

Everything felt flat.

I TRIED to distract myself by embracing village life. It took all the courage I had to overcome my fear that everyone would try to burn me in the street, but the alternative was staying in the cabin, staring at a Caleb-shaped dent in my chintz chair. Every time I headed to the book group, or volunteered at Cole's bird sanctuary, or helped Alex take her painting into the Halt gallery, it got a little easier. I hadn't had a panic attack in weeks.

Today was no different from any of the days before it. I awoke, lonely, and boiled the kettle for tea. I went into the village to join Alex for a look around the Crookshollow witch-craft museum, then I picked up some groceries and came back to the cabin. I settled myself down at my desk with a cup of tea and a box of Jaffa Cakes, and tried to muddle my way through the first red herring in my mystery.

Minutes turned into hours while my fingers flew over the

keys. The story was starting to come together. I started to think I might be able to fix the main character with a few edits.

I was interrupted by a scuffling in the bushes outside the window.

My head snapped up. *What's that?*

Something darted through the trees. It looked like a huge animal, the size of a dog. My heart pounded against my chest. *Could it be ... a wolf?*

I stared out the window, searching the trees for any sign of movement. I don't know how long I watched, it might've been hours. But there was nothing. *Did I imagine it? Am I so desperate for Caleb that I've started seeing him everywhere?*

Tears rolled down my cheeks. *Damn, I thought I'd cried enough to flood the ocean already.* I reached for my fifty-third box of tissues.

A knock at the door startled me from my thoughts.

I glanced out the window. It was Margaret. She was holding a bottle of wine and a teacake, her walking stick pressed hard against the porch. I flung open the door. "I thought you could use some company, dear," she said, giving me a sympathetic grin.

Great. I was so pathetic, even an old lady felt sorry for me. I wiped my face with the back of my hand, hoping Margaret wouldn't notice the tears. I didn't really want any company, but what could I say?

Plus, a woman learns never to turn away free cake.

"Sure thing." I plastered a smile on my face, and held open the door.

Margaret bustled inside, plopped herself down in the ruined chair, and flicked on the tiny TV I'd bought to help fill my days. She turned the volume way up. "Get us some plates, would you? And some glasses for the wine."

I moved to the kitchen to find the things, while Margaret punched the volume on the TV up even higher.

"Have you read this month's book club choice—" I started to say.

"Shush!" Margaret silenced me, gesturing to the TV. "Not during the news, love."

She must really be getting deaf. That TV is up so loud, the walls are shaking.

I set down the glasses and poured the wine. On the TV, a round of adverts finished, and the news jingle started playing. Great, just what I wanted to see – murders and massacres all over the world. I cut myself an enormous slice of cake and settled back for an evening of grimacing.

"... in national news, a remarkable arson case in the small hamlet of Old Garsmouth was closed today—"

Old Garsmouth? I leaned forward, cake poised at my lips. The old familiar tight feeling in my chest returned. Why was my old town on the news?

"—where two men and a woman confessed to an arson attack on a local resident's home. The arson at black resident Rosa Parker's property five months ago had all the markings of a suspicious case, but no arrests had so far been made, with local police claiming lack of evidence. However, this week, three local residents have come forward to confess to the crime. We cross now to our local correspondent, who is standing outside police headquarters, where the suspects are being released on bail—"

I stared at the screen, my heart in my mouth. The footage was taken in front of the main station in Leeds, where a woman was being escorted inside through a small crowd of reporters snapping away. "Susan, just a few words!" one of them yelled.

Susan? Susan was one of the arsonists?

The news flashed to a press conference, where DI Martin –

the officer in charge of my case – stood behind a lectern, flanked by supporters. "I'm pleased to announce that with this confession, we can officially close the door on this heinous crime. We'll be charging all three suspects on multiple counts of arson and assault. Unfortunately, we haven't been able to contact the victim, but we're assured she will receive notice justice has been served."

A reporter called out, "What made them confess?"

"We wouldn't have been able to make this arrest without the help of Father Wolf," Martin said, gesturing to a black-robed man standing behind him. The inspector stepped aside, and the camera zoomed in on the face of the priest. The man lifted his face, and looked directly at the camera.

My chest tightened. My heart thundered against my ribcage. My jaw froze.

It was Caleb.

I gasped, my whole body frozen. Margaret reached out and clasped my hand, her bony fingers squeezing mine.

"Father Wolf, a few words!" one of the reporters yelled out.

Caleb nodded, and stepped up to the podium. "I can take no credit for this result," he said, his face serious. "For it is purely the work of the Lord. I was blessed to be able to administer to my flock by helping justice to be done. The village of Old Garsmouth has been very much divided in recent years. Too much hateful speech and petty vengeance for imagined slights. These three sinners asked for repentance for this crime, and I encouraged them to come forward, to cleanse their guilt by owning up to what they did to Rosa Parker."

The camera flicked to another screen, where Susan, her teenage son Stanley, and one of Sam's key advisors were shown in custody.

I can't believe it. I leaned forward, my heart pounding. *How is this possible? How did he get them to—*

Someone knocked on the door. "Go away!" I yelled, my eyes glued to the TV.

"I think you want to answer that, dear," Margaret said, dropping my hand.

I darted up and yanked open the door. There, standing on the porch, holding a giant bouquet of flowers and a box of Jaffa Cakes, was Caleb.

My knees wobbled. I couldn't believe he was really there. I reached out a hand to stroke his cheek, almost expecting it to land in midair. My fingers connected with his skin, and a surge of energy leaped from his body, sizzling against my skin.

"You ... " I couldn't form words. "You did ..."

"Hey, Rosa." The corner of his mouth tugged up into that beautiful grin, the grin that made the sun shine brighter. "Long time no see."

"I can't believe—" My knees buckled. I grabbed the edge of the door to keep from falling. Caleb darted forward and grabbed me, holding me against his broad chest. Heat swirled around us, and my skin burned with the fire of his touch. *After all this time, I can't believe he's come. I can't believe he did this for me.*

My legs wobbled, and I gripped his arms, struggling to keep myself upright.

"Easy," Caleb said, his husky voice like honey. "I wouldn't want you to fall, now."

"I can't believe you did this." I reached up to kiss him, but he pulled away.

"Rosa," he said, holding his finger to my lips. "Before you make a decision about me, I need you to understand why I left."

"You're here now, and I don't care—"

"You should care. So I'm going to tell you. You don't need someone to protect you, but after we had that fight, I realised that was the only thing I was doing. I was treating you like a princess that had to be kept safe all the time, because I didn't want you to ever have to be hurt the way they hurt you again. But in protecting you, I was smothering you. I wasn't giving you the freedom you needed, because I was too afraid of losing you. I guess ... you've seen the family I grew up with, and I think I carried around a lot more of that around with me then I realised. I had to leave because I had to find a way to show you that I didn't want to be just your protector anymore. I want to be your partner, your mate."

"You ... you pretended to be a priest for two months in order to bring my arsonists to justice?"

Caleb nodded. "Let me tell you, those robes are *damn* uncomfortable."

"I don't know if I approve the way you made a mockery of the Lord's servants, young man," Margaret admonished him from her chair. "But I definitely approve of your results."

I laughed. "So do I."

Caleb stroked my hair. "All it took was a lot of prayer, and a few well-timed shifts, and a claw to the throat. They were very willing to repent and do the right thing, in the end. They've confessed to charges of stalking, harassment and destruction of property."

"What?"

"They tracked you down here, supposedly to punish you some more. They were the ones sending you the texts, and they wrote the graffiti on the cabin wall. But enough about them. I've been going to a class."

"A class?"

"*Fundamentals of racial discourse through history.*" He grinned. "I've been taking it online, which is just as well, because I'm the only white guy in the whole class and I ask a lot of stupid questions."

The smile on my face widened as I imagined Caleb working his way through the course material, learning all about black history and colonialism and feminist rhetoric and white privilege. *I can't believe he's doing that, for me.*

"I'm starting to understand things, Rosa. I won't say that I'll always get it right, but I do want to understand. I guess ... I wanted to come back to tell you that, and to say that I don't expect you to ever forgive me, but if you did, I'd be here in a moment to—"

"Just stop. Stop talking." I wrapped my arms around Caleb's neck, and pressed my lips against his. My heart soared as his familiar scent enveloped me, and his tongue slid over mine. His strong arms around me fitted so perfectly. I never wanted to leave his embrace. I wanted to float forever in this perfect moment.

"I'll just get out of your way, dearies." Margaret grinned as she shoved past us, making her way through the door.

"Thanks for your help, Margaret!" Caleb called after her.

"Just pay your damn deposit on time, Caleb Lowe!" With that, she was gone.

"Deposit?"

"Yeah." Caleb scratched the back of his head, looking slightly guilty. "We can talk about it later."

I put my hands on my hips. "We'll talk about it right now."

"Well ... when I called Margaret to get her to help me show you the news segment, she *happened* to mention that one of her tenants moved out last week. This particular tenant had one of Margaret's deluxe cabins ... you know, the kind with two downstairs rooms, and a mezzanine bedroom?"

"Yes..."

"She said she'd keep it aside for me, just in case ..." His lips pressed against mine. "In case today went well."

"Are you telling me that you were so sure I'd take you back that you paid for a new cabin?"

"I wasn't sure at all. But a strong woman once taught me that when it comes to following your dreams, you have to be bold."

I laughed, wrapping my arms around his neck and pulling him in tight for another explosive kiss. "It sounds like the perfect place for a mated pair to make their new home."

He grinned that beautiful Caleb grin, and everything in the world seemed new and wonderful again. "It'll be the perfect place to write books and raise cubs."

"Cubs? Who said anything about cubs?"

"You don't want kids?" He looked worried.

I drew him in again, my tongue darting against his. "I want everything you got, wolf-man.'"

THE END

Sign up to Steffanie Holmes' newsletter to be notified when new books are available, and get a free Crookshollow story!

EPILOGUE

THREE MONTHS LATER

"*H*oney, I'm home!"

The cabin door slammed, jerking me out of the world of my book. I heard Caleb's boots clatter against the floor as he kicked them off. I couldn't wait to tell Caleb that I'd just heard back from an agent about my mystery manuscript. She wanted to represent it and try to sell it to a major publisher. I'd been staring at the email for the last half hour, unable to believe it.

"Caleb, come here, you won't believe what's happened. I'm—"

"Meow!"

What was that? That didn't sound like the door creaking—

"Meeeeeow?"

I whirled around. Caleb was standing behind my chair, the widest, cheekiest grin on his face. In his arms, a tiny black-and-white kitten clung to his sleeve like its life depended on it.

"You didn't." The little cat stared at me with wide eyes, its little nose sniffing the air. I reached out to pat it gingerly. It started purring instantly, and my heart melted into a puddle.

"I did." Caleb placed the kitten in my arms. It curled up into a ball in the crook of my arm, purring like an engine. "I walked past that *Witch's Familiar* pet store on the high street, and this little dude looked up at me from the window and made a face and I just couldn't leave him there. Don't worry, I got all the food and trays and stuff we need." He pointed to a stack of bags beside the door. "Plus some insect screens to put over the windows and a harness so we can take him outside without him killing all the local birdlife."

"Hey, little guy." The kitten clambered up my arm and stretched across my shoulder, batting at my hair. His little pink nose nuzzled against my cheek.

He is perfect.

Caleb tilted his head to the side. "Do you like him?"

One of the kitten's little paws got stuck in the curls, and I had to extract a strand of my thick, frizzy hair from around his little toe beans. "I *love* him. Caleb, thank you so much."

"Anything for my girl." He wrapped his arms around me, so the kitten sat in the V of our two bodies. Caleb kissed my cheek.

I stroked the kitten's silky fur until he was vibrating, his little eyes closed in ecstasy. He reminded me of the first time I met my beautiful Lennox. *We should call him Lewis.* "Does he have a name already? I want to call him Lewis."

"Check out his collar."

Disappointed, I ran my finger along the edge of the kitten's collar, until it snagged on a metal ring. I pulled the ring out to see what was written on the tag, only to discover there was no tag at all.

On the end of the ring was a glimmering black stone. A black diamond.

My heart stopped. I couldn't breathe. I stared up at Caleb, unable to believe this was real.

Caleb's eyes glinted at me, sparkling even more than the diamond. "I take it you're suitably surprised."

It's a diamond ring. He's giving you a diamond ring. "Um ... Caleb ... uh ..."

"Rosa Parker, you make me the happiest guy in the world. You are brilliant, and funny, and you keep me on my toes. I would be honoured if you would take me as your husband." He wiggled his eyebrows, and pointed at the kitten clinging to his chest. "I would get down on one knee, but I don't want to disturb our new friend."

Tears streamed down my face. My finger caressed the beautiful black diamond, but my eyes remained glued to Caleb. He may be a white guy and a crazy werewolf, but all I wanted was to wake up next to him for the rest of my life.

"Yes." My heart soared as the word flew from my lips. I knew it was the right answer. Happy tears poured from my eyes. "Yes. A hundred times, yes."

Caleb's lips met mine, his kiss passionate. Between us, the kitten purred with frantic vigour, and he tried to climb up the side of my face.

"Ow, you." I laughed as my tears slid over the kitten's fur. I reached up and peeled the creature off my face. I held little Lewis while Caleb undid the collar, and slid off the ring.

"You're going to have to put down the kitten to give me your finger." Caleb grinned.

"Not a chance." I switched Lewis to the other hand, and presented my finger to Caleb. He slid the ring on – it fit perfectly, the beautiful diamond sparkling against my dark skin. A black diamond for a black princess, because that's what I felt like.

"It's perfect." I kissed him again. "What should be do to celebrate?"

"We can think about that later," Caleb said. "Right now, you should probably rescue your manuscript from your new friend."

"What? Oh, no. Kitty, get down!" I tore myself from Caleb's arms and leapt across the room, scooping up the kitten just as he started to dance across my open keyboard. If he accidentally sent an email of gibberish to my new agent ...

Caleb laughed. "I think we're going to have a great time, the three of us. Maybe ..." He lifted an eyebrow to me. "Maybe one day, the four of us?"

"Maybe." I raised my eyebrow at him, the ache inside me swelling up again.

"On the bed, Mrs. Lowe," he growled, just the sound he knew that made my knees weak.

"Hey, I'm not Mrs. Lowe yet. I might even keep my own name, if it's going to be on the cover of my book. And besides, if we're going to try for a cub *now,* what will we do with our new friend?" I gestured to the kitten. "It would be rude to do that in front of him. We might warp his fragile little mind."

"He's gotta get used to it sooner or later," Caleb growled. "I don't intend to let you out of that bed for days."

I knitted my fingers in his, enjoying the heaviness of the ring against my skin. "That's an awfully bold statement, Mr. Parker. Perhaps we should see how much stamina you really have."

He flipped me on the bed, his hands snaking under my shirt as he smothered my lips in kisses. "Yes," he whispered against my lips. "Perhaps we shall."

THE END

In the next *Wolves of Crookshollow* book, tattoo artist and party girl Bianca Sinclair inherits a Victorian mansion from her grandmother, but only on the condition that she finds a husband. Enter sexy wolf shifter Robbie Maclean. Sparks fly in this unusual marriage of convenience. Read Inking the Wolf now.

Sign up to Steffanie Holmes' newsletter to be notified when new books are available, and get a free Crookshollow story!

WANT MORE CROOKSHOLLOW WOLVES?

Sink your teeth into the hot werewolf paranormal romance from *USA Today* bestselling author, Steffanie Holmes!

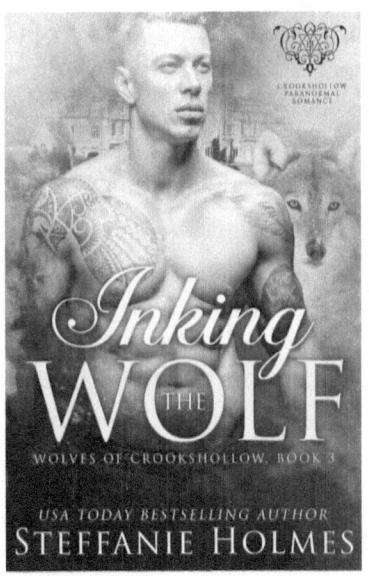

My best friend's a shapeshifter, and now we're getting married. Nothing could possibly go wrong, right?

When my Grandmother June died, I couldn't care less. That vicious old hag hated everything about me – from my blue hair and job as a tattoo artist, to the fact that I have no desire to give up my playgirl ways.

Now I learn she's left me Primrose House – a beautiful Victorian gothic mansion with a turret and a secret passage. The only problem? In order to officially take up residence at the house, I have to be married.

Enter Robbie, my gorgeous best friend and a wolf shifter without a home. We're getting fake-married, and he's moving into Primrose House with me to convince my parents that we're for real.

Robbie gets a free place to live, I get to keep Primrose House – everything's perfect.

Except ... when we kissed at the alter of our fake-wedding, something happened. To say "sparks flew" would be the understatement of the century.

That kiss didn't just spark, it set off an inferno.

I can't stop thinking about Robbie. How come I'd never noticed how hot he was? – those soulful eyes, that Scottish accent and hot shifter body ....

But he's my best friend, and my fake-husband. If I mess this up, I'll lose both Robbie and Primrose House.

I just have to control myself. I just have to resist to urge to repeat that kiss.

It can't be that hard to avoid falling into bed with your best friend, right?

Right?

Inking the Wolf is the third book in the *Wolves of Crookshollow* series by *USA Today* bestselling author Steffanie Holmes. It's a standalone book with a HEA, where a party girl and a down-on-his-luck shifter find more than ghosts in an old Victorian house. If you like your paranormal romance with a touch of the gothic, this book will have you howling for more.

START READING NOW

INKING THE WOLF

AN EXCERPT

"Come on, Bianca." A note of anger crept into Robbie's voice. "If this fake-marriage is going to work, we have to be completely *honest* with each other, remember? Are you just going to toy with me until you get tired of me, and then toss me away like you do with everyone else in your life?"

"That's not fair." I yanked my hand away.

"It's completely fair. You don't let anyone get close to you. You have hundreds of friends, but not one of them really knows you, not the way I do. Fuck, I'd do *anything* for you. Could you even say the same about *anyone?*"

I balled my hands into fists. This wasn't going the way I expected. "You think you have me pinned down, don't you. Well, we *do* have to be honest, don't we, Robbie? What about being honest about how *you* feel? What about all the times I asked you if you were okay with our arrangement, if there was any reason we shouldn't do it? But oh no, it's all my fault, because I foolishly expected a little honesty from my best friend."

"What do you mean, I haven't been honest?"

I shrugged, leaning back to rest on my ankles. I folded my arms across my chest and adopted the petulant expression that drove my mother crazy. "You like me. Everyone tells me so. You didn't tell me, and so I didn't know that I shouldn't snog girls in front of you—"

"I don't *like* you," he growled.

"Then why—"

"I thought it was obvious. I'm fucking in love with you, Bianca."

The words slammed against me, jolting through my body like an electric current. Robbie's strong hands grabbed my arms, yanking me onto my knees. His eyes blazed as his lips slammed against mine. Heat surged through my body, lighting every part of me on fire. *God, I want you. Touch me, Robbie. Tell me again that you love me.*

Robbie cupped my neck, pushing my head against his as he deepened the kiss. "Robbie, I can't—" I tried to say, but his lips smothered mine, chasing away my protests. I sank into the kiss, savouring every delicious moment, every surge of energy as it coursed through my body.

I fucking love you, Bianca.

The words pounded against my skull. Women and men had told me that before, and it was usually the signal that I had to end things. This time ... the words surged through my body, lighting up something dormant within me, something that desperately wanted to speak the words back.

START READING NOW

ALSO FROM THE WORLD OF CROOKSHOLLOW …

CROOKSHOLLOW GOTHIC ROMANCE, BOOK 4

Love so fierce it transcends even death.

When Elinor Baxter arrives at the dilapidated Marshell House to settle the estate of her law firm's oldest client, she can't help but feel a little spooked. The creaking gothic mansion is a far cry from her life as an adventurous party girl back in London.

Then she meets Eric Marshell, a man dressed entirely in black with a wicked smile and the ability to float through walls. Eric was the violinist in popular rock band Ghost Symphony until a hit-and-run accident claimed his life. Now he's trapped inside his mother's house for all eternity, and the only one who can see or hear him is Elinor.

Eric and Elinor fight their attraction for each other as they dig into the mystery of Eric's death. But when they uncover a dark and sinister plot that threatens Elinor's life, their bond draws them into a world neither of them understands. Can their love transcend the boundary between life and death?

The Man in Black is a steamy gothic romance by USA Today best-selling author Steffanie Holmes, Set in the English village of Crook-shollow, it's a standalone novel of love, redemption, and second chances. If you love clever BBW heroines, crumbling gothic mansions, and brooding rockstars who know what they want, then this book will have you shivering all over.

READ NOW: The Man in Black

OTHER BOOKS BY STEFFANIE HOLMES

This list is in recommended reading order, although each couple's story can be enjoyed as a standalone.

Nevermore Bookshop Mysteries

A Dead and Stormy Night

Of Mice and Murder

Pride and Premeditation

Memoirs of a Garroter (available May 2019)

Briarwood Witches series

The Castle of Earth and Embers

The Castle of Fire and Fable

The Castle of Water and Woe

The Castle of Wind and Whispers

The Castle of Spirit and Sorrow

Crookshollow Gothic Romance series

Art of Cunning (Alex & Ryan) - READ NOW FOR FREE

Art of the Hunt (Alex & Ryan)

Art of Temptation (Alex & Ryan)

The Man in Black (Elinor & Eric)

Watcher (Belinda & Cole)

Reaper (Belinda & Cole)

Wolves of Crookshollow series

Digging the Wolf (Anna & Luke)

Writing the Wolf (Rosa & Caleb)

Inking the Wolf (Bianca & Robbie)

Wedding the Wolf (Willow & Irvine)

Fallen Sorcery Fae (shared world)

Hollow

Witches of the Woods

Witch Hunter

Coven

The Curse (coming in 2018)

Want to be informed when the next Steffanie Holmes paranormal romance story goes live? Sign up for the VIP Readers Club at https://www. subscribepage.com/briarwoodprequel *to get the scoop, and score a free bonus epilogue to enjoy!*

ABOUT THE AUTHOR

Steffanie Holmes is a USA Today bestselling author of steamy historical and paranormal erotic romance. Her books feature clever, witty heroines, wild shifters, cunning witches and alpha males who get what they want.

Before becoming a writer, Steffanie worked as an archaeologist and museum curator. She loves to explore historical settings and ancient conceptions of love and possession. From Dark Age Europe to crumbling gothic estates, Steffanie is fascinated with how love can blossom between the most unlikely characters.

Steffanie lives in New Zealand with her husband and a horde of cantankerous cats.

Steffanie Holmes Mailing List

Want free books, exclusive giveaways and exclusive sneak peeks at upcoming Steffanie Holmes paranormal romance books? Sign up for the mailing list to get the scoop.

Join the conversation! Learn more about Steffanie:
steffanieholmes.com